This wasn't the R & R she'd been hoping for....

She had come out here for peace, quiet and the restorative benefits of painting and solitude. Instead a total stranger had walked her into something that harkened back to Iraq. She really ought to just pack up and go somewhere else.

But she knew she couldn't, wouldn't do that. She hadn't been exaggerating when she had said she would never abandon a fellow soldier, and she meant it. She got the feeling Craig didn't have a whole lot of help, so unless they found a reason to call in the Feds or ATF or something, she would do what she could to help. She was going to have his back.

She heard Craig draw a breath, as if he were about to say something, when she suddenly realized that the edginess running along her nerve endings no longer had solely to do with him.

"Shh," she whispered almost inaudibly. "We're being watched."

Conard County: The Next Generation

Dear Reader,

This story was born of a confluence of things. It began as a memory of the "water wars" I saw when I sold real estate in the Rocky Mountains. Things like that can get extremely touchy and very litigious and expensive. It can even get dangerous and ugly. But as I toyed with the idea, I needed a reason for the water problem, and I began thinking about all the headaches this could cause the forest service if water was cut off to forest service land.

And voilà, I had my hero, a law enforcement officer with the Forest Service, a man who found his peace and meaning in preserving public lands for the future. And my heroine, a woman with a traumatic past who had come to the mountains to heal and paint. From there it was one easy step from water being the problem, to the guy who was building a militia on his private land.

I hope you enjoy this story of two people melding their very different lives as they face an unexpected threat together.

Rachel

RACHEL LEE

Rocky Mountain Lawman

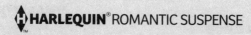

HARLEQUIN® ROMANTIC SUSPENSE

ISBN-13: 978-0-373-27826-8

ROCKY MOUNTAIN LAWMAN

Printed in U.S.A.

Books by Rachel Lee

RACHEL LEE

was hooked on writing by the age of twelve, and practiced her craft as she moved from place to place all over the United States. This *New York Times* bestselling author now resides in Florida and has the joy of writing full-time.

To my dear friend Linda, who helped with research and saved my sanity on more than one occasion. Sometimes we get sisters by birth, and other times we discover them. Thanks, Sis.

Prologue

Buddy Jackson sat at the fancy dining table his great-grandmother had carted out here from back east almost a century ago, a table that looked out of place amidst the mostly rough-hewn surroundings of the cabin his grandfather had built and his family had added to over the years.

His wife and kids were out tending the garden as they should be. The growing season here was short, and there was no time to waste.

Across from him sat Cap MacDonald, a guy he'd met last year at a gathering of "Preppers," as they called themselves, people who were preparing either for the collapse of society or the end of the world. All of them, of course, assumed that they would survive the cataclysm. Buddy had no doubt of it; he was living in the middle of nowhere. Little could reach him here on his mountainside.

But Cap had somewhat different ideas, and they appealed to Buddy. Cap didn't just want to survive, he wanted to *win*. To be in control afterward. What's more, he made a good argument for self-protection and keeping the parasites out after the troubles started.

Cap had even grander ideas, though. Buddy had been prepping for a long time, and sometimes he got tired of waiting for the moment that would prove the brilliance of his foresight. Cap wasn't prepared to wait. He spoke of how it was their job to bring it all about.

That sounded okay to Buddy most of the time, and the fact that Cap was pulling together a small militia didn't seem like a problem. If the revolution was coming anyway, what was the point of waiting for it?

But something was bothering him now.

"You heard," he said to Cap, "about that hiker they found dead about four miles from here?"

Cap shook his head. His hands were busy cleaning the AR-15 he always carried. "What about him?"

"He was dead."

Cap shrugged. "People die out here in the wilderness. You aren't stupid, Buddy."

"No." Buddy dropped it, but he didn't stop thinking about it. He knew Cap took his guys out to walk through the national forest that surrounded his land on three sides. Nothing wrong in that. But he also had figured out that Cap was capable of killing. That was one thing Buddy didn't know about himself, and he'd been glad to have someone join him who wouldn't hesitate to defend the compound if necessary.

But surely that didn't extend to some hiker wandering around in the woods? Of course not.

After a minute or two, he finally stopped thinking about it. The revolution hadn't begun yet, and Cap couldn't have had any reason to hurt a hiker, one who wasn't even prowling this property.

No reason at all. Must have just been an accident.

Chapter 1

Skylar Jamison sat near the top of a rise with a gorgeous view of a narrow river valley below and the soaring face of the Wyoming Rockies ahead of her. Fields of wildflowers in brilliant reds and yellows dotted the grassy slope where she sat, and she could see them in the valley below, as well as in patches on the mountains.

From here she beheld a vast panorama of beautiful nature mostly unmarred by human presence.

That's why she'd come here. She needed to refresh herself, rediscover her joy in painting after a bad breakup. The pristine wilderness of the national forest around her washed away the sludge that seemed to have mired her heart and soul.

She sat on the grasses on a paint-splattered light-weight tarp. Before her was a small easel holding a canvas on which she had daubed some of the incredible colors around her. Beside her lay a box of oil paints, some rags and a small plastic bottle of citrus cleaner for her brushes. When she was done for the day, she'd wrap her brushes in a cleaner-soaked rag and plastic until she returned to her motel room and could rinse them. On the other side of her was a camera with several lenses. Painting outdoors might inspire her creativity, but the light changed swiftly, and when it was especially good she'd snap photos to capture it, so that she'd have a visual reminder for working later.

Up here, despite it being summer, the air was a bit chilly, and she had wrapped herself in an old sweater she didn't mind ruining with paint. The quiet breeze tickled her cheeks and occasionally rustled the grasses around her, a great background to her rambling thoughts.

A fluffy cloud blocked the sun temporarily, changing the light drastically, flattening the contrast and perspective. Something about the change gripped her and she reached for the camera, taking a number of quick shots.

"Hey!"

The sharp, annoyed cry was so unexpected that she nearly dropped her camera and swung around. A burly man was striding out of the woods just behind her to the left. He wore woodland camouflage head to toe.

She gaped, uncertain how to respond.

"What the hell do you think you're doing?"

Still shocked by the unexpectedness of the man's arrival and his apparent irritation, she sat frozen. One of the things she'd always hated about herself was her occasional slowness to react. It might have saved her some trouble at times simply because she thought first, but at other times it was potentially dangerous.

The man strode closer, and there was nothing casual in his approach.

Suddenly galvanized, she jumped to her feet, still holding the camera.

"I asked what the hell you're doing!"

He was getting so close that nervousness assailed her. Instinctively, she braced herself in a defensive posture in case she needed to protect herself. They were all alone up here, miles from anywhere.

"Painting," she finally said.

"That looks like a camera to me."

She wondered what the hell was going on, but surprise began giving way to anger as she measured the implied threat in his voice and his approach. "So?"

He got close enough to see the canvas and hesitated. Finally he said, "We don't like spies around here. You find some place else to take your pictures. I mean it."

He glared at her for a palpable second, then turned and strode away.

"What the hell?" she said aloud to the now empty hilltop. "What is going on?"

The grasses, trees and mountains didn't answer. The breeze kicked up a bit, chilling her. She looked around, trying to re-center herself. Same hill, same mountains, so why did she feel she'd just slipped realities?

"Idiot," she muttered finally. Probably some cranky old curmudgeon who thought he owned the entire state. Defiantly, she picked up her camera and looked through the viewfinder and her telescopic lens. Mountains, trees, grasses, wildflowers. A cabin.

She turned the camera back. She hadn't really been looking that way because the lighting was bad and didn't appeal to her, but examining more closely now she saw what appeared to be some kind of homestead across the valley on a higher elevation. She could have zoomed in more, but decided not to. Spy? Really?

Damn it, she thought, this was national forest land. She wasn't trespassing and had every right to be here. But did she really want to get into it with that nut?

Annoyed, she squatted and began to pack up. There were probably a hundred places where she could get a view just as good without the hassles, and who needed the hassles? The stubborn part of her defiantly wanted to remain, but she'd come out here for peace, not conflict. God knew, she'd endured enough conflict for a while.

She unscrewed the lens from the camera, slipped it into its case, then put everything in her camera bag. It took a little longer to put up her paints, soak the brushes and wrap them in cloth and plastic. When she was sure everything was secure in her backpack, she started to fold her tarp.

Irritated in ways she couldn't quite put her finger on, she damned the man for destroying a perfectly beautiful day. Part of her wanted to stay put, just to show him, but given the isolation out here, she had to admit that might not be wise. *Just find another place, Sky.*

God, she was learning to *hate* men. Such a sense of privilege, as if they were masters of the universe. She had a right to be here, too.

She was stuffing the tarp in her backpack when she saw another man emerge from the trees from the opposite direction, this one riding a horse. She tensed at once, then recognized the colors of the U.S. Forest Service. A ranger. She decided to stay right where she was and give this guy an earful about what had just happened. After all, wasn't it his job to make sure the public wasn't harassed on public land?

She wasn't at all clear what these folks did, but she was sure of one thing: at the ranger station before she'd come up here, a very nice woman had told her she was free to go anywhere she liked in the forest, but advised her to file a description of her planned activities and check in when she returned, just in case.

"If we need to rescue you," the woman said cheerfully, "it would be really helpful to have some idea when and where to start looking."

Raising her hand, Sky waved at the rider. At once he turned his mount a little and began to come directly toward her.

God, he looked iconic, she thought. A big man on a big horse under the brim of a felt Stetson. There was no mistaking that long-sleeved light olive shirt with its patches and brass nameplate, or the dark olive jeans. And soon there was no mistaking the glint of a badge on his breast, or the gun holstered at his waist. Or the shotgun in the saddle holster. She guessed he wasn't an ordinary ranger. What the heck happened in these mountains?

When he got close enough, she could see a square, sun-bronzed face, some dark, close-trimmed hair. Not his eyes, though, in the shadow of his hat. He rode easily, as if he'd been born in the saddle, seeming to sway with the horse's every move, relaxed and comfortable. Broad shoulders, narrow hips. And armed.

That kept grabbing her. She wondered if she was foolish to come out here without some kind of protection.

He reached her at last, raising a finger to the brim of his hat. "Something wrong, ma'am?"

"Maybe. This is forest land, right? Open to the public?"

"Yes, ma'am."

"Then why would some guy come tell me to go someplace else?"

He glanced across the valley. "Big guy? Burly?"

"That's him."

"I know him." The ranger shook his head. "I'll take care of it. He won't bother you again."

"What is he? Some kind of nut?"

"I suppose you could argue that." For the first time he smiled faintly. "Isolated places sometimes grow cranks. Are you getting ready to leave?"

"Believe it. I don't like being treated that way. Besides…" She hesitated. "He unnerved me a little. It's very lonely out here." Something she'd been enjoying only a short time ago.

"It can be." Rising a bit in his stirrups, he scanned the area. "How long ago did he bother you?"

Sky tried to measure it. "It had to be at least fifteen minutes. I started packing up as soon as he left."

He looked at her things. "What do you do?"

"I was trying to paint. I'm an artist."

"Taking pictures?"

"Sometimes. To capture the light."

"Well, that might do it. All right, I'll have some words with him. In the meantime…" He swung down from the saddle. "Let me help you carry your things and make sure you get safely back to your car or your campsite."

Before she could do more than thank him, he'd swung the strap of her heavy camera bag over the pommel of his saddle and picked up her backpack, holding it with one hand and his reins in the other. "Which way?" he asked.

She pointed to where she'd left her car, grabbed the

box containing her supplies and canvas, and together they started walking. He didn't seem to be in any hurry, sticking to a leisurely pace.

Sky, for her part, was starting to bubble over with questions. She just didn't know if she should ask him. But finally one burst from her.

"Are you some kind of cop?"

He glanced at her, just before they entered the shadow of the trees, and at last she caught a glint of dark gray eyes. "Some kind. I'm in law enforcement for the service, but I'm also a biologist. So I wear a few hats. I keep an eye on the wildlife while patrolling for violators, I do search and rescue, firefighting." He gave a laugh. "Short staffing makes everyone a jack-of-all-trades, I guess. Anyway, I guess you could say my main job is protecting visitors and employees. Whatever's most needed on any day." He paused. "I'm Craig Stone, by the way."

"Skylar Jamison. Sky for short."

"Nice to meet you, Ms. Jamison."

"I was certainly glad to see you. That man made me really nervous, and I don't get unnerved easily. What is he? Some kind of hermit who thinks he owns the woods?"

"It's a little more complicated than that. Are you aware that when we turn land into national forest or parkland we don't throw out people who are already living there?"

"I hadn't thought about it."

"Well, we don't evict people. They get to stay the way they always have if they want to, or we buy them out. The guy you met owns a spread inside the forest here."

"Is that what I saw across the valley?"

"Part of it. He owns a fair piece."

"Does he make a point of bothering people?"

"Not usually. He's got his property posted and doesn't like trespassers, but..." He paused. "Something's going on over there lately. I usually mind my own business when it comes to his property, but maybe it's time to have a few friendly words. I'm certainly going to make sure he doesn't drive people off public land, or scare them. Maybe I can even find out why he was bothered by you at all."

"He called me a spy."

Craig turned his head and looked straight at her. "Really?"

"His word, not mine."

He fell silent as they continued to walk. The sound of the horse's hooves were almost entirely muted by the deep pine needles under the trees, then would become louder again as they scuffed through leaves. "How often have you been out there?"

"This was the third day."

"Do you use that camera a lot?"

"Like I said, to capture the light as much as anything. It's changing constantly, and sometimes there's something about it I really want to catch for later."

"I wonder if the camera got to him. Well, I'll find out. Either way, if you want to come back to this spot, you can. I'll make sure of it."

"You may have a lot of guns, but they won't be around when I'm out there alone."

That elicited a laugh from him. "True, but I don't think Buddy runs to violence. A little nutty maybe, but I never heard of him hurting anybody. But if you like, I know some other vantages as good as that one I can show you. Well away from Buddy."

"I may take you up on that." Although the idea of ceding ground to a crank annoyed her no end. She knew perfectly well that she could deal with that guy. He hadn't even been armed that she could see. She just didn't want the conflict. This was supposed to be a break.

"Feel free. Just leave a message for me with Lucy at the station. She'll radio me."

"Thanks. So you're a biologist, too?"

"Focused on wildlife mostly."

"What kind?"

"If it walks, crawls or flies, I'm probably on it. Our mission is to protect everything in these forests for future generations. It's not always easy. We humans seem to have some problems getting along with nature."

"No kidding! So I bet you know the names of all the wildflowers?"

"Sure. You want to know what they are?"

"Actually no," she admitted. "I see them a different way, categorize them by colors and shapes. Names might change what I see."

"An artist's eye?"

"Maybe so."

"Then why did you ask?"

She gave him a sidelong glance. "Because you're the first person I've ever met who might actually know the official names of everything in the woods."

He flashed another truly attractive smile as they reached the service road and her battered sedan came into view. He helped her load her car, then closed her door after she climbed in. She rolled down the window and started the engine.

"Drive slow. We've got some logging trucks driving a little crazy up here."

She looked up at him, drinking in again his good looks. "I didn't see any."

"We're doing some thinning to prevent disease and clearing some deadfalls. If you stay around awhile, you'll see them. Drive safe." He gave the top of her car a friendly rap, then stepped back, remounted and watched her drive away.

Glancing in her rearview mirror, she saw him. Dang, that man looked good enough to eat.

As soon as there was nothing left but a cloud of dust, Craig pulled the radio off his belt to call his boss. "Hey, Lucy."

"What's up, Craig?"

"Buddy. He's done it again. I'm going to have to go talk to him, probably in the morning. Night's drawing near."

"Want me to send someone to meet you?"

"I doubt that's necessary. I'm just going to remind him that the public has a right to be on public land."

"What's going on with him?"

"Damned if I know, but maybe I can find out. I told a lady artist to let you know if she wants me to find her somewhere else to paint."

"He bothered *her?* Craig, I don't like it. I can see him getting mad at a bunch of rowdy campers, but a woman alone who's just painting?"

"And taking photos." Craig paused. "It's the photos that might have been the problem, and that's what worries me. Why would that bother him?"

"Are you *sure* you don't want some backup?"

"I never had a problem with Buddy before."

"Nobody had a problem with him before. But don't forget that dead hiker we found at the beginning of the summer."

"I seriously doubt Buddy was involved in that. Misadventure."

"Misadventure my butt," Lucy said bluntly. "I'd feel a whole lot better if the medical examiner could ascertain cause of death. I know it probably wasn't Buddy, but you take care. The guy's getting weird."

Craig tucked the radio away and looked at the sky. The day was waning; it would take him a while to get to Buddy Jackson's place, which meant there wouldn't be much light when he got there. Definitely best to wait for morning, especially if he wanted to be able to see anything.

And seeing what was going on at Buddy's place suddenly seemed like it might be important.

Sky drove carefully down the service road, avoiding some ruts and keeping an eye out for logging trucks. The sightlines were short along this narrow, winding road, and she could see why Craig had warned her to be on the lookout. A truck could be on her almost before she saw it.

Her meeting with him had gone a long way to easing her anger, though. So this guy Buddy was apparently a harmless nut. Okay, she could deal with that. And she wanted to go back to that spot, because it had evoked images in her mind that she wanted to get on canvas. The colors had been gorgeous, the valley steep and full of character, the shadows almost haunting. While her paintings were more impressionistic than realistic, she knew she wouldn't capture what that spot evoked in her if she relied mostly on memory and even photographs. There was a *feeling* she had while sitting there that didn't follow her when she left.

Buddy had sure blown that up this afternoon.

On the other hand, she'd met Craig Stone. He was handsome, yes, but what appealed to her was his quietude. She sensed serenity around him, an ease with himself and his place in the world that she could only envy. Did spending a lot of time in the woods do that?

She almost laughed out loud, however, when she thought about that calm and peace that seemed to suffuse him and compared it to the fact that he was packing both a rifle and a pistol. She had wanted to ask him about that. What dangers was he prepared for? Bears? Wolves? People? All of the above?

She'd heard over the years that occasionally rangers got killed on the job, but she didn't think it was very common. Well, if she saw him again she would ask him.

In the meantime, if that peace she had felt in him came from being in the woods, she wanted some of it for herself. She'd gotten an inkling of it during her few days on that hill painting, but she just wished it would stay with her. Instead, by the time she got back to town, it seemed to have vanished.

When her thoughts started to run on Craig Stone and whether she'd see him again, she sharply reined herself in. Hadn't she come here to escape all that? Hadn't she just about decided men weren't worth that kind of effort? She was supposed to be nursing a bruised heart, not seeking another one.

Man, she definitely needed some Zen and tranquility. Just for a while. Time to gain perspective, time to ease the wounds, time to replenish the batteries so she could return to her rehab work fresh and ready to aid the vets who needed all the help they could get dealing with their scars, both visible and invisible.

She made it down the mountain without meeting a

logging truck, and pulled into the ranger station. It was a nice-looking log cabin set just inside the entrance to the forest. Two stories high, it appeared big enough for a few rangers to live there for the summer.

Inside the lobby there were some comfortable rustic chairs, some rugs on the plank floor, carousels holding pamphlets and a long counter behind which the ranger on duty sat. A glass-fronted case displayed souvenirs but the only ones that caught Sky's attention were the little stuffed Smokey the Bear dolls. Before she left, she'd send one to her niece who lived in Hawaii.

The ranger, a woman, rose from a desk and smiled. "I hear you had some trouble from Buddy today."

"It wasn't exactly trouble. He was just rude." Sky felt a little embarrassed, wondering if she'd overreacted to the guy. He hadn't actually threatened her, he'd just told her to get lost. Still, she thought there was something a bit menacing in the way he'd approached and yelled at her, making a wild accusation.

The tall, dark-haired woman's name badge said she was Lucy Tattersall. "Well, Craig will get him to lay off. By the way, do you want Craig to show you some other places that might be good for your art?"

So Craig had apparently radioed the entire thing to Lucy. Now she *did* feel embarrassed. "He didn't have to make a big deal about it," she protested. "A guy was rude to me. Apparently he's a little quirky. But I'm not running from that. I'll paint in the same place tomorrow. In fact, I'll paint there until I've gotten what I want from the location. It's beautiful."

Lucy's dark eyes sparkled. "You go, lady." But then the sparkle faded a bit. "Just be careful. Buddy's never been a real cause for concern, but things can change, you know?"

"I'll be fine. If he gives me any more trouble, I'll report it." She smiled at Lucy. "I guess I got my backbone up. Public land and I'm the public."

"Exactly," Lucy agreed. "Buddy has always had an aversion to trespassers, which I can understand. It's *his* land, not forest land, and some of our hikers overlook that. But if you see him again and manage to get on his good side, maybe he'll talk to you a bit. He's got some interesting stories to tell. So same place tomorrow? Be sure to check in before you go."

Sky walked out and climbed into her car with the definite sense that Lucy hadn't told her everything. But why would she? Sky was a stranger and the rangers probably never gossiped, except possibly among themselves.

Glancing at her watch, she realized she had time to clean up before she met with a local veterans group. Somebody back in Tampa had apparently let the VA up here know she was going to be in the area, and the first day she was here she'd been approached to speak with the local support group about what she did as an art therapist.

At first she had been annoyed because she was supposed to be taking a break from all of that, but now she found herself looking forward to it. It would only be an hour or so, depending on how much they wanted to hear, and since she didn't have any personal involvements here yet, it shouldn't be too painful.

In fact, it might prove to be part of her healing.

Chapter 2

Craig camped under the stars that night, on a back slope so Buddy wouldn't get the idea that he was observing him. He could have gone to one of the empty cabins scattered around the forest, provided for the needs of rangers and researchers alike, but when the weather favored it, he preferred to be outdoors.

Over a small fire, he made coffee and heated up some freeze-dried food. The forest sounds changed at night, and he loved the contrast. The wind kicked up a bit, rustling through nearby trees and carrying a wolf howl from a long way away.

The migration of a wolf pack down from Yellowstone still tickled him, although it was over two decades now, and it did create some trouble with surrounding ranchers. The Thunder Mountain pack, however, stayed small, and if it had split, the new pack had evidently migrated elsewhere. So eight wolves prowled this forest, on average, and right now they had some pups they were taking care of.

Moose, elk, bear and pronghorns all thrived here, and were doing better since the wolves' arrival. Forage had increased for all of them, and even the birds had multiplied since they got to pick over wolf leavings. By and large, this had become a healthy, thriving forest despite past scars left by men's gold mining and lumbering, and occasional holdovers like Buddy Jackson.

Which brought him back to Skylar Jamison and Buddy's strange reaction to her. The camera, he had already decided, had to be at the root of Buddy's concern. But why would Buddy be bothered if someone took a few photos? Why would he use the word *spy?* In short, why was Buddy acting like a man with something to hide?

How had he even known Sky was there and taking photos? Was he watching the area through some kind of telescope himself?

None of this made Craig feel particularly easy. Buddy had always been the independent and slightly quirky kind of cuss you'd expect to want to live in the middle of nowhere with his family. No problem there. Some folks were just built that way. But clearly something had changed since last summer, and it was something he needed to look into.

Spying? The word rang serious alarm bells.

Well, he'd do what he could to deal with that in the morning. Meantime he could indulge in more pleasant thoughts, like that cute little artist.

All right, she wasn't little. She was a bit taller than average, and she moved and walked with the ease of someone whose body was in tip-top shape. From what little he could see of her under that baggy, ugly sweater and paint-stained jeans, she seemed to have a nice figure. But her face, even smeared with a daub or two of oil paint, had been winning. Blue eyes, curly brown hair escaping from a ponytail, a face that immediately made him think of a Madonna. Which was something he didn't often think about.

Apart from everything that had been going on, he'd sensed an aura of sorrow around her. A feeling that life hadn't been treating her well recently. Not that he should care. He would do his bit by keeping Buddy out of her hair and in a few days she'd be gone. The way everyone else left.

Lucy had chided him once. "You really need to marry a forester."

"Are you offering?"

That had sent her off into gales of laughter, the more so because Lucy didn't run to men.

The thing was, though, Craig didn't feel lonely. At least not often. Overall he was pretty content with the way things were. He'd long ago figured out the average woman needed far more year-round attention than he could provide, but he loved his life and wasn't about to give it up. The thought of a picket fence made him shudder. So he settled for a few good friends and the companionship of the wilderness. He didn't have a whole lot to complain about either.

The night didn't promise to grow too cold, so he doused the fire with his leftover coffee and climbed into his sleeping bag, pillowing his head on his saddle. Nearby his mount, Dusty, stirred occasionally in the horse version of sleep.

He stared up at the infinite stars and thought of all the people before him who had lived just such a life, from shepherds to cowboys to hunters, and knew he was in good company. It was a great life, and yes, it was missing a thing or two, but they didn't fit. *Que será,* and all that.

He drifted into sleep with visions of Sky dancing around the edges of his thoughts. Simple thoughts, for the most part, because his life was largely a simple one, mostly untethered and unconfined except for the dictate to protect this forest and all its inhabitants.

The next thing he knew, his eyes were popping open to a flaming sunrise sky. Yawning, he sat up and debated whether to try to start another fire and make some coffee. He liked starting his days with coffee, but he'd pretty well put paid to that by dousing his fire pit last night. It was still wet, and an unusual dew clung to everything.

Rising, he made his way to a nearby stream, washing up with special soap that wouldn't pollute the water, then donned a fresh shirt and underwear. While he didn't exactly look perfectly creased, that was to be expected when he didn't touch base overnight. Good enough for what he had to do, anyway.

He saddled Dusty, fed him a handful of oats and promised him better grazing in just a little while. He kept his promise as soon as he reached the spot where Sky had been painting. While Dusty ate his fill of the tenderest shoots of green, he surveyed the valley and across it, Buddy's place.

It sure was a long distance, he thought again. So what the devil had bothered Buddy?

Pulling out his binoculars, he scanned the area around Buddy's place. Even with their aid, he couldn't see a whole lot of detail at this distance, certainly nothing to ring alarm bells.

So what had bugged Buddy? That telephoto lens and

the resolution it could probably provide? If so, Buddy was up to no good. And how had Buddy become aware of it anyway? Just seeing someone return to the same hilltop a few days running shouldn't have been enough to bother him, not at this distance.

Smothering another yawn, he capped the binoculars, let them dangle from the strap around his neck and urged Dusty toward the trail he knew was in those woods. Maybe Buddy would be neighborly enough to offer coffee. Somehow he doubted it.

Before long, he sighted a few hoofprints that told him someone had ridden up this path recently. Probably Buddy yesterday. At least he was keeping his ATVs to his own property. They'd had a discussion about that just the year before last. ATVs did a lot of damage to the ecosystem, and weren't allowed in this forest except in a few places. One or two ATVs wouldn't have been a problem. The problems began when you got a lot of people with them, which seemed to happen nearly everywhere they were allowed.

By the time Craig reached the valley, the sun had fully risen over the eastern foothills and had begun reflecting off the top of the mountains ahead of him. He'd approached Buddy's place from this direction any number of times, and figured by now they saw him coming.

When he reached the creek that tumbled through the valley, though, he frowned. As far as he knew, they'd had a normal snowpack this past winter despite its being warmer, so why the hell did the water seem slower and not as deep as it had only a few weeks ago? He'd have to check that out. If a beaver dam or a deadfall cut the water to the valley by too much, a lot of life would suffer.

Given the warmer winter, they were apt to lose a

whole lot of moose and elk to ticks as it was. They didn't need to be going thirsty on top of it.

Dusty picked his way carefully among the wet rocks, reaching the other side without having even wetted his knees. Not good.

Craig could feel that he was being watched. The certainty settled over him but it wasn't a comfortable feeling. In the past he knew his approach had been watched, but it hadn't made him uncomfortable. For some reason this time it did, and his guard went up although he kept his posture relaxed.

Something sure as hell was going on. The question was what. His instincts insisted on kicking into high gear.

Keeping his pace slow and lazy, he began to wind his way up the narrow track that led to Buddy's place from the valley. The man had a wider road that connected to a county road, but it was out of the way for right now, and not the way he wanted to approach. He wanted this to appear like just another of his friendly visits, visits he made in a neighborly fashion a handful of times every summer.

But as Dusty climbed steadily, he felt as if he were approaching an armed enemy encampment. He told himself not to let his imagination run wild because Buddy had said something a little off the wall just yesterday. But the feeling wouldn't leave him alone. It was such an unusual notion that half of him resisted, sure he must be losing touch with reality. The other half, however, couldn't let go of it.

Yet nothing seemed to have changed. Not one thing that he could see. The atmosphere had changed somehow, markedly. How was that possible?

At last he reached the first signs posting Buddy's

property. There was no gate to bar the way, although rusty barbed wire stretched away in each direction. He passed the signs by only a few feet, though, and waited. He knew Buddy would show up shortly. He always did, and Craig treated those no-trespassing signs with respect.

Up the hill in front of him, he could make out signs of Buddy's house, a log cabin, really, and the out-buildings, mostly hidden by trees. He stiffened ever so slightly, though, when he glimpsed what appeared to be a new cabin under construction. Buddy didn't have that large a family.

Changes. They might signal something, might explain Buddy's sudden increase in paranoia. He wondered if he could find out what was going on.

Soon he heard the roar of Buddy's ATV coming down the winding path. When it rounded the last corner he saw his first cause for worry: Buddy wasn't alone. A stranger rode behind him, a camouflaged stranger carrying a rifle. God, what was Buddy into now?

Buddy pulled to a stop and turned off his engine. "Craig," he said with a nod.

"Buddy." Craig looked pointedly at the guy behind him. "You need someone to ride shotgun now?"

"Just my friend, Cap. I'm allowed to have friends, right?"

"Never said otherwise. You've just never greeted me with a rifle before."

"Been having a problem with trespassers. Seeing a gun makes them pay attention to the signs."

"Guess it would." Nor was there a damn thing illegal about it. "Nice to meet you, Cap. Craig Stone, Forest Service."

Cap gave the shortest of nods. Craig intuitively disliked the man. Something about his eyes, hard eyes. If he learned nothing else, Craig was learning that Buddy was changing *something*.

"You here for a reason?" Buddy asked.

"Actually, yes. You know the public has a right on public lands, Buddy. You can keep people off your property, but not out of the public forest. So if that painter lady wants to come back today, or tomorrow, or any time, she's allowed to be up on that hill without you bothering her."

"She was taking pictures of my place."

So there it was. Craig paused a thoughtful second. "I asked her what she took pictures of. She's trying to capture the light for painting later because it changes so fast. She hardly even knew you were here until you bothered her. So tell me, Buddy, there's nothing about your place that you'd have to worry about being photographed from damn near a mile away. Is there?"

"Of course not!"

Cap seemed to second Buddy by spitting tobacco on the ground.

That answer was too emphatic by a mile, Craig thought, though he let absolutely nothing show on his face. "Didn't think so," he said amiably. "Anyway, just leave the tourists alone. You didn't need me to remind you. As for the lady painter, I'll tell her to point her camera in a different direction if it's got you so worried."

Buddy shifted on the seat of the ATV. "Naw," he said finally. "If she's just a painter…"

"Well, I saw her canvas. So did you, I imagine. She'll be here a few days then move on like everyone else. It's not like she's settling in across the valley."

"I guess not.

Craig started to turn Dusty, then paused. "Say, have you noticed any deadfalls or new beaver dams? Water seems low in the valley creek."

Buddy hesitated. "No, can't think of one. I'll keep my eye out, though."

"Thanks. You know how much damage too little water in the valley would do. We'll probably lose enough elk and moose as it is."

"Ticks are gonna be bad," Buddy agreed. "Too many already."

"Yup. Anyway, if you see me poking around, that's why. I've got to find out why the creek is drying up." He touched the brim of his hat, nodding to both men, and completed Dusty's turn.

Sunlight glinted off something in the undergrowth, and his eye followed it swiftly. A trip wire? Just a foot outside Buddy's fence?

He reined Dusty, feeling the men's eyes on his back as if they were hot laser beams. He didn't turn. "Buddy?"

"Yeah?"

"Trip wires are only legal if all they do is set off an alarm."

"I know that!"

"Then have a good day. And make sure they don't run too far past your fence. Public land again."

Without looking back, he rode slowly away.

Now he was absolutely convinced that problems were brewing, and he was going to have to get to the bottom of it. Soon.

He hadn't liked the look of that Cap guy, either. Hell's bells. Trouble was coming to his forest. He knew it as sure as the sun was pushing toward midday.

* * *

Sky liked being in Conard City almost as much as she liked being out in the forest. The place had a worn charm, sort of like fading elegance, especially downtown. The downtown was old enough to bring to mind images of women in long skirts, maybe some of them sporting Edwardian stylishness, swishing along the streets. There were even hitching posts left around the courthouse square, and the courthouse looked as if it had been lifted right out of New England.

She liked to sit on the benches in that square, amidst the gardens that the city carefully tended, and now, the second morning after her encounter with Buddy, she even received nods and greetings. Some old men played checkers at a stone table with benches beneath a huge cottonwood, and she wondered if that table had always been there or if it had been put there for them.

Her artist's eye was taking snapshots, and mentally framing them as if for a canvas. Maybe someday, if she was here long enough, she'd ask those old guys if they'd mind if she took a photo of them.

She was dressed for painting again, and she liked the fact that nobody looked askance at her splattered jeans, shirt and jacket. It was a fact of her life that sooner or later most everything she owned showed signs of oil paint. Sometimes she joked that it just jumped out of the tubes at her.

She had carried her painting supplies with her and set up her portable easel with a blank canvas on it. On the bench beside her, she spread out her tarp and then opened her box of brushes and tubes of oils. At home she preferred a sturdy acrylic palette, but when traveling she used one covered with tear-off papers, like a stiff pad. The farther she got from a studio, the more problematic cleanup became.

Looking around, she thought about the colors she wanted for undercoating the canvas. Though the viewer would never see them, at some level they satisfied the brain, as if while they might appear invisible, they weren't.

But even as she sat there staring at the stark white canvas and trying to pick tones and hues from the world around her, she knew she was chickening out. She ought to go back to the woods and paint what she had wanted to paint, not hide out here in the center of town.

She shouldn't let that crank drive her off. When had she ever been one to give ground anyway? Four years in the army, some of it in a combat zone, had stripped her of ordinary fears. One man with an attitude wasn't enough to run her off, not anymore.

But then she realized what she really wanted to avoid: Craig Stone. Her attraction to him had been immediate and strong, and she didn't want that. Not now, maybe not ever again. And certainly she didn't want to grow any feelings, even purely sexual ones, for a man who clearly wasn't going to be around except every now and then. Heck, given his job, she might never run across him again.

So why hesitate? As men went, that made him pretty safe, didn't it?

She was used to being very clear about things, at least in her own mind, but the lousy breakup with Hector had left her uncertain in some way she hated. Worse than uncertain, she realized. Unsure. Very unsure. As if she didn't trust her own mind and feelings anymore.

After her time in Iraq, where she'd been caught up in some pretty ugly stuff, she'd had a certain amount of post-traumatic stress. Of course she had. Damn near everyone had it to one degree or another. For some it was more crippling than others, was all.

She'd been fortunate. She'd come home with a bunker mentality, a tendency to jump at every unexpected noise and a total loss of any sense of safety. But she had come back without disabling flashbacks, and after about six months she'd been able to drive again without seeing every oncoming vehicle or object alongside the road as a potential bomb. She knew how lucky she was, especially after spending the past few years working with vets who were a whole lot less lucky.

She didn't often have nightmares anymore, she functioned, she felt safe most of the time and an inclination toward explosive outbursts had been gone a long time now. War was a life-altering experience, and not all its effects would vanish, even with years, but she believed she'd come back as far as she ever would.

This square, for example. There'd been a time when she would have found it extremely uncomfortable here, surrounded by strangers who walked by, with cars moving along streets, windows that stared blankly back at her and doors that could conceal any kind of threat. But here she was, feeling pretty much fine, although maybe a smidge less comfortable than she had felt alone on that hillside with pretty good sight lines. So maybe this sense of uncertainty was all the breakup's fault. Hector certainly hadn't added to her self-confidence any.

Which still left the question of why she was sitting here in the square when the place she really wanted to paint was that hillside from yesterday. That rocky valley and creek had called to her, suggesting both nature's strength and mystery. This lovely but tame park didn't do that.

Still, the morning eased by, the people shifted, cars left and new ones appeared. Birdsong emanated from nearby trees. A wandering dog came up to sniff her, then decided she didn't have anything worth pursuing, like food. It wandered on and was greeted by the guys playing checkers.

She still hadn't pulled out a brush, the canvas sat blank in front of her, and she finally accepted that something about that Buddy guy had triggered problems she had believed she had overcome.

She was sitting here paralyzed, emotionally and physically. The way it had sometimes been after she returned from the war. Lost in some place where even thoughts seemed to fall silent, where time passed unnoticed. Just plain lost.

She tried to whip up some anger, either at Buddy or herself, but it wouldn't come. Moving meant action, and action meant taking risks. Anger was dangerous if it grew too big. She understood all about it.

She had hunkered down again in the silent, safe cave within herself, but even acknowledging it didn't free her from it.

Damn. But the word floated through her mind with little emphasis, as if it came from some place far away. *Dissociation.* She understood that, too. The only question was for how long. Or how she could shake it.

Some portion of her mind managed to remain detached from her detachment, odd as that sounded. It allowed her to observe what she was doing, and started commenting. A learned skill from the therapy she'd gone through after her return.

The problem with her current dissociation was that it provided a comfortable place to be. A safe place, beyond reach. The other side of the problem, however, was that it held her paralyzed and uncaring, and therefore useless. And the observer part of her even rustled up a little annoyance that some jerk in the woods could have put her here again by doing something as insignificant as yelling at her. Man, he hadn't even threatened her, he had just told her to go away and called her a spy.

Still, she didn't move. The day progressed around her, the afternoon arrived with warmth and she was beyond noticing much except the way the shadows moved with the passing hours. She even quit paying attention to the activity around her, instead closing her eyes. It would pass. It always passed eventually. That was one thing she had had to learn to believe, that it would pass.

The morning after his meeting with Buddy, Craig drove a service truck into town to pick up his laundry and dry cleaning, and shop for some fresh food. Freeze-dried and other lightweight foods didn't satisfy him indefinitely. Tonight he was going to stay at one of his favorite cabins in the forest and cook. And maybe even heat up enough water to take a comfortable gravity shower rather than the icy ones he was used to.

Oh, he could have come into town more than he did, but the fact was, he liked his job enough to want to be in the woods as much as possible. And nobody hassled him about it as long as he filed his reports on time. That had taken up most of last evening at the ranger station.

He tossed his cold groceries into an ice-filled cooler in the back of his truck, then headed toward the sheriff's office. He and Dalton were going to have a little chat about Buddy. Not necessarily a big deal, but Dalton had jurisdiction and might be able to learn more about what Buddy was up to. For his part, Craig was confining himself to hunting for what might be damming some streams while keeping a long-distance bead on the Jackson place. Problem was, his duties were going to carry him farther afield. They always did. It was a big forest he had to keep an eye on, from humans to animals to growing things. He couldn't stay in one area too long without overlooking other important things.

But now he was concerned about Skylar Jamison. Maybe he should hunt her up and make a strong suggestion that she paint elsewhere. Who knew what kind of paranoia Buddy was ratcheting up with his new friend.

When he got to the sheriff's office finally, he saw her sitting in the courthouse square with her painting stuff. At least she would be easy to find, and he didn't have to worry about her being out on that hill before he could talk to her.

Inside, the dispatcher, Velma, sent him straight back to the sheriff, Gage Dalton. Dalton had a small office, his desk overrun by a computer on one side and papers on the other. He almost looked glad for the interruption.

"What can we do for the forest service?" he asked.

Craig dropped into one of the wooden chairs facing the desk. "I'm not exactly certain, but I am uneasy. I'm sure you know Buddy Jackson."

"Most folks do. And most folks stay clear. It's not that he's done anything wrong, he just makes people uneasy with all that doomsday stuff."

Craig nodded. "I've been thinking of it as basically harmless."

Gage straightened a bit. "But not now?"

"Damned if I know. That's why I stopped in. Twice this summer he's tried to chase off visitors. Last month it was a group of campers. Two days ago it was an artist who was sitting across the valley and painting. He called her a spy and told her to go away."

"Spy?" Gage repeated the word disbelievingly.

"That was my reaction. The word was over-the-top. So I paid Buddy a visit yesterday morning to remind him he can't drive the public off public land. Just a neighborly reminder, but what I saw bothered me."

"Such as?"

He told Gage about the Cap guy, the AR-15 and the trip wires. As he did so, Gage began to frown. "I can see why you're uneasy. And Buddy's out of your jurisdiction."

"Exactly. But he's in yours. Those trip wires especially bother me. They're just outside his fence, which means they're most likely still on his land, but you know the law about them."

"I surely do. Warning only. Well, I guess I'll have to mosey out that way and have a little chat with Buddy. See if I can do some snooping. The problem with these preppers is that they're so secretive. They don't want anybody to really know what they're up to."

"Of course not. Innocent folks who haven't prepared might come looking for help."

"Only they don't phrase it that way," Gage said grimly. "It's not people looking for help. It's thieves looking to steal and kill. I didn't think Buddy had gone quite that far, but I'll look into it."

"Thanks. I'll let you know if I get wind of anything."

"Same here," Gage promised.

As he emerged into the main office, Craig glanced out the window and saw that Sky was still sitting in the same place. In fact, it looked as if she hadn't moved at all.

"You know her?" Velma asked, her voice scratchy from years of smoking.

"I've met her."

"Well, I'm starting to worry. That girl has been sitting out there since early this morning, and she hasn't moved much since she set up her painting stuff. She's been sitting like that all day. Think I should send someone over?"

"I'll go," Craig said. "I need to talk to her anyway. She's probably just lost in thought."

"All this time?" Velma shook her head. "I hope you're right."

So did he.

"Sky?"

Startled out of her inner silence, she opened her eyes and saw Craig Stone squatting in front of her. Where had he come from?

"Sky are you all right? I was just in the sheriff's office across the street, and the dispatcher was getting worried. She says you haven't moved in hours."

Talking felt like too much effort, but the concern in those gray eyes managed to touch something inside her. "Relaxing," she said heavily. It was hard to get the word out. But a tendril of panic began to penetrate her cave. She didn't want to have to explain what was really going on. She didn't know if she could. This guy probably wouldn't even be able to understand.

"No," he said after a moment.

She watched, still not caring, as he packed up her stuff. "Let's go," he said.

"Where?"

"Someplace quiet."

She couldn't even work up the energy to argue. The observer scolded her, but she didn't care. It would pass on its own. It always did.

She didn't resist as he led her to a forest service truck across the street and helped her in. He tossed her belongings in the back, then climbed in beside her and drove them out of town toward the forest.

"Why?" she managed to ask finally.

"Because I know a thousand-yard stare when I see it."

Wow. That should have evoked a response, but it didn't. She drew a breath, a deep one, trying to sync herself to reality again.

"There's a cabin I'm taking you to," he continued as if they were having an ordinary conversation. "It's one we keep for foresters and researchers. I was going to stay there tonight. Got a hankering for a real meal and a real shower. There's plenty of room, it's peaceful and nobody will bother you."

Except him. He'd walked into her cave. Oddly, she didn't feel any irritation.

Nor did he try to draw her out. The rest of the long drive, he didn't say a word. The shadows had grown lengthy by the time the truck bumped up to a small cabin in a clearing that was only slightly larger. She saw his horse in a small corral, grazing contentedly.

It wasn't until he parked and came to help her out that things began to come together again. Chilly pine-scented air and the quiet of the forest reached her. She was coming back.

For the first time since that morning she felt something: a massive wave of relief. The world began to take on depth and reality again, no longer seeming like a colorless play she watched from a distance.

Inside the cabin, she sat in a rustic but well-padded chair while he built a fire in a woodstove. Soon the heat began to reach her, and she took another long breath.

She was back. Looking around, she took in the basic decor, evidence that this was a temporary dwelling used by those who didn't demand conveniences. He had a lit a few oil lamps and was now heating some cast-iron cookware on top of the woodstove.

"I hope you like steak," he said. "I've got some fresh broccoli I picked up today, but not enough to qualify as a meal."

"I like steak."

He turned from the stove. "You're looking better."

"Sorry."

He shook his head. "No apologies."

"This doesn't happen anymore. At least not for years now."

He pulled a bench over and studied her. "Buddy?"

"I guess. I thought I was fine. I went to the square to paint this morning, then…I don't know. It's been a long time."

He nodded, seemed to hesitate as if not sure whether he should press her. Finally he rose again and went to cook dinner.

Delicious smells wafted around her.

"Sorry the mashed potatoes are instant. We have to make some sacrifices, and I wasn't expecting company when I shopped."

"That's fine." And it was fine. Everything was fine again, fine enough that she stood up. "What can I do to help?"

"You can help later. What I'd like to know is what's going on with you."

She supposed she owed him at least something since he'd cared enough to charge in like Lancelot on a white steed. Well, olive forest service truck. "I'm a veteran. It's been a long time, but sometimes I just…go away inside myself."

"And Buddy caused that?"

"I can't say for sure. I haven't…dissociated like that in years. Maybe it was talking to a veterans group the other night."

"You did that?"

"I work in rehab with vets at home. Somebody told them I was coming up here and they got in touch with me. Although, it doesn't bother me at home. I mean, I deal with vets and their problems five days a week. But the thing is, if it was Buddy yelling at me, I should have reacted when it happened."

He didn't answer for a minute as he turned the steak and stirred the broccoli. "Maybe it was thinking about coming back out here to paint that set it off."

"Frankly, it shouldn't have happened at all. It's been *years!*"

"I believe you," he said quietly. "I'm really sorry it happened. It must have felt like having a rug yanked out from under you."

His understanding was nothing short of amazing. She said quietly, "It took me years to trust my own mind again."

"I know."

"How can you know?"

"I have a brother who never could."

"Craig…"

"Sh." He turned from the stove, smiling. "Let's just enjoy dinner, shall we? You can tell me as little or as much as you want. Or we can talk about all the names of the wildflowers and plants."

Just like that, reality zipped its seams back together and she laughed. Everything was okay now.

Except for the fear, long buried, that this might happen again.

Chapter 3

After dinner she helped him wash up in a kettle of water he had heated on the stove. The simple task was welcome, and it felt good to be focused again.

The thing was, she didn't know what to talk to him about. He'd stepped in and rescued her, but he had also seen a weakness in her that embarrassed her.

Yes, she knew it was normal, given where she'd been. It hadn't happened in a long, long time. There was no reason to think it might happen again anytime soon. But at the same time she had just cratered the trust in herself that she had worked so hard to regain.

He was right about one thing: she felt as if a rug had been pulled out from beneath her feet, and worse, he'd seen her take the pratfall. Not even Hector had ever been faced with that, and they'd lived together.

This guy was a stranger who was now more intimately knowledgeable about her than a guy she had thought she might marry.

Lovely.

He brought out a well-worn pack of cards and they sat at a rough wooden table to play pinochle. They hadn't been playing very long, however, when he said, "You're worrying. I can feel it. Worrying isn't going to help."

She struggled to meet his gaze. "You don't understand."

"Then tell me."

She resisted the thought of exposing herself in that way. He'd seen too much already, and she didn't want to lay it all out there where it would be painful even if he didn't react the wrong way. This wasn't a therapy session, after all.

"I'm fine," she said firmly. "Just fine. It won't happen again."

He frowned faintly but didn't press her. "I went over to pay Buddy a visit. I don't think he'll bother you again."

"Thank you." She hesitated. "It wasn't that scary, you know. I've been through far worse. It was just unexpected and weird."

"I'll give you that."

"I hope I didn't cause you any trouble."

He put his cards down and went to get the tin coffeepot from the stove. He topped off both their mugs before putting it back. "Buddy may be causing himself some trouble."

"What do you mean?" Interested, and now on relatively safe ground, she was able to look at him as he once again sat across from her.

He gave a small shrug. "Well, if I knew exactly what

was going on, I'd have a better answer for you. Some things have changed at his place, not for the better, it seems to me. Right now I can't tell you much except that I did ask the sheriff to pay a visit to get a sense of things."

Sky hadn't considered that. "Jurisdictional problems?"

"Buddy's not part of my forest." One corner of his mouth lifted. "I can involve myself only when he does something outside his own land."

"What didn't you like?"

He sighed, reached for his cup and sipped coffee. "He's got a new best friend, a guy I didn't like on sight. That doesn't happen often. Nor am I usually greeted with an AR-15 when I visit."

Sky felt a cold twist of apprehension. "That's not good."

"It might mean nothing. Buddy's a prepper."

"What's that?"

"Oh, he's been preparing for Armageddon or the end of the world, or revolution for a few years now. A surprising number of people do, so by itself it doesn't mean much. Storing up food, learning to live off the land, all that. It's a quirk, but it's a harmless quirk for the most part, or at least I thought so with Buddy. He showed me around a couple of years ago, and he's pretty damn self-sufficient. I was impressed, honestly, although it's not a way I'd choose to go."

"But you must be pretty much self-sufficient, as much time as you spend in the woods."

His smile widened a bit. "I can get by, but that's short-term. Buddy's prepared to get through an entire year."

"Wow. That must be expensive."

"Some of it is," he allowed. "But Buddy hunts, makes his own jerky and cans a lot of the produce from his garden. It's quite an operation and keeps the family awfully busy." He gave a laugh. "If I were Buddy's wife, I'd probably be demanding overtime pay."

"I can see that." She felt an answering smile curve her mouth. "Children?"

"Six. They all work hard, too, and they're home-schooled. Nice kids."

She thought it over. "I don't see anything wrong with that, if that's the way you want to go. God knows I've seen enough people suffer because they couldn't be self-sufficient."

His smile faded. "You've been in war, right?"

She nodded. "Iraq."

"Me, too. See, that's what bothers me about preppers."

"How so?"

"They really don't know what they're proposing to survive. Buddy might do better than some because he's in the middle of nowhere, out of line of fire except for nature. But so many of these folks really don't have the least idea how damaging and chaotic a real war is. How little safety there is for anyone. If we have some really big catastrophe, nobody's going to be safe. And if any of us are going to survive, we're not going to do it alone in a mountain stronghold."

"Probably not," she admitted. "I've talked to enough Afghanistan vets. To be safe, you have to keep moving constantly. Buddy looks pretty well planted in place."

"Exactly. Anyway, Buddy, if he ever needs to, could probably survive some relatively small social upheaval, but anything major…it's going to be rough on anyone. And I've seen enough of the world to know that survival is more likely when you have a community working together. People helping people, not fighting each other."

She nodded agreement. "But now he's got this friend who worries you."

"Yeah. He goes by the name of Cap."

Sky chewed her lower lip. "That's an unusual name. Do you suppose it's a rank?"

"I'm wondering. And he was the one with the AR-15."

She met those gray eyes again and felt an unwanted shock of desire. Where had that come from? It was the last thing she needed. She dragged her gaze away and told herself to cut it out. "Militia?" she asked finally, hoping her voice sounded normal.

"It's possible." Craig put his cup down and rested his elbows on the table. "Thing is, I don't know. I didn't like the look of this Cap, I didn't like being welcomed with a semiautomatic rifle, and I didn't like the fact that he's got trip wires outside his fence now."

Sky felt color draining from her face. "Trip wires?" She whispered the words. Such things evoked horrifying memories for her. She battered down the blackness that tried to swamp her.

"I reminded him they're legal only as an alarm. He said that's all they are, but I don't know. A year ago, I'd have believed it. Right now, with Buddy getting paranoid enough to bother you and some campers a few weeks ago, I'm not sure of anything anymore. Hence a visit from the sheriff. Sky, maybe you should think about painting somewhere else, away from Buddy."

She thought about it. She thought about it hard because her first instinct was to get stubborn. She didn't run from things, but this wasn't her fight. She'd come out here for peace, not a battle.

But she had run away today inside herself, and she didn't like that. She had to do something to prove to herself that she could handle things, even the Buddy Jacksons of the world.

"No," she said finally. "I'm going to paint where I want to paint, and he'd better not bother me again."

"You don't have to prove anything."

"Yes, actually I do. To myself."

Their gazes met again and locked. Craig returned her stare for a while before finally compressing his lips and nodding. "Okay. He probably won't bother you again anyway. He knows I know about it, and that means others probably do, too. You should be safe now. But…" He hesitated.

"But you're concerned about this Cap guy so I should still be careful."

"You should always be careful alone in the woods."

Something about the way he said it caused another chill to snake through her. "You're really worried."

"I haven't exactly reached REDCON Three yet, but I'm heading that way."

She knew exactly what he meant. Half his attention would now be on Buddy's activities, alert for anything that might pose a threat. "Then I'll just observe RED-CON Three myself. I should be fine."

"Your call." He pulled the cards together and tucked them back into the battered box. "I've got a spare radio you can use. No cell reception in these mountains, but the radio uses a COMSAT link, so you won't have any trouble getting in touch with me or the office. It also has a GPS Nav system."

"Are you sure that's necessary?"

"Maybe not, but I'm going to insist on it. I need to do some poking around. The water flow in the valley creek has dried up some and I need to find out if any of the feeder streams are blocked. And while I'm out there looking for that, I'm going to put a better eye on Buddy. Something about his place is making me uneasy."

That sounded odd coming from a man who created a first impression of self-contained serenity. She supposed that she ought to take that as a serious warning.

But for right now, she was just relieved that she'd made a decision, that she was out of her private cave. That made her aware that she owed this man something.

"Thanks for what you did earlier. Bringing me out here."

His smile was enough to make her melt. "You'd have done the same. Sorry this isn't the Waldorf."

"This is perfect. It's a helluva lot better than a tent in a sandstorm."

That drew a huge laugh from him, one that caused his eyes to sparkle and tipped his head back. "God, I'll be happy if I never have to deal with that grit again. Give me dirt any day."

He brought in two sleeping bags from the truck. "I keep a spare handy in case. I haven't used this one so you don't have to worry. Sorry there are no cots."

"Hey, the ground is great. A floor is even better."

"Yeah, at least there isn't a rock in exactly the wrong place." He spread out both sleeping bags. "No pillows," he apologized.

"That's what I have a jacket for."

"If you want, I'll take you into town for clothes in the morning. I didn't even think of stopping to get you a change. Hell, I didn't even think that you'll want your car if you decide to stay out here."

He was nice, she thought as she climbed into the sleeping bag and zipped it up. Very nice. "What about your shower?"

"It can wait. I don't think I stink too much yet."

He didn't stink at all. He smelled like pine and fresh air, with a hint of wood smoke. All of it good.

Their sleeping bags were necessarily close in the tiny cabin, but soon Sky was comfortable, having punched her jacket into the right shape for her head. Firelight seeped out of the stove, casting dancing shadows around the darkened interior of the cabin.

Much nicer than a tent in a sandstorm, she thought. In fact, it would have suited her well for a long time.

She felt peace creeping into her, the serenity she had sensed around him at their first meeting, and she wondered if it was contagious, or if it was just the surroundings.

Everything seemed awfully far away right now, but not the kind of far away she'd experienced earlier. This was ever so much better.

She turned her head and looked at him. Firelight reflected from his eyes, telling her he was staring at the ceiling, his head propped on his saddle.

"Craig?"

"Hmm?"

"You mentioned your brother."

"Yeah." The fire crackled, and for just a second or two the room grew a little brighter. "I was a marine. He joined up two years after me. I got out just before stop-loss started. He didn't."

"I'm sorry."

"He wanted to make it a career. He would have stayed anyway. But it got to be too much for him. He was at war for an awful long time, Sky."

"Too many were." She knew the toll that had taken, too. She'd worked with men who'd spent the better part of six or eight years in combat zones. Unimaginable. "Is he getting better?"

"He's gone."

She sucked a sharp breath. Words wouldn't come as her heart started to crack.

"I'm sure he's better now," Craig said. Then he turned on his side, giving her his back.

Sky stared at that back for a long time before sleep finally snuck up on her.

Morning arrived with watery light pouring through the cabin's one dusty window and the smell of perking coffee. Stirring, feeling really good, Sky allowed herself the luxury of stretching and slowly waking up.

The cabin was empty, and for a moment she wondered if Craig had left. He had a job after all. But no, he'd said he'd take her into town this morning for clothes and her car.

Then the door opened and he walked in. For an instant he was framed against the brighter morning outside and the towering pines. In that instant he looked almost mythical, so tall and strong, and clad in his forestry uniform.

And so damn sexy. That sexiness didn't just come from his good looks and powerful build either. She was drawn to that serenity, that inner strength he seemed to have. He felt like an emotional oasis in the midst of a stressful world.

She sighed, telling herself to quit being fanciful, and pushed up on one elbow, tossing her hair back from her face.

"Sorry if I woke you. I was out taking care of Dusty."

"Dusty's your horse?"

"None other."

"Well, you didn't wake me. I woke all by myself. That coffee smells good."

"It smells about ready, too. Want me to bring you a mug there?"

"Actually, I need to get up and move. But thanks." She pulled the zipper down on the sleeping bag and stood up, padding in her socks over to the table.

He looked so pressed and creased this morning that she felt grungy by comparison. Same clothes as yesterday, and worse, spattered by paint. Maybe she carried the individualistic artist thing a bit too far. But then, honestly, she couldn't seem to keep clothes for long without getting paint on them.

"I look like a hag," she announced.

"That's not possible." He joined her at the table. "I could lend you a hairbrush if you're desperate and don't think that's icky."

"After four years in the army, little seems icky anymore."

He smiled. "Ain't that the truth. Cereal for breakfast, I'm afraid."

"That sounds so good. I'm ravenous. Something about fresh air."

"The air's fresher outside," he joked. "It might make you even hungrier." But he didn't jump up immediately to get breakfast and she was grateful for that. She wanted her coffee first, and then maybe she'd be capable of helping him.

Feeling around in her pocket, she found a scrunchy and pulled her hair back from her face into a loose ponytail.

"I'm sorry it's chilly in here, but I let the fire go out overnight."

"We wouldn't want a forest fire."

"Exactly."

"I'm fine, really." She looked down at the arms of her shirt. "You must wonder why I'm always covered in paint."

"Actually no. You're an artist. Why, do you get asked a lot?"

"It annoyed my ex-boyfriend. Somehow that little black dress I tried to keep in the closet for important occasions always managed to get messed up like everything else. I joke that the paint jumps out of the tubes at me. Maybe I'm just sloppy."

"Well, I've painted some. Not oil painting but other kinds. The funny thing about paint is that it seems to go everywhere, and you don't notice it on your elbow, or the sole of your shoe, or wherever, until you've messed up something else."

She flashed him a grin. "You *do* understand."

"Yup."

"If I catch it soon enough, sometimes I can get it out. But too often the pigment is a permanent stain anyway." She shook her head. "I look for cheap clothes because I know that before long they're going to be painting clothes."

"That's hardly a crime."

"Well, it feels grungy when you look like you just stepped out of a recruiting manual."

He laughed. "Only because I picked up my stuff from the dry cleaner yesterday. Besides, I have to meet certain job standards. It's not always easy when I'm out in the woods for days on end."

"I wouldn't think so. Life was easier in some ways when we wore cammies."

"Not if you were getting them splattered with paint, too."

He made her laugh, and he did it so easily. She liked this man. She felt a sort of bond with him already, probably because they shared some background, but bond aside, she just liked him. He seemed to have a naturally upbeat nature, and if she had a choice, that's how she wanted to be, too.

He finally got the cereal and a quart of milk from the truck and a couple cheap plastic bowls and metal spoons from the cupboard. The silence felt companionable as they ate and then washed up, this time in cold water.

"Let's get you back to town," he said as he rolled up the sleeping bags. "On the way I want to talk to you about the wisdom of coming back into Buddy's vicinity to paint."

"I thought I'd given you my opinion."

"That doesn't mean I won't press mine again."

"Not a quitter, huh?"

"No more than you."

"Dang marines," she said, but not seriously. That just drew another laugh from him.

Sky was an appealing woman, and he liked what he'd seen of her personality so far. It troubled him, what had happened to her yesterday, for her sake. He couldn't imagine what it must be like to believe you had left all that bad stuff behind only to have it rear up without warning while sitting in a perfectly safe place on a warm, sunny day. That had to leave her feeling insecure.

So he could understand why she didn't want to give

ground to Buddy and his outsized paranoia. It would mean giving up something else, and of course she didn't want to do that. She wanted to face things and get on with life.

And she was probably wondering if Buddy had been the cause of her slip at all. Two days later must make it seem unlikely to her.

He damned the fact that he spent so much time alone. It made him a dull conversationalist. He wasn't one to just make conversation anymore. Maybe he never had been, but days spent alone in the company of the forest, days during which his only human contact might be radioing in to headquarters, had an effect. For the first time he wondered if it was a bad one.

With Sky sitting on the bench seat beside him as he drove back toward town, he felt the silence like a weight. Ordinarily he found silence to be a great companion, but now he felt it like a failing. She must be uneasy inside herself, but he couldn't think of a thing to say to distract her or just amuse her.

Damn.

She was the one who spoke first, though. "Just how edgy has this Buddy got you?"

"Edgy enough that I'm not going to ignore him for a while."

"Is that really reason for me not to paint there again? You said you warned him to leave me alone."

"You and anyone else rightfully on public lands. But he already knew that."

"And that's part of what's worrying you."

"Yes," he admitted. He glanced at her as they drove along the dirt road, and felt the punch of attraction again. *Easy, boy,* he told himself. *The woman's fragile.* Maybe not too fragile, but after yesterday he couldn't count on it. Not that her possible fragility seemed like a problem, except that he didn't want to hurt her in some way with a misstep.

Sky didn't answer as they rounded a bend and gravel crunched beneath the tires. When she spoke at last, it was revealing. "I have to do it, Craig. I'm not sure that's what set me off yesterday. If it was, it was one heck of a delayed reaction. But I need to know I can face things."

She needed to know it wasn't going to happen again anytime soon. He could understand that easily. He'd watched Mark, his brother, fight the same battle and never win, not ultimately. He wanted Sky to regain the security that had been shattered yesterday.

So okay, he thought, he'd have to keep a close eye on her without hovering. From a distance so she didn't feel as if *he* didn't trust her. Damn, how was he supposed to do that? Well, he had plenty of reason to be poking around in the vicinity of Buddy's place, looking for any blocked streams. He'd already given Buddy a heads-up on that, so theoretically there shouldn't be a problem. It would be a way to assure Sky that he was working, not hovering.

So that's the way it would be. Relieved that he'd settled that, he drove right past the headquarters building and on toward town. "You're staying at the motel?"

"Yes," she answered.

"Great place." His tone was a tad sarcastic, unusual for him. Probably a sign that he was getting wound up about things.

"It's not so bad. I've been in worse." Then she laughed quietly. "But your cabin was nicer."

He managed a chuckle in response, but the difficulty of producing it was another warning. Okay, so his isolation was about to be disturbed in a couple of ways.

His days of communing with the woods were going to be disrupted, thank you very much, Buddy.

He stifled a sigh for fear Sky might misinterpret it.

"Okay," he said. "I said I'd give you a radio. Keep it with you all the time, especially when you're in the forest. I want you to promise me that if anything feels even the least bit wrong you'll radio me."

"I can do that." She paused. "You *are* at REDCON Three."

"I'm rapidly getting there."

"Because of me?"

Yeah, because of her. She threw another factor into the Buddy equation, and he was already unhappy with that. "It's Buddy," he said, which was at least partially true. "He's acting out of character. I'm not going to be entirely easy until I know what's happening over there."

"I can help with that."

He almost jammed on the brakes. "Sky, stay out of it. Nobody knows the dimensions of the problem, or if there's a real threat. Nobody. It's not your responsibility. Don't get in the middle."

"I'm not going to turn tail. I'm not going to *do* anything except paint and pay attention. But you're sadly mistaken if you think I'd leave a comrade to face this alone."

When had he become a comrade? Well, of course, when he'd told her he had been a marine. That was going to complicate matters, because he knew that code too well. There'd be no talking her out of this if that was the tack she was taking.

Nor could he see any way to argue with her about it. There were some things the military just stamped on your soul, and that was one of them.

Another complication.

"I won't do anything stupid," she assured him. "I have no desire to. But I'll just be alert and keep my eyes out, okay? I can do that while I paint without being obvious."

He supposed he was going to have to be content with that. But then he got to thinking about what might have set her off yesterday. If she could figure it out, that could be important. He absolutely hated the possibility that it might happen to her all alone in the woods.

"What were you thinking about yesterday morning?" he asked.

"What? Oh, you mean when...it happened?"

"Yeah. Maybe there was a trigger of some kind."

She fell silent long enough for him to wonder if he had offended her. But eventually she spoke, just as they were reaching the outskirts of town.

"Truthfully? I seem to remember thinking how peaceful it was in the square, and how nice to be able to look at all those blank windows and closed doors and not have to wonder what was behind them."

Blank windows and closed doors. "That may have been it," he remarked. "Think about it."

"Perhaps," she said presently. "It could be. It was a funny way for my thoughts to turn, but then I'm usually busy with something and don't pay attention. Yesterday I wasn't busy at all."

"I'll tell you a secret I've never told anyone else." He felt her eyes on him. "When I first got back, I couldn't stand closed doors even inside my own apartment. It took a while."

"Yes," she answered quietly. "And driving. It was six months before I could drive without seeing everything on the road as a threat."

"Yeah. I remember that, too. Once burned and all that."

He wheeled the truck into the parking lot at the La-Z-Rest Motel, next to her car. "If you want, pack up enough stuff so you can stay overnight at the cabin. I can show you the way back later. It's not far from where you were painting, believe it or not."

"Thanks, I'll think about it. Your bosses won't give you trouble?"

"Not if I tell her first."

He bent across her, getting a whiff of deliciously womanly scents that drove his libido into high gear. Crap. The downside of spending so much time by himself was a certain group of unsatisfied needs. But now was definitely not the time.

He pulled a radio out and handed it to her. "You've probably used these before."

She looked it over. "It's very similar to one I had in the army."

"It's almost identical. The government tends to buy big lots." Despite his every resolution and all his good common sense, he couldn't stop himself from touching the back of her hand and then squeezing her shoulder. "Keep in touch. I want to know where you are, okay?"

For an instant he saw a flash of rebellion in her face, but it vanished quickly. Evidently, she understood the sense in his request. "Will do."

He sat with his motor idling while he watched her disappear into her motel room.

Trouble, he thought. For the first time he wondered who was going to give him the most: Sky or Buddy.

Then he put the truck in gear and backed out. Time to get to work.

* * *

Buddy watched Cap's three guys unload nonperishable food from two box trucks into his beat-up barn. The barn would serve for now, until they finished the new cabin and its underground cellars.

What almost nobody knew was that beneath Buddy's own cabin, over the years he'd built an underground bunker for his family. Nothing fancy, but bit by bit he'd strengthened it until it could stand against anything but a direct nuclear attack, not that he was expecting one of those here on his remote mountain.

But now Cap and his guys were joining Buddy, and that meant more food and necessarily a bigger bunker, or at least an additional one. Buddy didn't mind. He kinda liked the way Cap thought, and he liked the control Cap exerted over his men, as he called them. They jumped to do what he said like good soldiers.

But it also gave Buddy a chance to impress Cap, because building underground on the side of a mountain had certain problems. Buddy knew how to deal with them, and Cap didn't. So Buddy might not have an army of his own, but he was an expert in some things. That meant Cap needed him.

As the thought drifted across Buddy's mind, he felt a quiver of unease. It had seemed like such a good idea to join forces with Cap and his group. It helped with a lot of things, like the guns, the ammo, the expense, even the food.

But on the other hand, from time to time it occurred to Buddy that Cap could just take over. That he could decide to run the show, maybe even get rid of Buddy and his family.

Each time he had the thought, though, Buddy told himself he was being too paranoid. Cap had never done anything even to hint that his thoughts ran that way. Hell, if that's what he wanted, he could have taken over already. Instead he was building an additional bunker and cabin, and bringing in plenty of supplies of his own, not using up Buddy's.

So no reason to regard Cap with suspicion. He had no reason not to think the guy was a man of his word.

Preppers had to stick together, after all. If they started turning on each other, no way they'd survive the coming apocalypse.

Nobody was really sure what form that apocalypse would take. Sometimes he and his wife and now Cap would sit around in the evening and talk about all the possibilities, each worse than the next. Cap seemed to lean toward revolution, and Buddy considered that a definite possibility.

He only got edgy when Cap kind of hinted that maybe they should just go ahead and get the ball rolling. But every time he said something like that, Cap would then laugh as if he were making a joke.

The guy had a weird sense of humor.

The three men had just finished carrying the last boxes of MREs into the barn when the sound of an approaching engine reached them. While the trees muffled noises for the most part, the facing hills had a contradictory effect, bouncing sounds back this way.

"Pull those trucks behind the barn," Cap barked at his guys. "Make yourselves invisible."

The three guys hopped to. Buddy enjoyed that.

Cap looked at him. "You expecting somebody?"

"No."

"What about that ranger?"

"Craig? He never comes from the county road. Ever.

Besides, this is my property. The Forest Service stays off it."

Cap nodded. He felt the sling of the AR-15 hanging over his shoulder. Buddy found it strange that the guy was never more than six inches from his gun, especially out here where there was damn all to be worried about most of the time, but that was Cap.

"Maybe I should get out of sight," Cap said.

"Naw. You're my friend. But you might stash the rifle until we know what's going on. For all I know it's a UPS delivery." That was a joke, because UPS dropped his stuff in town with a friend willing to hold them for him. He didn't get deliveries out here.

Joke or not, it got Cap to put his rifle out of sight. Buddy couldn't say why that relieved him, but he knew he wasn't ready to be looking for trouble. Talking to that painter at Cap's prompting had brought him a lot more attention than he really wanted.

The vehicle that eventually rounded the final bend of his driveway and emerged from the trees was a sheriff's SUV. Buddy tensed immediately. The deputies stopped by occasionally, but rarely. Usually neighborly type calls to see if he needed anything.

But coming so soon after his face-off with the artist, he was expecting no good. He grew even more tense as the vehicle crossed the clearing and he saw the sheriff himself at the wheel. Definitely not the usual call from a deputy.

Gage parked and climbed out, crossing the remaining twenty feet. "Morning, Buddy," he called out. "You all doing okay?"

"Just fine, Sheriff," Buddy answered. His heart had begun racing and his palms felt a little damp. He didn't like this.

Gage looked at Cap. "Howdy."

Cap as usual didn't say anything, so Buddy filled the silence, trying to sound casual. "Gage, this is Cap, friend of mine."

"Pleasure," Gage said easily enough, then returned his attention to Buddy. "Hate to bother you, but you know we found that hiker last month. Until we figure out what happened to him, we're just checking on folks to make sure they're not running into any trouble."

Buddy relaxed a hair. "Haven't seen a damn thing unusual." Then he decided that if the sheriff had heard about that painter lady, it might be stupid to ignore it. Might make him suspicious. "I got worried about some woman who was across the valley. Felt like she was keeping an eye on me. Craig Stone says she's just a painter, though."

Gage nodded. "I heard. Just a painter. I can understand why you'd be uneasy after that hiker, though. We're all uneasy."

Buddy relaxed even more. "So you guys are worried?"

"Not exactly. Not yet. But I wouldn't be doing my job if I didn't check around from time to time, not until we're sure it was just an accident. There's a lot of woods out there for a bad guy to hide."

"True."

Gage looked around. "You're building a new cabin. Something wrong with yours?"

"I need some place for friends to stay."

Gage cracked a smile. "I understand that. Sometimes I wish I had a guesthouse."

"Yeah."

"Not that I can do much in town. Sometimes I wish I had a spread like yours, Buddy."

Buddy swelled with pride. "We can do a lot up here, Sheriff. Let me show you the garden."

It never occurred to Buddy that by walking Gage around to show off a few things he might be revealing more than he thought.

Cap would have something to say about that later, but right now, Buddy just felt good. And proud.

Chapter 4

Sky returned to the hill overlooking the valley to paint. Her mood had changed dramatically, though, and she didn't quite see anything the same way. The colors didn't sparkle the same for her, and even the changing play of light didn't capture her interest.

She lay back on her tarp, staring up at the deep blue sky overhead, and realized that her desire to recenter herself with this trip had been interrupted. First by that Buddy guy, then by her dissociation the day before, and now by the memory of the way she had responded when Craig brushed her hand and squeezed her shoulder. Simple, meaningless touches, but they'd hit her like an emotional explosion.

Too much had hit her. As an artist, she knew how easy it was to get blown out of the water sometimes. To lose touch with that creative spark inside her. She knew just as well that sometimes the only way to handle it was to make herself pick up a brush and smear color on canvas, even if it would never amount to anything.

But she didn't reach for her brushes or paints. Instead she lay there trying to sort her way through all that had happened, trying to figure out what had triggered her and why the hell she wanted to be attracted to a man, any man, so soon after her breakup.

Rebound? Maybe. Looking for some reassurance that she was an attractive woman and a good lover? Most likely. But the rest of it?

She closed her eyes, thinking over yesterday morning, trying to put herself back in the courthouse square and get in touch with what she had been feeling. It was the blank windows and closed doors, she decided. Craig had been right about it.

Her awareness of those doors and windows should have alerted her to the fact that she was slipping in time. She hadn't consciously lived with that fear in a long time. In Iraq it had been different. Covered windows and closed doors had become menacing to her. The need to know what was behind them had often been nerve-racking. She knew exactly what Craig had meant when he said that for a while he couldn't stand closed doors even in his own apartment.

It was an odd thing when she thought about it rationally. For most of her life, a closed door had been a protective thing that kept the world at bay. So much better with a lock, to keep threats out, not that she'd lived in fear. Still, a closed door had been comforting, a bulwark.

Then Iraq. Walking and driving down streets where she couldn't see what was happening in those secret interiors had taught her a whole new way of thinking and feeling. A way she had believed she was past.

Apparently not.

Sighing, she sat up and looked around the valley. Good sight lines. Even Buddy's approach had been shocking only because she hadn't been expecting it. Now that she was on higher alert, or REDCON Three as the military called it, she wouldn't be caught unawares again.

No, she wasn't allowing herself to become entirely lost in thought, not now, not anymore. She heard every little sound, and her eyes moved restlessly, checking out every movement. Like in Iraq.

Not good. She couldn't live in this state again, not if it wasn't necessary. But maybe it was.

Craig certainly seemed to have some concerns about Buddy now, and after the way the guy had shouted at her and called her a spy, she shared them. Even if he was only slightly unhinged, it was best to take care.

But she wasn't going to cede ground, and she wasn't going to turn tail, and she sure as hell wasn't going to walk away while Craig dealt with this.

Again, rationally, that seemed like an extreme reaction. It was *his* job, after all, not hers. She was supposed to be on vacation. Yet she saw how alone he was out here most of the time, and she wasn't going to bow out. While he could probably get reinforcements if he needed them, the fact was he didn't have them right now.

So she was going to sit here, being an extra pair of eyes for him, keeping watch on things across the valley.

Probably exaggerating her own importance, she thought wryly, but old training just wouldn't lay down and die. Hadn't she just faced it again yesterday?

Call it sentry duty, she thought. Early warning system. Beside her on the tarp lay the radio, itself like a sudden arrival from a past she'd tried to completely leave behind.

Though women weren't supposed to be combatants, war had changed enough that it was unavoidable. Riding as part of a supply convoy, being shelled by RPGs at a base…women in uniform were as much a part of that as any man. Hell, they'd even given her a weapon to carry, and taught her how to use it. She'd been in a couple of firefights, certainly not as many as a scout patrol, but she'd been caught up in them anyway, in narrow streets with boarded windows and locked doors. She hadn't been safe from improvised bombs on the roads, either. She'd been in two convoys that had been hit, and she'd lost more than one friend.

So she had some scars. One of them had evidently been opened yesterday. Maybe the unexpected encounter with Buddy had softened her up in some way, lowered her guard against her own memories. Add to that talking to some of the vets at that meeting, which had dragged up a few memories, and then looking at those doors and nearly blank windows along the street had finished the job.

That was probably it. She'd just better keep her guard up for a while. While it was just an unfortunate confluence, not likely to reoccur, she sure didn't want to go away inside herself again. She needed to be able to trust that she wouldn't do that. Absolutely needed to.

Yeah, she had something to prove all right. To herself.

She picked up her camera, pulled the lens cap off and used the telephoto lens to sweep the valley and Buddy Jackson's place across the way. It was an act of defiance she needed to make. Spying? She'd show him.

Unfortunately she didn't see a damn thing. Not

even anybody walking around Buddy's property. Some
spy. Almost laughing at herself, she trained her camera farther up the valley. She kept hoping she might
spot a wolf, although she had been assured she probably wouldn't even know they were around unless they
howled. Still, she hoped.

But her small act of defiance lifted her spirits. She
capped her camera and set up her easel with the canvas she had daubed paint on a few days ago. Her spirits lifted even more as she looked at the colors she had
chosen. Amazing, but when she looked out over the valley she saw those colors had changed in just a couple
of days, some growing brighter, some darker.

She was ready to paint again.

Craig was working his way slowly along Buddy's
side of the mountain, checking streams that ran down
narrow gorges to the valley below, all the while trying
to get closer to Buddy's property. He wanted to see if
those trip wires wound around the entire perimeter,
and if so, what they were attached to.

Seemed like a stupid thing to do for an alarm. In
these woods those wires were apt to be bumped by a
lot of things that weren't human, not exactly what he
figured Buddy was worrying about.

Damn trip wires seemed extreme any way he looked
at it. Hikers and hunters could read Buddy's signs and
wouldn't misinterpret the barbed wire fencing.

Giving a mental shrug, he kept Dusty heading
slowly up the rugged slope beside the brook, although
at this point he could fairly well say this brook wasn't
dammed. But it kept him riding within sight of Buddy's property. Between the trees he glimpsed the fence
and the trip wires when the sun reflected from them.

A long time ago, the property had been cleared of trees right along the boundary on both sides. At least Buddy had let some of the brush grow back to stabilize the soil, but not so much that Craig couldn't catch sight of the wires.

He was just ambling along, checking his watch from time to time, thinking that soon he'd head on back and see if Sky had come out to paint and if she wanted to stay at the cabin again. He kind of hoped she would. She'd been easy, undemanding company, and it had been nice to share the place with her. A change.

A snort from Dusty brought him out of his woolgathering and he looked around immediately. Some animal? Dusty rarely reacted to anything except wolves or bears, but he saw none.

However, as he glanced toward Buddy's place he saw two things that troubled him. That movement among the trees on Buddy's property appeared to be a man in a camouflage. Maybe that Cap guy. Buddy ought to tell him that camouflage worked better when you held still.

But then he saw something else, and drew rein. Dusty halted, shaking his head and pawing once.

"Sh, sh…" He patted Dusty's neck and slid back on the saddle just a bit, a cue to hold still.

Something was being built just inside the fence. All the way out here, two-by-fours were rising in a skeletal shape.

Damned if it didn't look like a watchtower.

His neck prickling with the awareness of being watched, Craig turned his attention away from the watchtower as if it didn't interest him at all. He dismounted, holding Dusty's reins, and walked away from Buddy's property toward the gorge, pretending to look down into it for obstructions. Cover. Act like it didn't matter what the hell Buddy was doing on his own property.

But as he pretended to scan the gorge up and down and the tumbling stream below, his mind was totally focused on that structure behind him.

It would have to grow a lot taller to see over the old-growth trees, but as that wouldn't have done a lot of good anyway, unless you were expecting trouble from above, its only purpose could be to post a guard on the fence line.

He'd known Buddy for three years now, and never before had the man gone to anything like this extreme. Something had changed, and Cap's arrival seemed to be part of it. He had to find out who that guy was. Or Gage did. The balance had been changed somehow.

What the hell were these guys up to? Why in the world would they think they might need an armed perimeter? The possible answers to that question didn't settle Craig's mind at all. Nothing was going on around here or anywhere nearby that constituted that kind of threat.

Unless someone on Buddy's side of the fence was doing something illegal or, worse, planning something illegal. It sure wouldn't be the first time such things had happened.

He remounted and rode farther up along the gorge, acting as if it were all he was interested in. He found a place to cross it, then came back down the other side, taking his time, acting as if he hadn't a thought in the world except to check the water flow.

But all the while he was turning possibilities around in his mind, none of them good.

* * *

Sky carefully placed her canvas in its carrying box as the afternoon faded, leaving the light flat and unattractive. She hadn't seen Craig at all that day, or anything else for that matter. But she *had* hoped, foolishly, that Craig would show up.

But why would he? she asked herself. After her withdrawal yesterday, he'd be wise to avoid her. No guy could possibly be interested in a woman with that kind of problem.

But then she scolded herself for even thinking of it. Damn, she'd just been through an emotional wringer over a breakup, finding out her boyfriend thought she was a lousy lover and that he'd been cheating on her. Hadn't she come out here trying to convince herself she wanted nothing to do with a man ever again?

She could have laughed at herself for her inconsistency except right now it didn't feel funny. What the heck was going on with her?

She felt even more foolish because she had packed up enough of her things so she could accept his offer of spending the night at the cabin. But he'd have to show her where it was, and evidently he wasn't going to.

But why would he? She hardly knew the guy, but it was painful anyway. He hadn't had to make the offer if he didn't mean it. That seemed almost cruel.

She wouldn't have thought him the type, but as she'd amply proved, she was no judge of men. Apparently she couldn't tell a nice one from a creep.

Sighing, trying to buck herself up and convince herself not to take things so hard, she finished packing up and began her trek back to her car. The trail through the woods was quiet except for some birdsong and ordinarily soothing, but evidently nothing was going to soothe her today. Silly or not, she was feeling rejected.

Of course, Craig could have just gotten busy with something he couldn't just drop. He probably had all kinds of duties he needed to fulfill. Then she wondered why she was making excuses for him. He was just a near-stranger who had been nice to her a couple of times. She had no right to expect more from him.

She was putting her supplies in her car when she heard a truck approaching. She straightened and watched as a forest service vehicle came around the bend in the road and pulled up behind her.

It was Craig, and he climbed out with a smile. "I was afraid I'd miss you," he said cheerfully. Evidently he didn't begin to imagine the emotional loops she'd been running through as the day passed. Why would he? She was nobody special to him.

"I was just leaving," she said. She hated the way her spirits lifted at the sight of him as much as she hated the way they'd spent the day nose-diving because he hadn't showed up.

"Did you want to spend the night at the cabin?"

"I'd been thinking about it."

"Good." His smile broadened. "Let's get going. Food will be slim pickings, though, since I didn't get to town."

"I filled a cooler with enough for two," she admitted, now that it seemed safe. Odd to realize that she hadn't been feeling safe because she had thought he might be avoiding her. That was over-the-top, surely.

Maybe she ought to just get into her car right now and drive to another state before she grew any more foolish than she already had. But running from things wasn't her style.

She followed him a mile up the dirt road until they

took a left turn into a narrower, bumpier track that she remembered from the other day. Vaguely. She had only been starting to emerge from her psychological isolation at that point and was certain she couldn't have found her way back here.

Dusty was already in his corral, grazing contentedly on rapidly thinning grasses. A water trough near the cabin had been filled, and some kind of feed had been poured into a concrete basin.

"He looks happy," Sky remarked as she climbed out of her car.

"He's always happy," Craig answered. "He's got a good life, plenty of exercise, open spaces and food. I'm kind of like him myself."

Maybe so, Sky thought as Craig insisted on carrying everything inside—her painting supplies, her suitcase and her cooler. As the evening crept up on them, it began to grow chilly. Sky grabbed her jacked off her backseat and pulled it on. Quite a contrast to Tampa at this time of year, she thought. You could have two or three seasons in just one day here.

"Want me to start the fire?" Craig asked as he came out of the cabin yet again.

"How fast is it going to cool down?"

"Air's thin here, so pretty fast. Let me get some more wood and kindling."

She walked around the cabin with him to help, and carried three split logs inside. "Don't you guys keep food here?"

"Not much. This cabin isn't often used unless someone wants to be out here for a while studying something. So there's not a whole lot beyond what I'd call an emergency kit. Survival stuff. I don't like to use it before we're ready to restock for another year."

That made sense to her.

They dropped six logs beside the stove in a wooden box, then Craig went out to split some kindling. Once again she followed him, feeling a bit like a puppy. He was good at splitting wood and asked her to carry a few handfuls of splinters and dust inside while he gathered up thicker strips of wood.

Sitting on the chair she had occupied the night before, she watched him build the fire with quick, practiced movements. "How would somebody do that if they didn't know how?"

He glanced over his shoulder as he squatted in front of the stove. "There's a small propane torch in one of the cabinets. Even a tyro could get a blaze going."

She chuckled, and was glad to realize her mood had improved dramatically. For all the wrong reasons, but it was still an improvement.

With the touch of a single match, the tinder caught and soon flames were dancing along the thicker strips and igniting the bark on the split logs.

Craig remained squatting, watching until he was sure it was burning well, then closed the stove's door.

"So how did your day go?" he asked her.

"Absolutely nothing happened. I didn't see anything, either."

"Good. I guess Buddy got the message."

"Apparently. What about your day?"

"That was a little more problematic. I tried to radio you to tell you I was headed your way, but you didn't answer."

"Really? The radio didn't even crackle all day. Oh, sheesh!" Rising, she went over to her bag and pulled it out. "I can't believe I did that! It was off."

He straightened and gave her a crooked smile. "I guess you *really* didn't want to be disturbed."

But she didn't find it amusing. Still holding the radio, she returned to the chair and sat staring at it. This wasn't good. "This isn't like me."

Craig pulled up the split log bench and sat close, facing her. "Maybe it's the altitude change. We're just about eight thousand feet here."

"Maybe." But she doubted it.

"Talk to me, Sky. I'm sure I'll understand at least some of it."

He probably would. The question was how much of herself she wanted to expose.

"Okay," he said after a minute. "I'll tell you something about me. Fair enough?"

She nodded and reluctantly looked up from the radio. She didn't want to gaze at that attractive face again, into those gray eyes that seemed almost bottomless at times. He drew her, and she was uneasy about that pull. It couldn't possibly lead to anything good, not in the long run.

"I'm thirty-four," he said. "I separated from the marines at twenty-two, then went to college. I studied biology and I'm a thesis away from my master's in wildlife conservation."

"Really? That's impressive."

"It'll be impressive when I finish the thesis. I'm planning to spend the winter on it. I've been collecting data since I joined the Forestry Service six years ago but the university is starting to get impatient with me." Another of those half smiles. "Can't say I blame them. Anyway, never married, never felt the urge. Most women can't stand the way I live my life."

"Why not?"

"Because I'm in the woods a lot. Even in the winter. Too much of a free spirit, I guess."

"I can understand why you like it out here. I like it, too. If I made enough from my painting, I'd get myself a cabin just like this one and paint full-time."

"Yeah?" He seemed to like that. "You wouldn't go crazy from isolation?"

"I hardly notice isolation when I'm painting. Maybe that's one of the things that drove my ex-boyfriend crazy about me. He said I didn't pay him enough attention." She resisted mentioning the lousy lover part. "Between my work with veterans, which sometimes drained me, and the times I'd lock myself in my studio endlessly, he felt neglected."

Craig tilted his head a little, clearly thinking about it. "The guy sounds selfish to me."

"He sounds ordinary," she argued.

"Maybe so. I guess I'm strange. I wouldn't have a problem with any of that, maybe because I'm the same way myself. I occasionally stay in the field for a week or more at a time. Sometimes I get radio calls asking if I'm still alive."

Sky felt her mouth tip into a small smile. "For me it was a knock on the door."

"Ha!" He slapped a hand lightly on his thigh.

"But what exactly do you do in terms of law enforcement? Is it dangerous?"

"Not usually. I run across campers and hikers, check them out, make sure they aren't headed for trouble, that they've got the proper permits if they're planning to hunt or fish. Sometimes I run across poachers. That's a little more dangerous."

"What in the world do they poach? Elk? Moose?"

"Some of that, of course, but my biggest headache

comes from bears. There's a demand in Asia for bear parts—paws, claws, gall bladders. Lots of money in it for a poacher."

"I never thought of that!"

"Most people don't. These types go far beyond someone who kills an elk for food. They can kill dozens of bears on a single trip."

"I admit I don't much like bears. Well, actually I'm afraid of them. But going after them like that is wrong."

"Bears will mostly leave people alone if we don't get in their way. But to go out and kill dozens of them just for small pieces that can bring a lot of money— that goes way beyond killing to eat, or even killing for a single trophy."

He gave a slight shake of his head. "Then we have any number of people who, if left to their own devices, would drain every stream and creek of fish. There's a reason for size and catch limits. We do what we can, but somehow we always wind up having to restock in some places."

"What other things do you deal with?"

"The whole gamut, basically. Right now I'm worried that there isn't enough water in the stream in the valley where you're painting. We had enough snow, the spring thaw didn't start much earlier than usual, so there's no obvious reason that stream should be running so dry so early. It looks more like late July or early August. That suggests there may be some obstructions causing problems on the feeder creeks. So far nothing."

"You have a full plate."

"Keeps me busy," he admitted. "But I like it most of the time."

"How much trouble do poachers give you?"

"Most skedaddle, figuring they can come back.

They're only likely to get angry when I confiscate their booty or equipment, or want to arrest them."

"Do you often?"

"Every now and then, if I have evidence. The ones who really tee me off are those who use traps."

"Traps have always struck me as so inhumane."

"I agree with you."

Relaxing, she was finally able to put the radio aside. The cabin was warming, and she slipped off her jacket. When he fell silent, she guessed he was waiting for her to do her share of talking. She wasn't quite ready yet, though.

"So these trappers. They can hurt more than animals, too, right?"

"They sure can. They cover the traps with pine needles so they're not obvious. They could just as easily trap a hiker, but so far we've been lucky."

"Do you have help?"

"It's a big forest. I only cover part of it. And if we catch wind that something big is going on, we work in teams."

"Good. It's got to be dangerous enough facing down a couple of poachers, never mind a larger group."

"You'd know."

She supposed she did. Benefit, if you could call it that, of having been in a war zone. "It's funny, but I never thought about this stuff. I think of national forests as peaceful places where people going hiking, fishing and camping. I don't even think about the hunting, and never poaching."

"No reason you should."

"When I first saw you I thought you were pretty heavily armed and I wondered what happened out here. Now I know."

His smile was almost as warm as the fire. She liked the easy way he smiled, and wished she could emulate him.

"So you're on vacation?" he asked.

"I guess you could call it that. A little R and R of my own." And this was it. The questions would start coming and she'd have to decide how much she wanted him to know. Then she wondered why it should even matter, since she probably would never see him again. There was nobody safer to confide in than a stranger. But she deflected anyway. "Any more problems with Buddy?"

She saw it happen. His face closed, and she sensed his withdrawal, telling her that he realized she was putting up barriers. And if she was going to put up barriers, so was he. An unexpected ache struck her then. Man, surely she didn't *really* care yet what this man thought of her.

"Well, he's building a watchtower along his fence line. Seems a little extreme." Then he rose and went to open her cooler, keeping his back to her as he checked on what they could make for dinner.

She was being hypersensitive, she told herself. Way too much. It wasn't as if she had some deep dark secret in her past. Well, except for her ex telling her she was a lousy lover, and there was no reason to broadcast that. But Craig had already seen the one thing she most didn't want others to know about her, that she could dissociate, however rarely. If she had any real secret, that was it.

"My boyfriend broke up with me a few months ago," she volunteered. "It was ugly. I started to feel dead inside, you know? Eventually it struck me that I was holding back with the vets I was working with, and that wasn't fair to them, or even helpful, so I decided to get away from everything. Try to find the parts of me that seemed to have gotten either gutted or worn out."

He pivoted as he squatted, and looked at her over his shoulder. His expression was kind. "You picked a good place to refresh. Well, except for Buddy."

"Yeah, there is that."

He turned back to the cooler. "You spared no expense, I see."

"I figured since you were kind enough to offer me lodging for a few nights, a mini banquet was the least I could do. I hope it's possible to cook on that stove, though. For all my military training, I never got much past heating an MRE."

He laughed and rose. "Trust me, nobody can outcook me on a woodstove or open fire."

"Show me how?"

"With pleasure."

But something had changed, and she was quite certain she was responsible for it. She had caused him to grow cautious with her shutdown, and now that she had she wished she could backtrack and be more open. Yet she didn't know where to start. There was a lot of her past she didn't want to look at, and working with vets had made her more of a listener than a talker. So what now?

What now proved easy with Craig, though. He walked her through cooking chicken breasts with some of the Marsala wine she had brought to drink, boiling pasta in a small pot, roasting some yellow squash and zucchini on a flat pan. "Not a whole lot of spices to work with, but we'll manage."

She wondered if she was going to remember any of his tutelage at all, because her awareness of him as a man seemed to be overwhelming her thoughts. Each accidental brush of their hands or arms made flame leap to her nerve endings. A deep ache was trying to grow between her thighs, and it seemed far more important than how to cook on a woodstove.

While they ate, she managed to suppress the longings he awoke so easily, or at least bank them like the fire in a stove. All the while, she knew they were apt to burst into flame again. Desperate for a different line of thought, she tried to bridge the gap again. "Did you always want to be a forester?"

His gray eyes twinkled in the lamplight. "Well, I can vaguely remember wanting to be a fireman, then a policeman. Or maybe it was the other way around. At one point I was determined I was going to be a truck driver."

"When did that change?"

"I was about twelve at the time. We were on a vacation, Oregon I think, and I saw clear-cutting for the first time in my life. Don't ask me why, but that offended me at such a deep level I mentioned it, and my dad responded that they'd plant new trees."

"But?"

He shook his head. "I looked at the big old trees, and those huge swaths of scars over the mountainsides, and thought about how long it was going to take for those big old trees to grow back. I'd be an old man, I figured. Then I started wondering about what all the wildlife did after the loggers came through. The birds, the bears, the raccoons, the beavers, all of it. Then it began to rain as we were driving through one of those cuts, and I watched soil start to wash away."

She put her fork down and studied him. "You were very aware for a twelve-year-old."

"Maybe. I don't know. I just know by the time we

finished that trip I was into it. Researching everything I could find about the effects of clear-cutting and so on, and before long I'd made up my mind I was going to save forests."

"That's wonderful. Truly. But how did the marines fit in?"

"Military family all the way back. Tradition. Every son must serve. Frankly, it never occurred to me to do anything else. It was how I was brought up. What about you?"

"Much more mundane. I needed a job, my father wasn't well and the army seemed like the answer as well as a place where I could do something really useful."

"Some answer. Did you always want to paint?"

She picked up her fork again. "This chicken is really good, Craig. Thanks. As for painting..." She looked back over the years. "I guess it's something I've always done. It's always been when I was happiest, usually. I'm not sure it was ever a conscious decision, but I know one thing—if I can't paint, I get unhappy very quickly."

It was, she thought as she listened to herself, a very boring story. But only on the surface, because there had been nothing boring about her tours in Iraq, and there was certainly nothing boring about working with vets who had serious problems.

But at least he didn't press her for more detail. Boring as it all sounded, why would he?

After dinner and dishes, he suggested they sit outside for a while. The night woods seemed magical to her, with a whole different atmosphere than the daytime. The air had grown cold but she hardly cared as she stretched out on her tarp on a bed of pine needles and looked up at a sky so full of stars she could hardly believe there were so many. She had seen them before, of course, in the desert when the air was clear and there were no lights, but it was a hard thing to remember exactly, just because of the sheer volume.

"It's so beautiful here," she remarked. "So peaceful. It's hard to believe anything bad could happen here."

"Depends on what you mean by bad. Nature can be as ugly as it is beautiful."

"So you don't romanticize it?"

"No way. I just love it the way it is."

She liked that attitude and figured it was probably the best one to have about most things. Of course there were exceptions, but she didn't want to think about the ugly side of life right now. She was enjoying the stars and company too much. And that awareness she had been tamping down sprang to life again. Damn, he was close, but not close enough. "I have a friend who has one of those fancy cell phones with a GPS. She points it at any place in the sky and it will tell her what stars she's looking at."

She heard him stir. "Let me guess," he said with gentle humor. "You'd rather not know the names."

"What good would it do me? The names are artificial. The beauty isn't."

"Like wildflowers?"

"Exactly." A shiver ran through her as a cold breeze snaked under her jacket.

"Want to go inside?"

"Not yet."

"Then let me help keep you warm."

He startled her by curling up beside her and slipping his arms around her. He did it so naturally, as if it were something they'd done before, but she froze anyway. Was he making a move? Part of her hoped he was, and part of her feared it. But already she could feel a warm tingle between her legs, feel her nipples grow firmer as if reaching for a touch. All sense seemed to be slipping away, and even the stars seemed suddenly filled with aching anticipation.

"It's funny," he said. "Given my job, I'm a categorizer. I have to be able to describe every damn thing in order to understand and report on what's happening. I can't imagine seeing things the way you do."

So he wasn't making a move. Disappointment washed through her, but at least it allowed her to relax, at least a little. "Labels have their uses," she finally said. "I imagine it wouldn't do you much good to report that something spongy and green seemed to be eating holes in trees."

His body shook a little, probably with a silent laugh. "I think I'd get fired." Then, "Sh. Listen."

She heard nothing at first except the sigh of the breeze in the trees, and the hoot of a distant owl. Straining her ears, she waited, holding her breath as much as possible.

Then, from a long distance, she heard a lonely howl. "Wolf?" she whispered.

"Sh. Wait."

Half a minute later, the howl sounded again, but this time before it finished, another joined it. Then another. Each one was differently pitched, making an incredible harmony. As she listened, she could almost hear the howls moving even farther away. Then, rather abruptly, they stopped.

"Wolves," he said, answering her finally.

"That was so eerie, but beautiful. How many?"

"Just a few of them. When they harmonize like that, it sounds like there are more. If you wait, it shouldn't be long before the coyotes start. They often let the wolves know they're around, claiming territory."

"Is it different?"

"A lot higher pitched, with yips. More like a dog than the wolves' howls."

She had totally relaxed into his embrace, feeling warm and secure, and now it seemed natural to turn her head a bit so that her cheek rested on his shoulder. After a while, it appeared the coyotes had no urge to stake their claim. She didn't care, though. It suddenly seemed like staying right here forever would be a great thing to do.

A man was holding her and she wasn't nervous. The night was quiet and soothing, and even the chilly air felt good on her cheeks. Why in the world would she ever want to leave these moments behind?

Then the brief fantasy crashed. "Better get you inside," Craig said. "You're going to turn into an ice cube."

The only thing that saved her from protesting was knowing how much she would reveal. She didn't want to be vulnerable to a man, not ever again.

She did a fairly decent job of convincing herself of that, too, as she rose and folded her tarp.

Just an interlude of watching stars and listening to wolves. Not one thing more.

Chapter 5

Craig knew he was being a fool, especially when it had felt so good to hold Sky in his arms while stargazing, but after a night in adjacent but separate sleeping bags, he made the offer anyway.

"If you like it that much here," he said as he got ready to head out for the day, "I can arrange for you to use the cabin for a while. As far as I know, nobody's scheduled it for anything special."

"Won't that inconvenience you?"

"Me? Nah. I can share the floor when I need to." Yeah, right. And spend half the night, as he had this past one, thinking about how good that woman had felt lying beside him in his arms. It was enough to drive Buddy and Cap out of his thoughts. Well, almost. They were still out there like some kind of toothache that was going to need more than a little aspirin before long.

"I've got to go to town," he remarked. "I'll stop at

the station and clear it with them. Then if you want, I'll bring back some food tonight. You're welcome here."

He watched her hesitate and wondered if she was thinking this might be as ill-advised as he was. Damn, he found her attractive, but he wasn't all that sure she felt the same. She'd also told him she was recovering from a recent breakup, so she was fragile in more than one way. If he had a brain in his head, rather than his groin, he'd stay clean away.

Half of him hoped she'd turn him down. Best to cut the link between them before it got tangled in knots and it became a real mess when she went home. That was a sensible idea but he was almost holding his breath anyway.

"I'd like that," she said finally. She gave him one of her rare smiles, one that lit up her face and seemed to light the world around her. "It's great out here. But only if you're sure I won't be in the way."

In one sense she was going to be in the way until she left the state. In another, she wouldn't be a problem at all. He'd managed to build a life where he didn't experience a lot of internal conflict, but here he was, diving in head first. Genius.

"It's cool," he said. "Besides, you're determined to come out here every day anyway. Might as well save the gas. I'll just get enough food and ice for a few days."

As easy as that, it was settled. Well, having her stay there was settled easily. Actually dealing with it was apt to be something else. Maybe he needed to take a look inside his own head and figure out where he'd slipped a cog. Of course, he could always camp out in the open, the way he usually preferred.

As he bumped down the service road with Sky in his wake because she wanted to do laundry and pick up a few things, it occurred to him that after having invited her to stay at the cabin, she might be offended if he took to sleeping under the stars.

Crap, he'd blown it all to hell. He'd failed to keep a safe distance, and now he'd put himself in a position where he might hurt someone unintentionally. Bright, Craig, very bright.

For the second day running, returning to downtown Conard City made Sky uneasy. She told herself to relax, that what had happened to her sitting in the square two days ago wasn't likely to happen again. And it wasn't.

But the uneasiness lingered. She tried not to look at the blank windows or notice the closed doors as she hurried about her errands. She even tried to think about her encounter with Buddy, and how she had probably overreacted, and how unlikely it was that he'd try something again, no matter what he was up to.

Sometimes letting people know about incidents like that provided a measure of protection. If anything happened to her, she knew the first place they'd look. And thanks to Craig, now so did Buddy.

The Laundromat was quiet that morning and she was able to wash all her clothes rapidly while she read a book. Unfortunately, as she folded her things, she noted again that everything carried the marks of her art. Everything.

She sighed, stuffed it all back into her suitcase and car, then headed down the street to the department store. Freitag's Mercantile. The name spoke of another era, and she liked it.

Unfortunately, while she had assumed when leaving Tampa that she wouldn't need much in the way of warm clothing—it was summer after all—apparently folks in this part of the world believed it was summer, too, which meant there wasn't a whole lot of warm stuff to look at. And she definitely needed warm if she was going to spend her nights in the forest.

A nice clerk named Glynda offered to help her, and Sky explained her problem.

"Thin blood?" Glynda's brown eyes twinkled. "Every so often we get someone from your part of the world. It doesn't help to tell them it's actually warm."

"For you, maybe," Sky joked.

Glynda laughed. "But I do have solutions. Layering. We've got some nice summer-weight sweaters, plenty of long pants, a few sweat suits…"

Sky might have splurged except she knew darn well that everything was going to have paint on it before this trip was over. Most of it, anyway. So she settled on some extra jeans, a sweat suit for wear in the evenings and a couple of those sweaters. Glynda even found her a warmer jacket. She hesitated, then reminded herself that she could probably wear it for a week or two in the winter and it would last forever. As long as she didn't paint in it.

With that done, she drove to the grocery at the edge of town, got more ice for her cooler, some reasonably healthy snack foods that shouldn't spoil and even some spices to use if she cooked. There was roughing it and there was roughing it. She'd had enough of the roughest of it in the army. These days she appreciated every creature comfort, however minor.

She stopped in at the station and Lucy gave her a key for the cabin. "Enjoy it," Lucy said cheerfully. "Nobody seems to want it any time in the next month, so have at it."

"Thanks."

Lucy leaned over the counter a bit. "Just be careful,"

she said more seriously. "Craig seems to think Buddy is just a harmless nut, but I'm not so sure."

Sky felt apprehension run along her nerves. "Any particular reason?"

Lucy hesitated, then shook her head. "Sorry, no. It's just a feeling. I guess I got worried when I heard he'd bothered you. Buddy never used to do things like that."

"So Craig says."

"And he's probably right. He deals more with the guy than I do. But just watch yourself anyway. Craig's still in town as far as I know, and I don't know when he'll be back. You've still got the radio he gave you, right?"

"Yes." And she'd better remember to turn it on this time.

"I monitor all channels, so you won't exactly be alone out there." Lucy smiled again.

And with that pleasant thought, Sky headed out toward the cabin to unload and then decide if she wanted to paint or do something else with the day. She was, she realized suddenly, free to do anything she wanted. It was a vacation.

Funny how that idea was only beginning to penetrate.

She'd managed to make most of her trip without thinking about Craig too much, but when she got to the cabin there was no avoiding it any longer. Her mind's eye kept throwing up images of him as she unloaded and carried everything into the cabin. Handsome. Well, okay, better than handsome because he managed to look really good without being at all pretty, or making her think he should be a movie star.

But more important was kindness. Reminding herself that anyone could be nice for short periods didn't help. He was nice. There was something about him that said he was a man comfortable with himself and with caring about others. Very different from her ex. Hector had seemed uncomfortable with strong emotions other than anger, and, like a lot of guys, poked fun at anything that might elicit tender feelings or tears. Guy-tough. Craig didn't seem to have a problem with that, but truthfully, how well did she know him?

After a sandwich she made from some bread and cold cuts she'd bought, she decided to return to her hilltop and paint. Besides, she had offered to be extra eyes for Craig, and so far today she hadn't done it.

She considered walking back down the road to the place she usually parked, then decided against it. If she needed for some reason to move fast, she didn't want her wheels to be nearly a mile away. And this time she remembered to turn on the radio.

She reached her hillside and quickly spread out her supplies and put her canvas on the easel. Today she wasted no time, but squeezed paint onto her palette and set to work. She needed to lose herself in her art, a good kind of getting lost within herself, and forget everything else. Most especially Craig. Heck, he probably wouldn't even show up today. From what she'd gathered, he didn't spend every night at that cabin and he had to cover a lot of territory. Buddy notwithstanding, his concern about the valley stream down below might take him quite a distance away.

In terms of immediate threats, and the size of those threats, she figured the stream was probably a top priority.

Pretty soon she was pleased with the way she had captured an impression of those wildflowers on the mountainside, surrounded by the deep green and shadows of the forest. Leaning back, she thought she'd done a good job of making the flowers appear to glow with a light of their own, creating a sense of mystery.

Feeling content, and realizing she was starting to lose the light, she began soaking her brushes and packing them away.

Then, on impulse, she picked up her camera and looked across the valley at Buddy's place. What she saw made her gasp.

She snapped a quick picture, scanned the valley with outward casualness because all of a sudden she had the worst feeling she was being watched. She snapped a few more photos, then began packing. She didn't want to walk through the woods alone, but there was no other choice. As she hefted her gear, she tried to arrange it so she could use at least some of it in self-defense. She could see no one around anywhere, hadn't heard anything, but that didn't matter.

No amount of evidence to the contrary could dispel the feeling that she was being watched, and that was one feeling she'd learned not to ignore in Iraq.

God, she didn't want to use the radio. Anybody might be listening. She just hoped Craig showed up.

Craig's visit to Sheriff Gage Dalton proved illuminating.

"Buddy seemed normal enough," Gage said, "but I didn't like that Cap guy."

"Exactly my reaction."

"I liked it even less when Buddy gave me a little tour. He's proud of what he's accomplishing in self-sufficiency, but you know that. Unfortunately when he was walking me around his garden, I saw some other things."

Craig leaned forward, his interest surging. "Such as?"

"He's bringing in an awful lot of supplies. Some trucks were coming toward me as I drove out there, and I could clearly see they came from Buddy's. There's nothing else up that road anyway, except for the ghost town, and that's pretty much off-limits.

"Anyway, he's filling up his barn, to judge by what I could see through a crack where a door wasn't completely closed. And then there are the footprints."

"Footprints?"

"I figure there are at least four other grown men out there in addition to Buddy and Cap. No evidence of women or children, though, other than Buddy's."

"How'd that strike you?"

"Probably about the same way it's striking you. Why would he need more men out there? He's been all about his family surviving a catastrophe. If he wanted another family out there, that would fit with what I thought I knew about him, but four men? That Cap guy in particular. I managed to get a photo of him I'm going to run through recognition software, but that might take ages."

Craig frowned, feeling his uneasiness about Buddy deepening. Worse, he felt a leap of concern for Sky. She was out there alone today. Not good, considering Buddy had already confronted her. The small comfort that came from knowing that Buddy was aware that others had heard about the confrontation grew smaller with each word that Gage spoke.

"Militia?" he said finally, hating the word.

"Possibly. I don't have enough to say anything for sure except I'd feel a whole lot better if I saw another *family* out there, not a bunch of men."

"I didn't like being greeted with an AR-15."

Gage nodded. "That's not typical either. I've known Buddy a lot longer than you have, and while I've always thought him to be a character—and Lord knows we've got enough characters in this county—I always counted him as harmless. I figured that if Buddy ever became a problem, it would be because the world was blowing up. Now I'm wondering if he's being used by someone with plans."

"Action type plans?"

Again Gage nodded. "Buddy's prey to conspiracy theories. Give him the right one, and you could manipulate him easily enough."

"Well, then, we don't want to do anything that might make him easy to manipulate. Make him think the government is after him. This is going to make watching him fun."

"I'm tempted to call a friend in ATF, but we don't have a thing to give him yet that would get him out here."

"Plus, if Buddy or his friend note that a lot of strangers are hovering around in the woods, it could make things harder." Craig sighed and stood up. "Okay. I've already made the excuse of needing to find out if some of the streams are blocked. That's how I saw that damn watchtower out there. But right now I'm concerned. The painter lady is out there by herself, and Buddy already confronted her once. I need to get back."

"Just watch your own back, too. I didn't like the feeling I was getting when I was out there." Gage shook his head. "I probably don't need to tell you, but when I was in DEA I learned never to ignore those feelings that something wasn't right. I've had that feeling ever since I talked to Buddy."

By the time Craig finished the food shopping he had promised to do, he was appalled at the amount of time that had passed. Despite his urge to get back to Sky as quickly as possible, somehow the hours had advanced, and now he still had a one-hour drive to reach the cabin.

His problem, he thought, as he drove as fast as he could back to the forest, was that he didn't have much of an internal clock anymore. His days were guided by the sun, not a wristwatch, and in town, farther away from the mountains, twilight came later. Once in the mountains, it fell fast because the sun generally vanished behind the peaks by about three. Down here, the lengthening shadows were a useless guide to him.

Even with budget cutbacks the service still had three full-time rangers, and a half-dozen seasonal foresters. There were some volunteers, too, mostly from the forestry college, but he didn't want to involve them. All he could really do, he decided, was tell Lucy to warn everyone to be on the lookout for anything unusual, and report it if they saw anything.

If Buddy and his new friend were converting his place into an armed camp, they might also be sending out patrols.

Why? Because that's what a good military commander would do, and he was definitely wondering about Cap. Militia, former military, whatever, he was willing to bet the guy wanted something more than a place to hunker down if the world went to hell.

The question was what was he planning. Supplies coming in by the truckload? Craig wasn't exactly versed on militias, but he knew for damn sure he didn't want one in his forest unless it played by all the rules and laws.

And then there was Sky out there on her own. Hell, he probably never should have allowed that. He could just imagine her firing up and saying she was able to look after herself, and he would mostly agree. She was the one, after all, who'd insisted on having his back.

On the other hand, he'd left a buddy out there alone. What the hell had he been thinking?

Maybe his problem was he just couldn't believe that things were getting dangerous. He certainly didn't have any real proof of it, except for Buddy's asinine behavior with Sky, but the uneasiness persisted and he needed to stop quashing it.

If it turned out that everything was fine, that nothing nefarious was happening, so much the better. But if he ignored his gut and something bad happened, he'd never forgive himself.

Time to be hypervigilant.

Lucy proved happy to put everyone in higher gear. Maybe she found it mostly boring to hang out at the station all day, Craig thought with mild amusement. Still, she was the one who wanted to go home every night, unlike some of the others. Something like new love, perhaps. Craig smiled inwardly. He supposed three months was too soon for a relationship to reach a state of calm.

Regardless, it wasn't like this place was overrun with visitors. It was a forest in the purest sense of the term, a preserve for the future. It had none of the attractions of a park and it was pretty much off the beaten path. With Yellowstone a couple of hours to the north, about the only people who wandered these woods were locals who wanted to hunt or fish, or some really determined hikers seeking isolation. Or poachers. Or, he thought with a grimace, logging trucks.

He had to dodge one his way up the road. As usual, it was moving too fast. A glance at its load told him it was carrying some fresh-cut lumber from farther north where they needed to thin out some trees that appeared unhealthy. He'd seen the devastation bark beetles alone could create so it was important to remove trees that created fertile ground for invaders. Not that they'd completely succeed. Mother Nature always managed to hold the trump card.

He passed the turnout where Sky usually parked and saw she wasn't there. He hoped he'd find her at the cabin. Driving a little faster than he should on the loose gravel, he headed up there.

They were going to have a talk, he decided. No more half joking about REDCON Three. It was time to move up the readiness scale, if only because his gut said so.

Sky made it back to the cabin without any trouble. Once inside, she dropped the wooden bar on the door, feeling a little silly. After all, nothing had happened, she'd just had a feeling. A creepy feeling, yes, but nothing more. But that photo she'd taken was burning a hole in her mind and she desperately hoped Craig would show up.

Then she dithered about whether to light the stove. It wasn't that cold yet, it was too early to think about cooking and she didn't want to cook anyway until she had some idea of whether she'd be cooking for one or two.

About the only comfort she had right now was that her radio hadn't done much but crackle with static during the day. Nothing was happening. Nothing at all.

She set up her canvas on the easel in one corner so the paint could dry more overnight, lit an oil lamp and tried to school herself to patience. Usually that wasn't a big deal for her, but today it was blowing up into one.

She had no idea whether she was impatient because

she might have news to share, or simply because she wanted to see Craig. And right at that moment she didn't care which it was.

Finally, she forced herself to sit and wait.

Craig pulled up beside Sky's car at the cabin, switched off the ignition and waited a moment, listening to the engine tick as it cooled down. His window was open, and the quiet of the woods was welcome. That quiet meant a lot to him, because here it was a safe quiet, and once quiet had meant danger, or worse, it hadn't been quiet at all.

Sky emerged from the cabin, standing on the little plank stoop that served only to catch mud when the weather got messy, and something about the way she looked seemed to reach out to him like a physical touch. He forgot all about the groceries and swiftly climbed out. Her eyes seemed too big, and there was a tension in her face. A tension and something more.

That something more drew him across the distance. Without a thought for common sense or anything else, he hauled her into his arms, holding her tight, pressing her cheek to his shoulder. "Are you all right?"

No words could describe how he felt when her arms wound around his waist and squeezed.

"I'm fine, really. Just edgy."

"Did something happen?"

"Not exactly. Well, no, nothing happened, but I have something to show you."

His interest piqued but not enough to make him let go of her. Not yet. She felt perfect in his arms, as if she had been made to fit against him just right. He'd had girlfriends before, even a serious relationship or two, but he couldn't escape the awareness that no woman had ever fit like this in his arms. Not once.

The feeling was so extraordinary that he totally forgot everything else. With his finger, he tipped her face up. Her blue eyes widened, then reflected a yearning that echoed his own.

That did it. Bending his head, he kissed her. His mouth barely touched her soft lips before a tsunami of hunger roared through him. Thought fell away as primal impulses took charge. A sense of amazement burst in him, almost like a firecracker, as he wondered how he could react so fast and deeply, but that went away, too, as his entire existence became focused on one thing only: Sky's soft, warm mouth, the way it welcomed him and answered him.

His blood started to pound, his groin throbbed. Desire rapidly swept him toward a place of enchantment, where everything else ceased to exist. Any second now, he would be lost in her.

But then he sensed something. A hesitation from her. An almost tentative and uncertain quality to her kiss. It acted almost like a dousing of cold water. What was he doing? He knew she was fragile, he could hurt her by simply being careless, by plunging ahead too fast.

Hell! Catching himself with difficulty, he lifted his head and looked down at her drowsy blue eyes, and her lips, just starting to grow a little puffed from his kiss. Behind the obvious desire he saw there, he saw something else, too: fear. She was afraid, maybe of him, maybe of being hurt. He didn't know. He just knew he couldn't push her into something she wasn't ready for.

So he tried a crooked smile and said huskily, "That was very nice."

Her eyes widened a bit, but her arms had loosened,

and reluctantly he let her go. She turned away quickly, leaving him to wonder what he'd done wrong. Kissing her? Or stopping? He swore inwardly and touched her arm.

She looked back and now her eyes were pinched. Crap, he had done something wrong. He wondered how the hell he could find out, but his brain was still half-thick with interrupted passion and he wasn't feeling terribly bright. No question occurred to him that might actually glean a response without making things worse.

"Sky?" It was a question, but she didn't answer. "I'll get the groceries I bought."

Her face relaxed a bit. "I bought some, too."

"Then we might have to be little pigs tonight."

The tightness vanished completely and she laughed. "I'm famished. I didn't eat much today, so I may shock you."

"I'd enjoy watching a woman with an appetite eat. Say, can I ask you something?"

She faced him fully. "Sure."

"Why is it that when I take a woman out to dinner she pecks at her food?"

"It's a social thing, I guess."

"What do you do? Eat before you go out?"

A giggle escaped her. "Actually, yes."

He just shook his head. "Don't do that to me. I like to enjoy my food and it's hard to do when my dinner companion is displaying anorexia."

She laughed, and the tense moments slipped behind them, although he still didn't have an answer to what had happened. Wires were definitely crossed somewhere.

He carted the food he'd bought inside, most of it non-perishable. Looking around he realized she had had the same idea. "We're stocked for quite a while unless we want something fresh."

"I didn't start cooking because I didn't know if you were going to be here," she admitted.

Again he thought he sensed a hint of trepidation. Was this all about her recent breakup? He guessed it was possible.

"Actually, I'm not going to be leaving you alone, not much. I may not always be in sight, but after talking to the sheriff today…" He let it hang.

"That's right!" She hurried to get her camera bag. "I saw something today. I hope the photo turned out all right because I think you want to see this. The viewing screen is small, though."

She pulled out her digital camera and begin clicking some buttons. Then she held it out to him.

He peered at the two-by-three screen. The photo had been taken from quite a distance, and even the telephoto lens hadn't been enough to make it huge. But what he thought he saw was enough to make him stiffen.

"I've got a laptop in my truck," he said. "Can you hook your camera up to it?"

"Of course."

He hurried out to get his laptop, checked to make sure he didn't yet need to put it on the car charger, then carried it back inside. He had a pretty good idea of what he was going to see even from the tiny image on her camera, but he needed to be sure.

He powered up his computer on the rickety table and Sky hooked up her USB cable to it. Moments later the picture appeared on the screen. In the enlargement, there was no mistaking it.

A row of four men stood in a straight line at attention, and all four of them had AR-15s slung over their shoulders.

In front of them stood the unmistakable figure of Cap, as if he were running a drill.

He lit the fire in the stove, as the evening chill was beginning to penetrate the cabin, but neither of them made any move to cook immediately, other than that Craig wrapped some potatoes in foil and put them on the stove's top. Nor did Craig say anything.

Eventually, Sky asked, "Did you get the same impression from that that I did?"

"I imagine so." He sat on the bench, looking over toward his computer where the picture still showed, then back at her. "I need to get this to Gage. I wish I had internet out here, but I suppose it can wait until morning. No need to press the panic button yet."

"Probably not," she agreed quietly. "But that looks a whole lot like a militia, or at least one that's getting started."

He nodded. "And not at all what I would have expected from Buddy. Either I seriously misjudged that man, or this Cap guy has found a way to manipulate him."

"But militias aren't necessarily a problem."

"Not necessarily. Not when they're the kind of guys who go out on weekends and play war games in the woods. When they start building armed compounds, though, they deserve some extra scrutiny."

"That does seem like an awful lot of firepower."

"Yeah." He fell silent as the two of them stood at the stove, cooking a steak and steaming some vegetables. The baked potatoes let out a hiss of steam.

"I'm not sure I timed this right," he said eventually. "I'm used to throwing my potatoes right into my campfire."

"We can eat in courses."

"Yeah." He flashed her a smile that didn't make it all the way to his eyes.

Sky basically muddled around in her own thoughts and emotions, a mix again. This man made her want things she thought she didn't want anymore. Then the kiss had ended so abruptly, she wondered if she had proved her ex right, that she was a lousy lover. Or if something else had made him draw back.

Then there was the whole thing going on at Buddy's. She was no ordinary woman with ordinary instincts, not after her tour in the army, and she wondered if she was leaping to conclusions about some men who were just playing soldier. Yes, that photo made her uneasy, but really, it might just be a game.

She glanced sidelong at Craig, who was turning the steak, and wondered if he had the same questions. Right now, though, if they were going to talk, Buddy seemed like the safest subject.

That or the classification of wildflowers.

Chapter 6

Sky wished she found Craig less appealing. She wished she knew how to kiss better because then maybe he would have kept on. Maybe she was nuts, but she felt that making love with him might turn into one of the best experiences of her life. She certainly wanted to.

But that was evidently going nowhere at all. Much as she tried to tell herself that was for the best, she couldn't escape a sense of disappointment. On the other hand, did she want to discover that her ex had been right about her?

Not really. Sometimes delusions were good things, and believing Hector had been wrong could be a useful delusion to carry. For all she knew, it might even be true. She certainly didn't want to learn that he had been right.

She checked the steaming veggies. "Just another minute."

Craig stuck a fork into the potatoes. "Well, these won't be far behind. The steak is on the edge of ready, too."

A short time later while they ate, she decided to tell him more. "I had the feeling that I was being watched out there."

"This afternoon?" He lifted his head to look at her.

"Yeah. Right around the time I took the photos. I tried to act like I was taking pictures of the whole valley, but that creepy feeling didn't quit. They might have been watching me through binoculars. Or I might have imagined it."

"You know better." He said it firmly.

"You're right, I do."

"If there's one human instinct that's rarely wrong, it's the sense that we're being watched. Hell. I need to poke around and see if I can find any evidence that someone was out there with you."

"I doubt you can find much. I didn't see anyone or hear anything, and I was alert for it. Pine needles are so thick in those woods they don't leave a good trail."

"Unless someone is on horseback and the hooves scuff them. Or someone is careless."

She pointed to the monitor. "Those guys don't look like they'd be careless. But they were down there, not anywhere on the hill where I was, obviously."

"That assumes they're the only ones working with Buddy."

She hadn't thought of that, and her heart quickened. "You think there might be more of them?"

"I wish I knew."

She frowned for a minute, arguing with herself. How much trouble did she want? This was supposed to be a little rest and recuperation, after all. But other instincts were kicking into high gear anyway.

"I'll wander in the woods a bit tomorrow, like I'm looking for another vantage for painting. I'll let you know if I see anything."

He shook his head. "I don't want you taking risks."

"Craig, I was a soldier, too. I think I know something about patrolling and self-defense. I'll be just fine. I'm not going to do anything to make anyone suspicious. Besides, I was hoping to find a ravine, something rocky and deep, to paint. I was going to be looking for that soon anyway."

He looked as if he were about to object, but instead forked a piece of steak into his mouth and chewed hard. The steak was nowhere near tough enough to demand that kind of attention, and she almost wanted to giggle.

"You've got to make me some promises," he said finally.

"Such as?"

"You won't wander too far, you won't go anywhere without your radio and if anything creeps you out, get the hell out."

She couldn't resist. "Are you going to throw me out of the forest if I don't promise?"

"Sky…"

She laughed quietly. "You usually seem so calm, I couldn't resist. Okay, I can promise that." And she could. It was basic common sense.

His expression relaxed. "Sorry. I guess I'm too used to taking command. I don't mean to underestimate your abilities. I just worry. I'm supposed to take care of the people in this forest."

She felt herself softening, too. She liked it when his face settled into gentle, calm lines. "I won't do anything stupid. But even if nothing else were going on, I'd be looking for a different vantage. I want something less peaceful and more energetic to paint."

He waved to the impressionist painting sitting in the corner on her easel. "That's not exactly pastoral. I can feel energy popping out of it."

"Really?" She looked at the canvas and smiled. "Thanks. I wasn't sure."

"You can be sure. I'm no art critic, but it's brimming with life. Wildflowers never looked so lively. And the shadows…" He thought a minute. "Somehow it feels almost haunted. Or haunting. Like the woods have spirits."

"You just made me feel like a million dollars. That's what I was reaching for."

"I think you got it." His gaze tracked back to her. "I spend so much time out here I get to feeling as if it's all alive. As in sentient."

She nodded slowly. "I was getting that feeling, too. As if there's some kind of consciousness out here. Different from ours, but very real. Don't Native Americans believe that?"

"Some do, at least, but I wouldn't venture to speak for them all. Have you ever read about Black Elk? He was an Oglala Sioux holy man."

"Afraid not."

"He wrote something that struck me deeply. I don't remember the exact wording, but it stayed with me anyway. Something about how when you cut a lodgepole pine you should always give the tree thanks for its gift."

Sky turned that around in her head, considering all the nuances. "I like that, too. And it would be a good way to live, always thanking the earth for its blessings. We might be better caretakers."

"I try to always keep it in mind."

She realized she had gotten a glimpse of this man's soul, and perhaps part of what made him seem so tranquil much of the time. For him, protecting nature wasn't just a job. He was protecting life of all kinds, taking care of the earth, and perhaps it seemed to him that his calling was at least somewhat holy. Not exactly a religion, but sacred in a way.

She liked that. She had seen enough destruction for one lifetime, and was more than ready to consider all life sacred. Even the rocks and trees, come to that.

After they washed up, he showed her how to use the gravity shower. Even though there was a holding tank into which she could pour some stove-heated water, she had a feeling the experience would be reminiscent of a few she had had in Iraq. Pull the chain, the water would be all the wrong temp, wash fast, pull the chain again...

"Or," he said, "you could continue to go to town anytime you want a real shower. I wouldn't advise the streams, though. That's really cold. But if you decide to go that route, there's biodegradable soap and shampoo on that shelf."

Not to mention she was beginning to wonder just who was wandering around in the woods. No, it would be the gravity shower or a trip in to her motel room. She had already paid in advance for an entire month.

Night had settled fully, and she decided to pull out her new jacket and stargaze again. The nighttime woods had a beauty all their own, one she probably couldn't justify in paint, but one she could feel all the way to the depths of her being.

She sat on her tarp with her knees up, arms wrapped around them. A few minutes later, Craig joined her with two cups of coffee. She noticed he put a safe distance between them.

"I love sleeping in the open," he remarked.

Well, that was a nice way of telling her she'd probably have the cabin to herself tonight. She almost sighed, then stopped herself. It was hard, she thought, to get to know somebody new. In fact, it was so hard she wondered if a lot of relationships lasted long beyond their expiration date simply because nobody wanted to go to that much trouble again.

But this was different. This was never going to amount to anything, so no effort was really required. Just take it for what it was and skip the social anxiety.

"So you'll be going to see the sheriff in the morning? What exactly happened?"

Craig turned a little toward her, sitting cross-legged. "Well, it turns out he was right. He saw evidence that there were at least four men there beyond Buddy and his family, and it bothered him that he didn't see them. As if they were trying to stay out of sight. And he didn't like that guy called Cap either."

"Sounds unanimous."

"Apparently. Anyway, when I was out riding along one of the streams looking for obstructions, I saw something *I* didn't like—a watchtower under construction."

She stiffened a bit, turning her head to look right at him. "What does he need a watchtower for?"

"Exactly what I was wondering. You know, Sky, I admit I've only known the guy for three years, but he never struck me as the sort who'd want to build an armed camp. At least not without some reason. Being out in the middle of nowhere like this mostly obviates the reasons. You tell me how many people are likely to show up at his place if a meteor drops out of the sky.

And if Yellowstone erupts, there aren't going to be any of us around anyway."

"What a thought!"

"It's true. Not likely in our lifetimes, but true anyway. Regardless, this is a pretty thinly populated place. Most of the ranchers are fairly self-sufficient to begin with. You take the townspeople, and I think this would be the last place they'd come. Besides, Buddy, being a prepper, isn't exactly advertising what he's doing. His family has been here forever, they've never been really sociable from what I hear and I doubt anyone thinks of him very often if at all. The sheriff and I know he's a prepper only because we see him so often and he's let a few things slip."

"So?"

"So I don't think he'd cross a single soul's mind if a catastrophe happened. People in town would pull together, the ranchers would hunker down and help who they could. But nobody would be on the way to Buddy's place. I'd bet on it."

Sky nodded and tipped her head back so she could see the stars and avoid looking at Craig. It seemed hazier tonight. She wished that haziness would encompass the man beside her, because every dang time she looked at him, the yearning blossomed anew. "I wonder if he's considered the downside to that."

"What do you mean?"

"If something bad happens and he needs help, nobody's going to think of him then, either."

Craig's laugh echoed off some nearby tree trunks and rocks. "That's a good point." He reached out, clasped her hand and squeezed, then released her. She regretted the loss of his touch nearly as much as she would have regretted the loss of air to breathe. She envied him suddenly, because if he felt the same attraction, he was doing a far better job of handling it. She tried to stiffen her own spine.

She forced her thoughts back to the subject at hand. "Maybe it was just brainwashing, but the army taught me we can all do a lot more and be a lot safer in a unit. Solo actors just got into trouble or caused trouble."

"I don't think that's brainwashing. I think it's true. Humans need community to survive."

"Says the guy who lives like a lone wolf."

He laughed, but shook his head, hard to see in the dim starshine. "Not entirely a lone wolf. I need my compadres in the service. In fact, they're coming in closer to help me keep an eye on this situation. Given that this is our busiest time of year, I can't get them all, but we won't be alone indefinitely."

"For busy this seems awfully quiet."

"We've got maybe seventy or eighty hikers out here now. I can't be exactly sure because not everyone checks in. Regardless, there's a whole forest to watch, not just this place, but we'll get some help."

She nodded, actually glad to hear that. "If we're going to play hide-and-seek in the woods, more people will help." Then she looked up at the heavens. "The stars seem dimmer tonight. Almost as if there's a haze. Is it going to rain?"

"There's none in the forecast but it's always possible since we're in the mountains. Weather can change fast."

"I wish I could capture how that sky makes me feel on canvas. But for once my imagination fails me. Every mental image I get would be blah, and no way would it do justice to what I feel looking up. That sky, even with the haze, seems so deep, so big. A canvas would confine it and flatten it."

"Maybe that's why there are so few paintings of moonless nights."

"Maybe so." She shivered a little, and hugged her knees closer. It was getting a lot colder out here.

"Want to go in?"

"Not yet," she answered. Not yet. The beauty out here was worth shivering a bit. Besides, once inside the temptation to give in to desire would simply grow.

Surprising her, he scooted over and drew her close to his side. "Maybe this will help."

Well, of course it helped. He might as well have struck a match to her. The chill vanished in a sudden wave of internal heat. Not good, she groaned inwardly. What the hell was happening to her? She couldn't remember having this much trouble corralling herself, even with Hector.

That thought brought her up short. Really? *Really?* She cast her mind backward, trying to remember what her initial days with Hector were like. She had certainly believed she loved him, she had found him attractive, but she honestly couldn't remember having felt like this. That attraction had been quieter, more under her control.

It hadn't struck her then, but it struck her now, that maybe that wasn't such a good thing.

Think about something else. Anything. Buddy provided an immediate source of distraction.

"This militia thing," she said. "What could they hope to accomplish? It's not like they could take over anything. Those things never end well."

"I guess it depends on what they want. Attention? Creating terror? I agree they won't get very far if they try something, but how far do you have to get to create an impact?"

"True. God, I hope they're not planning something." Such horrors were no longer abstract for her and it was beyond the scope of her comprehension that someone would willingly choose to cause such things except with extreme provocation. What provocation did Buddy have? Of course, there was still that guy called Cap. Who knew what motives he might have?

Come to think of it, she was getting awfully sick of Buddy and she didn't even know the guy. She had come out here for peace, quiet and the restorative benefits of painting and solitude. Instead a total stranger had walked her into something that inevitably harkened back to Iraq. She really ought to just pack up and go somewhere else.

But she knew she couldn't, wouldn't, do that. She hadn't been exaggerating when she had said she would never abandon a fellow soldier, and she meant it. She couldn't leave now. She got the feeling Craig didn't have a whole lot of help, so unless they found a reason to call in the Feds or ATF or something, she would do what she could to help. She was going to have his back.

No escaping that. It was a kind of loyalty that was rooted deeply in her, and it didn't require a personal relationship to validate it.

So here she was, sick of thinking about Buddy and company, not wanting to think about her attraction to Craig and just clean wiped out of conversation and other thoughts.

Lovely.

She heard Craig draw a breath, as if he were about to say something, when she suddenly realized that the edginess running along her nerve endings no longer solely had to do with him.

"Sh," she whispered almost inaudibly. "We're being watched."

He grew so still he might have been stone. He murmured, "I was just going to say that."

"Where?"

"Don't know. Sh. Eyes and ears."

She imagined that with Craig's arm around her, they must look like an ordinary couple just enjoying a starry night. On the other hand, they'd been talking about Buddy. Had they been overheard?

The thought stretched her nerves even tighter. A mistake so basic even a newbie should have known better. But who thought one of them would come to the cabin?

On the other hand, it should have occurred to them.

She tried to think back to when the sense of being watched had struck her, and how long before that they had fallen silent. She didn't know because she hadn't been paying attention.

Which made her mad, because she knew better than that. As long as there was any possibility that they needed to be cautious, she should never have dropped her guard. Never.

Worse, she had been the one to use exactly the wrong topic as a distraction. They had moved on to other things long before she started to feel watched, but no, she'd had to divert the subject back to Buddy.

She wanted to pound her head on something.

The feeling didn't last long. After a minute or two, the sense of being watched vanished.

"It could have been a bear or some other animal," Craig said quietly.

"Maybe. I wish I believed it. Me and my big mouth."

"Let's go inside," he said firmly.

This time she didn't argue. The night had lost its charm, and she was fairly angry with herself.

"I'll pick things up," he said as he pulled her to her feet. Then, tugging her close, he said quietly in her ear, "You keep watch."

At once she felt better. At least he trusted her that much. Right now she wasn't feeling all that trustworthy.

He folded her tarp as if he were in no hurry, and picked up the coffee mugs he had brought out for them. Then he lead the way inside, taking his time about it, and let her open the door since his hands were full. Only when they were inside did she say another word.

"I can't believe I was stupid enough to talk about that outside."

"We both talked about it. Don't beat yourself up."

"But I brought it up a second time." Annoyed, she kicked her foot at the floor. "Operational security. I can't believe I forgot it so fast."

"You're out in a national forest, for heaven's sake," he said mildly. "Not a war zone. Why should you even be thinking of things like that? I know I'm having trouble with it."

"I felt like I was being watched this afternoon. I shouldn't have forgotten that possibility so quickly."

"Consider where you are. There are lots of things with eyes out here that could watch you."

"Well, that's a creepy thought." Still, it settled her a bit. He was right. She had no reason to think Buddy's militia was watching them this closely. Why would they? Anyway, they hadn't been talking all that loudly, and the latter part of the conversation had been more generalized, about militias. "Okay," she said finally. "But I won't be so careless again."

"Fair enough. I won't either."

She looked at him from beneath her eyebrows, smiling faintly. "So the woods have eyes, huh? Sounds like a sci-fi film."

"So don't go out alone," he joshed back. "It's always the girl who goes out alone who meets the monster."

"Good point. Isolated cabin, nobody around, dark woods, yeah, I wouldn't last very long. I'd be lucky to be listed in the credits as 'girl number three.'"

"Which means you lasted longer than one and two."

The last of the tension seeped out of her and she laughed. "Sorry, I just got mad at myself for being careless."

"I was careless, too, like I said. So, okay, we'll follow reasonable OPSEC rules and REDCON procedures, but right now there isn't a whole lot of reason to be frightened of anything. I think Buddy and Cap would be happy if they thought we'd forgotten all about them, and that's the impression I intend to create."

"What about the sheriff?"

"I doubt he wants to stir the pot without some additional proof that something's going on. Mostly we're just going to have to keep an eye out and see what develops."

Then he pulled the zipper up on his jacket. "I'm going out to look around, check on Dusty."

A thought struck her. "Wouldn't Dusty have made some kind of ruckus if something was out there?"

He shook his head. "Dusty doesn't react to much except bears, wolves and snakes."

"I guess we know what wasn't out there, then. I'll come with?"

He shook his head. "We don't want to appear too alert if someone is out there. Let me just take an ordinary look-see, the kind I often do. I won't be long."

Of course he didn't find anything. She suspected that neither of them had expected him to, not in the dark. Probably an animal. It had to be an animal.

Because surely they were making too much of this Buddy character?

But then she remembered how he had accused her of spying, and warned herself not to go into a state of denial. Spying was something that worried a person only if they had something to conceal. Especially spying from so far away.

She was glad, though, that Craig didn't decide to sleep outside. He spread his sleeping blanket on the floor near hers and that simple choice meant more than it probably should have.

Oh, to hell with it, she thought. Just let it go. Nothing would come of this, and thus she had nothing to be worried about. In a few weeks, or sooner if she got the urge, she'd move on. The way she'd been moving on for a long time now.

Chapter 7

Three days later, Sky was convinced the problem, whatever it had been, was over. Craig patrolled but didn't find anything untoward. She went out and painted and no one bothered her. She wandered in the woods sometimes, enjoying the way light and shadow danced beneath the trees. She even found an absolutely perfect ravine, narrow and deep, full of large boulders, some of them still sharp in comparison to those worn by the water that raced through it almost but not quite like a waterfall.

The place was so full of power, the power of rocks, water and trees, that she fell in love with it. Ideas for paintings buzzed around in her mind, demanding expression.

This was what she had come all the way out here for, to find the essential creativity, to feel again the energy trying to burst out through her paintbrushes.

Enthralled, she snapped photos even though the light was dim in this tree-sheltered space, filtered and green for the most part although here and there the sun broke through to sparkle almost blindingly on water.

Moss covered a lot of the rocks, but the ones that interested her most were the ones that were bare. Rocks had always appealed to her in some way, the larger the better, and she thought these were gorgeous.

She was definitely bringing her gear back here.

She sat for a while on a flat-top rock with water rushing along one side of it, feeling as if she had fallen into a magical world. Well, these mountains seemed magical everywhere she went, but this place heightened that sense.

It was the kind of place that made her think a faerie could pop out from behind a tree, or even that a tree could slowly stir and talk to her. Fanciful thoughts, but they added to her pleasure. If humans had ever passed by here before, they had left no trace at all. It would have been easy to believe that she was the first person who had ever set foot here.

Part of the charm, she supposed, was that everything in the larger world seemed so far away. As if it were all the stuff of dreams, and the only reality surrounded her right now. Her thirsty soul reached for the beauty and soaked it up until she felt filled with it.

Hypnotized by the rushing water, she lost track of time. She didn't even notice that the light seemed to be lessening, deepening the secrets of the ravine and woods until that snaking, icy, breath-freezing sense of being watched crept up her spine to the base of her skull.

Damn, she was getting sick of that. It destroyed her mood as surely as if someone had fired a gun, and it made her mad. But mad at what? An owl? A raccoon? A mountain lion?

She muttered a cuss word under her breath, not that anything could have heard it over the crashing, rushing water. Hell, she couldn't even hear it herself.

But long training and honed instincts wouldn't let her ignore it. Grabbing her camera, she rose and started climbing out of the gorge. She half hoped she'd meet some idiot human so she would have someone to yell at.

But of course she didn't. Even if there was a person out here, there were too many places to provide concealment, even unintentional concealment. She'd forgotten her most basic training about keeping open sight lines, and she didn't care.

She was just mad, and dang it, she *would* come back here tomorrow to paint.

Near the top of the gorge wall, she caught a flicker of movement from the corner of her eye. At once she froze and slowly turned her head. Nothing. Absolutely nothing. Maybe a leaf had fluttered.

Except that the movement had left her with an impression of something considerably bigger. She resumed climbing again, but her senses were on heightened alert now. Anger had been forgotten in the possibility that whatever was watching her *didn't* want to be seen. There *were* predators out here, not all of them human, although she feared the human ones the most.

She needed her hands to climb this wall, and right now she didn't like not having them free. She quickened her pace to the top, and finally reached a point where she could stand without hanging on to rocks. Turning, she looked back.

The trees seemed to have closed in over the gorge, hiding it from sight once more. She could tell it was there only by the muffled sound of the racing, tumbling water. It was as if an invisible door had sealed behind her.

But standing there and looking back at the canopy of trees gave her the opportunity to look around. Nothing moved except gently swaying tree branches as the afternoon cooled and the evening breeze began to pick up.

But she was still in the woods, though they weren't as thick here, above the life-giving water. She began to trudge back to where she had left her painting supplies, sweeping the ground with her eyes, seeking any obvious disturbance among the carpet of pine needles and leaves. Nothing.

Maybe she was beginning to lose her mind in a whole new way.

Twenty minutes later she emerged onto the sunny hilltop where she usually painted in time to see the sun sink below the western peaks. Still so early, but she loved the way this premature twilight settled in. It would last a long time, but from her artist's perspective the light had lost its magic, growing flat, diminishing perspective.

She reached her supplies, which she hadn't fully unpacked yet since she had decided to hunt up a new place to paint, and bent to start picking them up.

She froze again. She knew how she'd laid things out. It was darn near an unbreakable habit to put everything in exactly the same place so she wouldn't have to hunt for things when she was working.

But something had moved. All of it had moved, she thought, but there was one thing she was absolutely certain had. She would have bet every last dime in her bank account that she hadn't left her palette on top of her paint box. The first place she always put that was right in front of her portable easel.

She had caught her hair up in a bun for walking through the woods. A few hairs at the nape had escaped, and now the breeze blew them about. Ordinarily she wouldn't have noticed, but right now they felt like the caress of icy fingers.

Somebody had touched her things. Probably gone through them. Her reaction to that was immediate and intense, and it wasn't fear she felt. She reached into her paint box and pulled out a couple of palette knives. They didn't look dangerous, but in the right hands, used the right way, they could be deadly.

She stuffed them in her pockets, then straightened, looking around the clearing. Then she saw bent grasses leading toward the woods she had just come from, but they weren't her path. So someone had come here and followed her to the ravine? And it was clear they had tried not to leave an obvious trail, otherwise she would have seen it upon emerging from the woods.

In fact, it could easily have been an animal that crossed the clearing, except for her palette. No animal would have done that.

What were the chances, she wondered, that whoever had followed her into the woods was still there somewhere? And if he was, how smart would it be to let him know what she had realized?

Slim and not at all, she decided, squashing down the anger that made her want to take off after the guy. He'd be long gone. Hell, even if he wasn't, he could see her coming. Finding someone in those woods wouldn't be easy.

Nor would it be smart to let him know he'd been found out. Damn it. Frustrated that her only smart move seemed to be to sit here for a while, then pack up and leave, she had to battle an innate need to act. She always wanted to act, and talking herself out of it wasn't easy.

But it was a lesson she had learned: sometimes no action was the best action.

That first day when Buddy had accused her of spying, the wise course had been to leave. She wasn't looking for trouble, the guy appeared to be a nut and standing her ground could have become costly at the time. It was one of those times she was grateful for her instinctive slowness to react in non-life-threatening situations, because a reaction at that time would have only caused trouble and solved nothing.

But the situation had shifted, and wisdom no longer advised her to cede ground. Well, maybe wisdom would but sometimes wisdom was wrong. If someone was taking this much interest in her activities, then there was very definitely something going on down there that wasn't entirely copacetic. Something they didn't want anybody to know about, even an artist who was just passing through.

That sounded like something a whole lot more serious than simply storing up food against some hypothetical Armageddon.

The suspicion swept her past simply being concerned about Craig needing backup. She had taken an oath long ago when she had donned an army uniform, and to her way of thinking, leaving the army didn't void that oath. If these guys were up to something bad, she still had a duty to protect her fellow citizens and the Constitution. That, too, had been woven into the fabric of her being.

A lot had become part of her during her years of service, like duty and honor and responsibility. Things like supporting her fellow soldiers no matter what, never shirking a job for any reason… Well, she didn't need to run through the whole list as she sat there listening for any unnatural sound. The point was, enough had happened to make this her fight, too. Quite enough. And unless those nuts in their compound across the valley turned out to be total innocents, it would remain her fight.

Finally she felt she had sat there long enough to make it seem like she hadn't noticed anything— assuming she was still being watched, but that feeling had gone away back at the gorge. Regardless, it wouldn't look hurried or worried now for her to gather her gear and head for the car.

She hoped Craig didn't stay in the field tonight. She needed to talk to him. She thought about calling him on the radio but decided against it. Radio silence right now might be wise. There was no guarantee the guys across the valley weren't monitoring the forest service frequencies, and given how paranoid they were beginning to appear, she thought it entirely possible.

She made her way through the woods and back to her car. For a few minutes she considered driving down to the headquarters building, or even going into town, but she really didn't need anything yet, and for some reason either option felt entirely too much like flight at the moment. She didn't like running, no matter what specious reason she might be able to come up with.

So she headed back to the cabin, hoping that Craig wouldn't suddenly decide to take it into his head to sleep under the stars. Considering he had said how much he enjoyed that, she was surprised he'd been joining her at the cabin every night. Summer, and the opportunity to sleep under the stars, wouldn't last forever.

Craig didn't like what he was finding as he poked around the streams in the vicinity of Buddy's property. Nothing was blocked by so much as a beaver dam, but that wasn't what got his attention.

No, it was the damn trip wires. They ringed Buddy's property, but at no time did he have an excuse to get close enough to find out what they were connected to. He was going to have to come over here after dark.

It was late afternoon, and he meandered along the valley stream, still wondering why it was so low. He'd expected to find a fallen boulder here and there, blocking one of the bigger streams, or even several blocking smaller streams, although as a rule the water soon overtopped such hindrances and found its way down.

He began to think somebody had dammed some rivers that he couldn't get to, and there was only one place around here that could happen: on Buddy's property.

Water was scarce enough around here. Water rights could be fiercely fought over, sometimes reaching a level a person might almost call a war. But Buddy didn't have anybody downstream of him to get riled, which left the forest service.

Damned if he could prove the diminished flow in the valley arose from a dam or anything except maybe, just possibly, part of the mountains hadn't had their usual snowfall. He took a few flow measurements to compare to the past few years, but they wouldn't prove anything either.

If Buddy had dammed a stream, he had violated his agreement with the service. He was damaging the ecology. Proving it, and figuring out how much right he had to intervene anyway, wasn't going to be easy.

Troubling him equally was that Buddy had never done such a thing in the past. Assuming he felt he needed to hang on to more water for the late summer and early fall when it would get really dry, what had changed from past years? The addition of Cap and his friends? Some so-called strategic thinking? Was he anticipating imminent apocalypse? If so, why?

Feeling frustrated and more than a little annoyed, Craig turned Dusty and headed back up the valley, intending to go to the cabin to meet Sky. Amazing how fast she had captivated him. He couldn't imagine not spending the evenings with her, and wondered if he was going to be able to go back to his solitary existence without pining for her company.

She was great company. Quiet, funny when she wanted to be and just plain comfortable to be with. The only time he got edgy around her was when he noticed she was an attractive woman. He'd been working on not noticing—unsuccessfully. It was sort of like telling himself not to think about the elephant in the room.

A quiet chuckle escaped him. He turned Dusty up the hillside, an unmistakable anticipation growing in him as he drew nearer to the cabin.

A movement to the side caught his eye, and he turned to look. He immediately recognized one of his fellow rangers, Don Capehart, riding toward him on Dusty's twin. He waved and waited for Don to reach him.

Don drew up alongside him, a blond man of about thirty whose skin didn't take kindly to the high-altitude summer sun. He was looking a little red and probably wouldn't tan, but he didn't seem to care. "Big doings?" Don said as they shook hands. "Lucy kind of filled me in."

"There's not a whole lot to fill in yet. Let's keep riding. There's a definite sense lately that everything we do around here is being watched."

"That doesn't sound good."

"I don't think it is. Buddy Jackson has trip wires around his entire property, and I can't get close enough to tell what they're hooked up to. If it's not just some kind of alert, getting close could be dangerous anyway."

"So you're thinking about looking after dark?"

Craig looked at him again. "You know me too well."

"Well, it's your job. Kind of my job, too."

"You're not law enforcement."

"So? You're not a firefighter either. That didn't keep you out of Spruce Valley last summer. Where are you headed?"

"To the cabin. My artist friend is probably already there. You should probably hear us both out."

Don nodded. "Fair enough. Some of the others are hanging out around here now. I wish we had more manpower."

"Take it up with Congress."

Don laughed. "Yeah, that works so well. I think we're at the bottom of the list anyway with the department."

"Can't blame 'em. We're not the busiest of forests, and we're relatively new."

"Keeping an eye on the loggers is practically a fulltime job. I caught them trying to cut some untagged trees yesterday. It's always fun to have a shouting match with a bunch of guys armed with chain saws."

Now Craig laughed. "How'd it go?"

"Well, the threat of losing their contract had to come

up. But they got to spew and cuss, and just generally vent. They calmed down, but I'm going to need to check on them again soon."

"Gotta love it. We spend months figuring out which trees need to go, and how many to preserve for the health of the ecology, and they *still* want to clear-cut."

"Hey, those are publically owned trees. Surely you've heard that."

"More times than I can count. They seem to forget they're not the entire public."

Don laughed, too. "I'm sure they're cutting more than they should. They always do."

"That's what happens when you go with the lowest bidder."

"You mean like us?"

They were still laughing and joking when they reached the cabin, acting like they hadn't a care in the world. When Craig saw that Sky's car was already there, parked beside his forest service truck, he felt his spirits rise.

Damn, he shouldn't let a woman who was passing through make him feel this way. He didn't want to feel loss when she left, didn't want his love of the forest's solitude to be dimmed by the transition of a single person through his life. But already it was feeling too late.

He sighed as he and Don took their mounts to the corral and cared for them. All too soon he heard a voice that he had become attached to.

"Hi," Sky called.

Saddle in his hands, he turned. Don, who had been checking his horse's hooves, straightened and looked around.

"You've been keeping a secret," Don said under his breath. "She's gorgeous."

"I'm surprised Lucy didn't tell you."

Don cracked a laugh as the two of them walked over to the fence rail. Craig balanced his saddle on it and brushed his hands on his pants.

"Sky, this is Don Capehart. Don, Sky Jamison, the artist you've been hearing about."

Sky put out her hand across the rail. "Nice to meet you. Will you stay for dinner?"

Don's smile was a bit too wide and warm for Craig's comfort. Yet he had no right to be bothered by it. That might have galled him most of all.

"I'd be delighted," Don answered. "In fact, I'll even help if you can wait to start until after I finish taking care of Tragic over there."

Sky's brow lifted. "Tragic? What a name!"

"He's Dusty's twin and I guess he got the name because he was so small as a foal that nobody expected him to survive. At least that's the story they gave me."

"You couldn't guess that now," Sky said.

"Not every runt is lost."

Feeling slightly disgruntled, knowing he had no right and that it was therefore stupid, Craig headed back to continue caring for Dusty. "How was your day?" he asked over his shoulder.

"Very interesting. I almost radioed you, then thought better of it."

He paused midstride and turned to face her. "What happened?"

"Nothing serious, but enough. Let's talk about it when you fellows are done out here."

He expected her to head back inside, but instead she put a hiking-boot-encased foot on the lower rail, leaned her elbows on the upper rail and watched them finish. Don didn't unsaddle Tragic, however, so at least he didn't intend to spend the night here. Small blessings, Craig thought sourly.

Then he wondered why he should care. If Don took her attention, his problems were over, right?

At last the horses were fed and watered. Stopping at the outside pump, the two men rinsed quickly in icy water, then accompanied Sky inside.

She had lit enough oil lamps to make the interior feel cozy as twilight deepened, and the fire was going strong. She had made coffee, too, and poured some for them. Then they gathered at the small table, the only place to sit other than the single armchair.

"So what happened?" Craig asked.

"It wasn't exactly a happening," she said. "I found this great ravine I want to paint, but while I was sitting there I got the distinct feeling I was being watched. So I headed back to the place where I've been painting, and found that someone had been through my stuff. I could even see where they had followed me from there to the ravine."

Don spoke. "Sure it wasn't an animal?"

"An animal would have knocked my things around, not simply moved my palette to a different place. Everything was disturbed, but only a little. If I weren't such a creature of habit in how I lay out my painting gear, I'd never have noticed."

Craig nodded. "I take it you drew a conclusion?"

She nodded. "If they're paranoid enough to follow a mere artist, those guys are up to something not good."

Craig looked at Don, whose eyes had narrowed. "I agree," he said.

Craig nodded. "I agree." He turned his attention back to Sky. "You shouldn't be out there alone."

"I doubt they've got more than one guy looking, and

trust me, they don't know what they're bargaining for if they bother me. I went through advanced infantry training and I had the opportunity to use a lot of it in Iraq."

He watched her eyes grow distant, and felt his chest tighten. He hoped she wasn't about to pull back into that place inside her, but then her gaze cleared. "They don't want to know what I can do with a simple palette knife."

He felt Don shift a little beside him, probably with discomfort. Don had never been in the military. But Craig looked at Sky with perfect understanding. These were the things that set combat vets apart: they *knew* what they were capable of. It wasn't always easy to live with, but they *knew*.

"Anyway," she said, brushing it aside, "I'm not worried about one of them."

"Probably no reason to be," Craig said. "They think you're out there just painting."

"They should believe it now that they looked through my gear."

He left it at that, although he wasn't as sanguine about it as he appeared. The whole idea that they were following her this way was problematic. Too much interest in someone they thought was just painting. Maybe having her stay at the cabin wasn't such a good idea. Maybe hanging out with her so much wasn't a good idea. What if he'd put her at risk?

He didn't say any more about it, but instead got busy with dinner. Sky wanted to help, but he and Don made a big show of waiting on her, which at least made her laugh at their foolishness. It was good to hear her laugh.

All the while he wrestled with telling her to clear out. Go to town, paint somewhere else. He doubted

she'd listen, but he had to be able to live with his conscience.

That moment when she had made the remark about
the palette knife troubled him, though. Not because
it wasn't true, but because this situation had cast her
back to a time she probably didn't want to relive anymore than he did.

There were times in life when you did what you had
to, but you didn't have to feel good about it. You made
some kind of peace, if you could, and moved on. And
now she was moving back because of that jackass and
his prepper fantasies about standing alone against a
world gone mad. A man who'd been relatively quiet
and harmless about it until this new crowd showed up.

Who was Cap and how many men had he brought
with him? It sure didn't look as if another family had
joined Buddy, but rather a small—very small—army.
In which case there might well be trouble of some kind.

Problem was, as the man had said, when the only
tool you had was a hammer, everything looked like a
nail. Some militia types could easily have that problem. All that firepower and paranoia induced a built-in
response. Even to solitary artists on the wrong hillside.
Had it gone that far?

He ruminated about ways he could approach Buddy
again without setting off alarms, but didn't immediately
come up with one. Gage had been out there just a few
days ago. Another visit so soon would ring alarm bells.

"You going out tonight?" Don suddenly asked.

They were done with dinner now and having cof-
fee at the table. "Not tonight," Craig said. "Tomorrow.
Maybe. I'm still trying to think of a reason to approach
Buddy again without making him nervous."

"Better to talk if we can. Did you ever find why the river is so low?"

"No, damn it, not yet. And I can't exactly prove it's too dry."

"It's too dry," Don said flatly. "We know that. But you're right, proving it is tough."

"I've used the flow meter a few times, in a couple of different places, but I need to compare it with past readings."

"It would be interesting to know if there's some place where the flow is normal."

Craig shrugged. "That's just as hard as anything else. It *seems* normal upstream from Buddy's place, but there's always a whole lot less water there anyway. Nothing yet I can pin on him."

"He might not even be responsible." Don shook his head. "How about I go over there. I can act like we haven't even discussed it and ask him if he's noticed anything. Tell him I've been traveling from downstream because the water volume appears to be down."

"I did that already. He claimed he didn't know anything about it. But it made a good excuse for looking over a lot of streams around his place. I don't think he'd go for it a second time. Would you?"

"Probably not. Okay, I'll think on it and see you here tomorrow night. If you're going over there, you're not going alone."

After Don said good-night and rode away, Craig found himself facing Sky, who appeared quite annoyed. "You're absolutely *not* proposing a solo night recon over there."

"Solo is the best way to go."

She cussed a word he'd never heard pass her lips before and stormed into the cabin. Wow, that was some reaction. He kinda liked the fire in her eyes. Almost as if an invisible cord pulled him, he followed her inside. He found her tossing another split log on the fire, which really didn't require it, but apparently she needed something to do.

He stood just inside the door, waiting for the thunder and lightning. He suspected she wasn't the type to keep silent if she didn't have to, and right now she didn't have to.

"Are you an idiot?" she asked him eventually, her voice far too calm.

"Not that I'm aware of," he answered easily, wondering where this was going and rather curious about it.

"You have the training to know better."

"I also have the training. Don doesn't. Good as he may be, I might as well take a rhinoceros over there with me."

He caught the corner of her mouth twitching, as if humor had almost overcome her, but then it thinned out again. He realized he was enjoying this.

"Craig...you don't know what those trip wires are attached to."

"I need to find out."

"For all you know they're patrolling the boundary every night. You don't even know how many of them there are."

"I need to find that out, too."

She slammed the stove door shut and twisted the lock. "Solo recon is a suicide mission. You know that. I shouldn't even have to remind you."

"Remind away."

Her eyes sparked as she glared at him. "What if those trip wires are hooked up to explosives? Have you considered that?"

"Absolutely. That's why I need to get close enough to look, and I can't do that in broad daylight."

"Doing it at night will get you turned into hamburger. What if those guys have C-4?"

"They could have dynamite for all the difference it will make. But I've got to find out more about what's going on."

"What made it so important? Water?"

"No. The fact they're watching you. You said it yourself, if they're worried about a painter, they've got something to hide, and people with something to hide are generally up to no good. *Somebody* has to find out."

"Then call the damn ATF. That's their job."

"I would if I had any evidence for them. What have we got, Sky? A lot of supposition, and some guys who are apparently creeping around in the woods and just generally acting like people who creep. Creeping and being a creep aren't illegal."

She glared for another moment, then a smile twitched at the corners of her mouth. "That's a lot of creep."

He had to smile back. "I'm not a writer. So, okay, seriously, what do we really know? Not enough to call the ATF. A few guys running around in camouflage with apparently legal AR-15s isn't going to make a case. Since I can hardly go up to them and ask if they've rigged those guns for automatic fire instead of semiautomatic, I've got to find something else. Or find out that they're not doing anything wrong at all and we can just ignore them."

"Ignoring them isn't at the top of my list," she admitted. "Not after today. Okay, I'll go with you on recon."

"No. You stay here."

Her chin set visibly. "If I were standing here in uniform, would you say that? Cut the chauvinist protective stuff. I'm trained, too."

He folded his arms. "You know, it was so much easier in the old days."

"These aren't the old days."

"No kidding. I'm not trying to be chauvinistic. I know better. The thing is, protection is my *job*. It's not yours. I've got no business dragging a visitor into any of this."

"If I recall correctly, Buddy dragged me into this."

Right then he had an overwhelming urge to drag her into his arms and kiss her until her lips were swollen, her body limp in his arms and her eyes hazy with desire. He didn't need a neon sign, though, to warn him this was exactly the wrong time to play caveman.

But she was something else, standing her ground like this, giving him what-for. He'd seen her in a time of weakness, and now he was seeing the steel core at her center. She was magnificent.

He suspected that wouldn't be a good thing to say right now either. So he waited.

When she spoke, her tone had moderated, but remained forceful. "If those guys aren't just playing, if they're up to something that could hurt someone, then it's *my* business, too. I took an oath and it didn't end the day I ditched my uniform."

She was boxing him in with arguments he couldn't dismiss. He knew exactly what she meant, just as he'd understood when she had insisted she wouldn't abandon a buddy. Some things just ran too deep.

But damn, it was frustrating when all he wanted to do was settle this issue without dragging her into trouble. Hell, there might not be any trouble, but at the moment he wouldn't bet on it.

She poured coffee and settled in the one padded chair. He poured himself some more, too, and took a bench. Staring into his mug, he thought it all over one more time. Each little piece and how they kept adding up. Any way he looked at it, a certainty gnawed at him that those guys were up to no good. He could not ignore it.

And glancing at Sky, he realized he wasn't going to be able to keep her out of it. He couldn't order her to leave, and as long as she remained she might be at risk. Today had pretty much made that clear.

He thought about asking her if she'd go somewhere else but he already knew what her answer would be. No doubt of it.

Sky was loaded for bear.

Chapter 8

The morning dawned hazy and gray, not a good day for painting. All contrast had vanished from the world, and the colors looked dark and haunted.

Sky stared out the window, for once not minding that weather was going to keep her from painting. Instead she thought over the night before. After her eruption at Craig, things had settled down. He hadn't treated her the way Hector had, giving her the cold shoulder. No, they'd simply moved on to other conversations and other activities.

They'd slept side-by-side in separate bedrolls again, and sleep had been elusive for her because her mind insisted on noticing how close he was, how easy it would be to reach out and touch him, draw him close, beg him to love her.

God, she wanted to feel desirable again. It had been so long now that she wondered if Hector hadn't been right about her.

She didn't even trust the heat she sometimes thought she saw in Craig's gaze. She must be imagining it because she wanted it so much. After all, he'd kissed her once, just briefly, and then had pulled back. She'd turned him off, not on. Let that be a lesson.

Funny how life didn't go the way a person wanted. Ever. Big plans, big dreams, and somehow they got gobbled up in reality. While she had never imagined herself as a Picasso or Pollack, she had still hoped she might be able to make a modest living with her painting. That hadn't happened yet, and like a great many artists, she supported her art with a job.

It was an important job, no question. She was proud and pleased to be able to help her fellow vets however emotionally wrenching it got. She had always wanted to do something that mattered, and that was certainly a job that was important. She figured she had done important things in the army, too, although sometimes that wasn't so easy to remember. But she had served and served well.

But after all she had been through, dreams of a husband and family seemed to be dissipating on the road behind her like dust devils after a car passed.

She knew Craig couldn't be the one she had hoped for simply because their lives were too divergent and he seemed happy with the solitude of the woods and his job. But dang, surely a fling wasn't out of the realm of possibility. Just a fling to let her know there wasn't something wrong with her.

But did she really want that question answered? What if the answer reinforced Hector's declaration? She'd never recover from such a judgment from two men.

So it was best to ignore her growing ache for a man

who showed little interest. She liked him a whole lot, he was fun to be with and that was the safest place to leave it. Better to indulge a private fantasy than take that risk again.

Other risks were far easier to take, like going on a night recon with Craig to find out if Buddy had something illegal attached to his trip wires. To find out how many people were in that compound—and yes, she was thinking of it as a compound now—and what they were up to.

It was possible that she was exaggerating the whole threat. Iraq had taught her to be sensitive to things she had never thought about before. Little signs. Little intuitions. Little niggles that something wasn't right. In theory she existed in a different world these days, but those instincts were surging again because of Buddy's odd behavior and the feeling she was being watched or stalked.

After yesterday, though, they should know that all she was armed with was an oil painter's kit. They should think there was nothing to worry about with her.

She guessed it would all depend on how much paranoia plagued them. The more paranoid, the more likely they were total wackos of one kind or another. Either they needed some serious psychiatric help, or they needed to be arrested.

"Good morning."

Craig's deep, husky voice coming from right behind her almost startled her. She hadn't heard him get up. Too lost in thought, she decided as she realized she could smell coffee brewing. He hadn't let the fire go out overnight, a good thing given that she'd probably be stuck here most of the day from the looks of it.

"Good morning," she replied without turning around.

"Dismal day."

"I'm never going to complain about rain again, after Iraq."

He chuckled quietly, then astonished her by gripping her shoulders and drawing her back a bit until she leaned against his chest. Such a hard, solid chest, and warm against her back. All of a sudden she wanted to melt into a puddle.

Then, almost tentatively, his arms wrapped around her, enclosing her waist, gently pinning her arms at her side.

She felt the warmth of his breath on her neck and tipped her head to the side, welcoming it. She held her breath in anticipation, surprised that he had made this move, hoping against hope that it wouldn't end here. That he would find her neck with his lips. That his hands, now loosely around her, would begin to move against her, trespassing in the most exciting of places. Exploring her. Learning her.

A heat was blooming deep within her, accompanied by an aching hope. All her fears of her own inadequacy burned away as every single cell in her body responded to building need. A kiss, a touch, oh, please!

His warm lips brushed her neck lightly. A shiver rippled through her and her knees turned weak.

"You're so tempting," he whispered. "So tempting."

Another rush of pleasure filled her, even as some little voice in her brain warned: tempting isn't the same as satisfying.

That thought once again acted like a cold-water bath. What was she doing? Had she lost her mind? Could she possibly handle another rejection? There might be lots of times she could be tough, but this was one area where she had become a raw nerve ending. This was one risk she didn't know if she could take.

He kissed her neck again, lightly, then lowered his arms. "I'm sorry, but if I don't get that coffee, I'll ruin it."

As quickly as that, the bubble burst completely. She remained frozen at the window, torn between relief and disappointment. Then she simultaneously realized two things, and they swept through her like a calming breeze.

She hadn't responded to his advance. Not in any way that he could tell. So she hadn't encouraged him to go further. He might have taken that wrong.

Or perhaps he was long past the stage of acting like a randy teen in the backseat of a car. Given the calm and serenity she had initially sensed in him, it was entirely possible that he wouldn't rush into anything, but would take his time to see how matters went. What they used to call courtship, in the days before people started falling into bed together on the first date. Old-fashioned, but she discovered she liked the idea. Time to test the waters. Moving slowly. Finding out if things were right. Avoiding a heart-wrenching crash.

Relieved, she was able to turn and look at him with a smile. This time when heat flickered in his gaze, she almost believed it was real.

"Looks like it's going to be a lazy day," he remarked as he fed them scrambled eggs and some slightly browned toast.

"Do you have to go out?"

"I'm overdue for a day off. I don't usually mind riding around in the gloom and rain, but today I may just stay tucked in. You can't paint in here, can you?"

"Not well. I really need the light."

"Oil lamps aren't going to cut it." He pushed his clean plate to one side. "I think we have a jigsaw puzzle or two tucked somewhere. But first I need to go look after Dusty."

"Does he mind the rain?"

"Not a bit." Craig grinned. "He's waterproof. But his dry feed isn't. I need to make sure it didn't get rained on overnight. I'll be right back."

Sky decided to take the opportunity to step outside with her camera. Rarely at home did she see clouds sailing as low as they seemed to at this altitude. They almost appeared close enough to touch.

The day had grown markedly cooler, not that it ever felt hot to her here, but the damp combined with the dropping temperature made her feel like a cozy day inside that tiny cabin beside the fire would be perfect.

She snapped the clouds as they raced past, appearing to graze the treetops. It created the sense that if she just climbed a little higher she might look down on them as if she were in an airplane.

Walking around the corner, she also took pictures of Craig and Dusty. He didn't wear his uniform today, but instead jeans and a thick flannel shirt. Only his felt Stetson remained.

She had no idea what she might do with these pictures, but she loved watching Craig with Dusty, the way they'd put their heads together as if communing, the way Dusty would nudge Craig and make him laugh. True companions, she thought, painted against a forest gone almost black in this light, with the deep gray of the clouds overhead.

Craig put some more feed in the bin beneath an overhang and added some water to the trough. Dusty nudged him again as if telling him to hurry, and the instant Craig stepped back, Dusty started to eat.

"I guess he was hungry," she said as Craig came out of the corral. He looked tranquil again, as if he'd shed every possible worry and felt content with life just as it was. She envied that, especially since she found contentment only when lost in her art.

"That's what he'd like me to believe, anyway," Craig answered.

"You really think he can reason that much?"

He lifted a brow. "I can tell you haven't spent much time with horses. Believe me, they think, they reason and I've even seen them lie."

"How in the world can a horse lie?"

"You'd be surprised. Take the time he got a stone bruise. A couple of hours later he was limping on the wrong foot. I checked it three times. No new injury, but he wasn't going to let up his demands for sympathy."

She laughed, but the sound seemed deadened by the woods around. Pivoting, she snapped some more photos at random, just for something to do. Her hands wanted to be doing something entirely different.

All of a sudden a push on her back caused her to stumble forward a step.

"Dusty," Craig said disapprovingly. "Leave the lady alone."

She swung around and saw Dusty at the rail, only inches away. He hadn't shown interest in her before. "Why'd he do that?"

"I think he's decided he wants your attention."

This close, she realized how large that head was. And what big teeth he had. The refrain from *Little Red Riding Hood* came back to her. "Um, what do I do?"

"Step a little to one side. They don't have the best

frontal vision, so you don't want to startle him. Then reach out and pat his neck. Don't touch his head. Not until you're friends."

She followed directions, then reached out slowly. Dusty regarded her from one very large brown eye, but didn't sidle away. She patted his neck tentatively and he nickered.

"He won't break," Craig said. "Pat more firmly."

Dusty tossed his head as she patted him, but didn't move away. She definitely got the sense that he liked it. A smile blossomed on her face and she patted him a few more times before he nudged Craig on the shoulder. From Craig he accepted a scratch right between his eyes, then he trotted back over to the feed bin and water.

"You've made a friend," Craig said. "Although I wouldn't try to touch his face until he's come to you a few more times. It's not like he's used to hanging out with loads of people."

She watched the horse for a few more minutes, although the chill was beginning to penetrate her clothing. Even the new jacket wasn't quite enough this morning. "How did it get so cold?"

"It happens at this altitude in the mountains. Come on, let's get inside where it's warm."

The cabin seemed especially toasty after the chill outside. Sky dumped her jacket over one of the two benches and stood near the stove, warming her hands. Gloves. She had never once thought of needing gloves. At home she might wish for them only a handful of times each winter, if that. Up here, she'd already wished for them repeatedly because as the afternoons cooled down, her fingers started to get awkward. Even if the diminishing twilight hadn't put an end to her work, the chill would have.

She sat on one of the benches with a cup of coffee. Craig stood at the front window for a few minutes.

"Pining to be out there?" she asked him. She hoped she sounded casual.

"Oddly, no."

"Oddly?"

He glanced over his shoulder with a half smile. "I usually love every minute of being outdoors in the summers here. I don't even mind being out in the winter, but when it comes to summer I hate to waste a minute of it. But I'm not feeling that way today. So yes, it's odd. I'm rather happy to be taking a day off, tucked inside with a lovely woman."

Lovely woman? Easy to say, she thought, looking away. She knew she was ordinarily attractive. It just hadn't worked out so well.

But one thing she certainly agreed with: it was nice to be facing a day here with him, without anything else that needed doing. "It's like a real vacation."

He abandoned the window and came to sit across from her at the table. "Being out here painting hasn't been one?"

"Certainly not since Buddy turned up. I guess I've been tense and on guard. That's not exactly relaxing."

"No, it isn't." He shook his head a little. "Part of me is impatient to get over there and find out what's going on. The rest of me is quite content to let it all go hang today."

A small laugh escaped her. "I can identify. You know, it's so different here from where I live in Florida. I honestly never thought about how early the sun would go down in the mountains like this. Or how fast it would get cold when it did."

"Three o'clock and the day's already dimming even though official sunset won't be until after eight. It's a long twilight."

"It has a fascinating effect on the light. It's not dark, but everything gets so flat even though the sky is still so bright. Then, almost as soon as the sun goes behind the peaks, the breeze picks up and the temperature starts to fall. It's very different from what I'm used to."

"What do you think of it?"

"I like it."

"Despite the light?"

"There's still usually enough time to paint. And I suppose if I wanted more morning light, I wouldn't have to go very far east to get it. Just out of the mountains."

"Not far at all," he agreed. He took another look toward the window. "I don't mind days like this. We're usually sunny and dry here, so it's great when it clouds up and moisture starts dripping from the pines. Even better when it rains."

Then he cocked his head at her. "What's the thing about painters and morning light? I've heard it before."

"The air is usually clearer in the morning so the light is purer. As the day goes on the light shifts to more golds and reds. It's not actually a necessity, but a preference, depending on what you want to accomplish. I know artists who paint by artificial light in their studios. It works. And honestly," she said with a wry smile, "not many people are ever going to see the painting in fresh morning light."

He laughed at that.

"If you want realism in a painting, those things can

become really important. I'm more impressionistic, and don't worry about it as much. But there comes a point when I feel like I don't have enough contrast and perspective, and that's when I stop. Like right now outside. I could paint it, even though it's flat and gray out there. I'm sure I'd come up with a good enough impression of what I can see, but it wouldn't speak to me."

"Speak to you?"

"That's hard. Um…" She thought about it. "Different strokes for different folks, I guess. Flat light doesn't give me the sense of energy I want. For others it might work fine."

"So it's something you feel as well as what you see?"

"Definitely."

He nodded slowly, clearly thinking it over. "I guess that's what makes an artist."

She had no idea how to answer that. If she came right down to it, she found it difficult to express what drove her, what satisfied her, what had always driven her to paint in a certain way.

"I'll bet you didn't have many light problems where you come from."

"That depends. For a lot of the summer the light is harsh and glaring. It softens in the fall, though. The Tampa area, where I live, feels really tropical. Looks tropical. The Gulf Coast is mostly a serene sort of place in terms of weather, water, beaches, palm trees. Then you go over to the east coast and the Atlantic, and it's very different, especially in the northern part of the state. A whole lot more energetic, in terms of the water and weather."

"I guess it's like the difference between the mountains and the prairie out here."

"Maybe. I haven't been around enough to know."

"So," he said, resting his elbows on the table and fixing her with his incredible gray eyes, eyes that now looked dark and mysterious in the dim light, "what brought you this way for your vacation? We're out of the way for most people."

"I was looking for out of the way. And I wanted mountains. Really big, huge mountains. Someone suggested western Montana, but then I found this forest online and it looked perfect."

"I need to show you around some," he said decisively. "There's a whole lot to see in these mountains. Great places to paint or take photos that I think you'd like."

Neither of them mentioned Buddy or that problem. She realized they were chatting as if this really *were* a vacation for both of them. But at the back of her mind hovered the awareness that he intended to do a recon over at Buddy's, probably tonight. That would be no vacation.

She definitely wasn't going to let him go alone, although if he rode out of here on Dusty, she had no idea how she could catch up. Didn't matter, she'd find a way. He absolutely shouldn't go alone.

Rain came sweeping through, a deafening drumbeat on the roof, heavy enough that the world beyond the window nearly disappeared. Craig made another pot of coffee for them and brought out a small stack of boxes that contained puzzles.

"You have your choice. There's one of those 3-D puzzles that I can guarantee we won't finish today. In fact," he added, looking at the boxes, "I can virtually guarantee we won't finish any of them in a day. Will that bother you?"

"Why should it?"

"Because some people don't like to do things they know they can't finish."

"I'm not one of them. But why so many puzzles?"

He set the boxes on the table and started spreading them out so she could see the collection. "Some researchers can stay here for weeks at a time. It gives them something to do on long evenings or when the weather's too bad. These have accumulated over a few years, from the look of it."

She selected the three-dimensional puzzle that looked like a castle on the Rhine. "I always wanted to do one of these but I never have."

The rain let up while they spread the pieces out. There was just barely enough room on the table for all of them and still have a little space to get started on the assembly.

Conversation turned desultory as rain swept through in bands and they worked to put the first pieces of the puzzle together. Sky enjoyed it. She seemed to have a knack for matching the colors, equaled by Craig's knack for matching the shapes. Surprise struck her when she realized the entire morning had passed so swiftly and that she was growing hungry.

"I need to eat," she announced. "Let's see what we have."

Cold cuts in one of the coolers and a loaf of bread provided the answer. She'd need to go into town tomorrow, though, Sky decided. They were getting low and the remaining ice would probably only make it one more day.

Of course, with only the one table they had to clear some of the puzzle pieces. It wasn't as if this place ran to conveniences like a counter. Well, why would it? It had a chemical outhouse and a gravity shower, and a woodstove. Not exactly the height of conveniences.

The rain became a steady downpour while they washed up afterward. Despite the oil lamps, the cabin seemed to grow even darker, almost nightlike. Craig slipped out to check on Dusty again, but this time Sky remained inside.

A long, lazy day, she thought. Enjoyable in its own right, but her awareness of Craig was growing steadily. Awareness of his masculinity, his wide shoulders, narrow hips. She had even grown fascinated by the strength of his large hands as he handled the puzzle pieces and wished they were handling her instead.

She sank onto the armchair and tried to reason herself back to reality and sanity. He had said she was tempting, then had turned to working a puzzle with her. Slow and gentlemanly were fine, but what if it wasn't that at all? That was a nice excuse she had manufactured for him, but it didn't help her one whit. Not really.

And it might not even be true. But then why had he kissed her, especially that kiss on her neck this morning? That had promised something he now seemed to have turned away from. It had been deliberate and deliberately sexual.

So what was wrong with her? But again she shied away from the question because she didn't want to know. The possible answer terrified her.

Chicken. Yes, all right, she was chicken. Hector had left huge scars. Only a fool would ask for another wounding.

Resting her elbow on the arm of the chair, she put her forehead in her hand, and picked absently at nonexistent lint on her new jeans. No oil paint there. Yet.

She needed to stop this. In a few weeks she was

going home, back to her life and her job. This was a momentary escape, and she shouldn't be complicating it with needs and wants that could only bring pain. Sooner or later they would, too. Because even if Craig didn't decide she was a lousy lover, she would be leaving anyway. Then what?

She should focus on her reasons for coming here, to heal from Hector and refresh herself for her clients at the center. Taking her life back, not giving it away in some mad fling.

She was far too old now to be thinking like a sixteen-year-old girl with a crush. Much as she had been trying to ignore these feelings since she had met Craig, they seemed to be growing increasingly insistent. Maybe, for her own sake, she ought to just pack and go find some other place to paint.

Maybe for Craig's sake, too. When she thought it over, she decided he wasn't feeling much more comfortable with any of this than she was. In fact, if it weren't pouring today, he'd probably mount Dusty and take off to his solitary woods, woods that seemed to give him so much peace.

He'd said he didn't usually mind being out in this weather. She stiffened a little as she wondered if he thought she needed a babysitter after yesterday. Well, it would hardly be surprising. He struck her as taking the "protection" part of his job very seriously.

How humiliating! She was perfectly capable of taking care of herself. She didn't need him to hang around. Unlike a lot of people, she was well-trained in self-defense, and it would take more than a couple of men to get the best of her.

She heard the door open and looked up as he stepped in. As soon as he closed the door and started doffing his wet jacket and hat, she said, "I don't need a baby-sitter, you know. You can go do whatever it is you ordinarily would be doing."

He froze, his eyes widening a hair. Then he dropped his hat on the cabin's one shelf and faced her straight on. "What the hell are you talking about?"

"You said yourself you don't mind being out in this weather. You must have things to do. You don't have to hang around here to keep me safe. I can do that myself."

His lips parted a little, then closed. He glanced down a moment, then returned his gaze to her.

"I know you can take care of yourself." He said it flatly. There was even an edge in the words, just a small one. "Are you trying to tell me to get lost?"

The question startled her, causing her to scramble around in her own thoughts. Was that what she was trying to do? Really? Or was it everything else she'd been mulling over?

"Sky?"

She didn't answer as she began to feel embarrassed by her own illogical thinking. She was trying to read tea leaves, ping-ponging from one idea to another feeling, ascribing motivations to him when she didn't know what they were, all the while dealing with the mess Hector had left in her heart and mind. Fear and yearning had mixed her up and now she was accusing him of things based on her own unsettling mental conversations—conversations that mostly made no real sense.

"Sky?" he repeated.

Her voiced was muffled when she answered. "Sorry. I don't usually make accusations based on one side of a private mental conversation. Certainly not one as mixed-up as I've been having."

She stared at her knees, hoping he didn't probe.

She heard him move, heard his boots on the wood floor, but she was still surprised when he knelt before her and seized her hands. He held them snugly until finally she lifted her gaze to look at him.

"I think," he said quietly, "that we need to talk."

"Go ahead." She certainly didn't want to do any talking herself. Everything she might say would only make her sound juvenile or crazy.

"Okay," he said after a few beats. "Me first. I am *not* babysitting you. I actually enjoy being with you. I like your company. I like your spirit. I was honestly glad to wake up this morning and realize I had a good excuse to stay here today. And there's nothing I'm supposed to be doing, because I'm seriously overdue for a day off. If anyone needs me for something important, I have a radio. Has anyone bugged me?"

"No," she said quietly, even as her heart lifted a bit. So he had really wanted to spend the day with her? That felt so good.

"However," he continued, "I'm aware that you're coming off a bad relationship. You told me just a little. So I'm tiptoeing because I understand that you're on the rebound, you're sore and hurt and I suspect you're seeing a lot through the lens of what happened with your ex. That's normal. We all do it. But I am not your ex."

"I didn't think you were!"

"Really? I get the feeling that sometimes you do. You may not realize it, but you've got yourself staked out with off-limits signs. Not every single moment, but they pop up. So I'm trying not to cross boundaries you don't want crossed. Besides, you're planning to return home. So why the hell would I want to get either of us into a mess that might hurt one or both of us?"

God, his thoughts had paralleled at least part of hers.

But at least he didn't say anything about her dissociation a few days ago. That would have wounded her.

"So you're fragile because someone just hurt you. I know that and respect that. Unfortunately, I can't help noticing how sexy and tempting you are. So I crossed the line a couple of times. I felt it."

He felt it? Oh, God!

"I wish we could have a lot more days right here doing exactly what we've been doing today. I'm relaxing with you and enjoying it, and I'd like to do it again tomorrow, but I don't think the weather will cooperate. So the sun will come out, my sense of duty will rear up and I'll get back to work."

She managed a nod as it began to penetrate that he'd said she was sexy and tempting. A warm glow started in her heart and between her legs, and it frightened her even as it gladdened her.

He tightened his grip on her hands. "Believe me, Sky, I'm not doing anything out of a sense of duty. Not today. I'm here because I want to be."

His hands holding hers felt so good. His skin was warm and dry, and slightly roughened from work. Not like Hector's soft hands. It gave her something to cling to. "Thank you," she offered tentatively.

"I don't know what that guy did to you, but it must have been some number. I see this wonderfully independent, outspoken, determined woman, and then I see something crumple inside you. Just every now and then. I don't even know who he is, but it makes me want to shake him."

"Hector," she managed. "His name is Hector. And you're right, he did a number."

"That's plain to see. I don't want to add to what he did, but I can honestly tell you that I want nothing more than to carry you to those sleeping bags and make love to you. I'd even," he added a little wryly, "like to think I could make you forget he ever existed."

What a beautiful thought that was. She ached for him to do exactly that. But she was frightened, too, and suddenly she loathed that fear. With all she had been through, how was it that a man had succeeded in making her afraid of life? Nothing else had.

"You're crumpling again," Craig remarked. He released her hands, brushed the back of his fingers against her cheek, then rose. "I'll get us some coffee. We're not done talking."

They weren't? But he had pegged her exactly, she realized. He had read her like an open book. She wouldn't have believed that anyone could see through her like that. She didn't know whether she felt uncomfortable or relieved that she didn't have to explain every little thing.

He handed her a mug and she cradled it in her hands, welcoming the heat. The stove was keeping the cabin warm, but for some reason, despite the actual temperature inside, whenever it got chilly outside her hands grew cold. Almost as if her body were adapting even though it didn't need to.

Craig pulled a bench over and sat close to her. "You said Hector cheated on you?"

"Yes." Then she blurted, "Worse than that. He said I was a lousy lay." She almost wanted to crawl under the floorboards as the words escaped her.

Craig swore quietly. "So basically he gutted you. By cheating, by claiming you didn't pay enough attention to him and by attacking you as a lover. That pretty much cover it?"

She nodded, but she didn't dare look at him. Not

at this instant. She'd just revealed one of her deepest scars and she felt more vulnerable than she'd ever felt on a too-quiet street in Iraq when they knew there were snipers around.

An odd thought, but one that told her she might be taking what Hector said way too hard.

"So he wanted you to pay more attention to him."

She nodded.

"Selfish. And you know what else that tells me?"

"No."

"The only lousy lovers I've ever run into were the selfish ones. I'd stake a year's pay that Hector was the lousy lover. Selfish. If you can stand it, think back over what it was like with him. I'd willingly bet that it was all about *him*. All of it."

"I don't know," she whispered. That revealed a whole lot, too.

"Was he your first?"

"My only."

"Then don't take his word for a damn thing. This whole picture says that Hector was the center of the universe and that anyone who didn't appreciate that fact wasn't good enough for him. How much time did he really spend trying to please you?"

She couldn't answer that, but the question made her start thinking. Other than the earliest days with him, she did seem to remember always trying to please him, and often failing miserably. Was that because of him or her? She didn't know.

Craig reached out for her hand and squeezed it. "I'm no lothario, although there may have been a time when I was younger that I strove for the title."

Out of the miasma of despair that had been filling her, she felt an irrepressible little bubble of humor. At last she was able to look at him. His expression was gentle. Kind.

"I've had more experience than you," he said frankly. "I've grown up a lot since then and I'm much more selective now. I can still say with absolute certainty that the only lousy lover is a selfish one. Inexperience can be surmounted but not selfishness. So quit beating yourself up over what one selfish guy said. I mean, for the love of Pete, he was cheating, demanding all your attention, and you'd believe him when he blamed *you* for not playing the planet to his sun?"

That was some way to put it, she thought. Her heart was lifting, thanks to him, and she turned her hand so she could squeeze his back.

He half smiled. "Anyway, you think about it, but one thing I can promise you. I'm spending this day with you because I want to. Not because I think you need protection, or anything else. Just because I want to enjoy a day with you."

"Even just doing puzzles?"

A truncated laugh escaped him. "Even just doing puzzles. If you decide to take down the no-trespassing signs, don't be surprised if I pounce. You've got my motor humming, woman."

Then he leaned over, brushed a kiss on her cheek, before rising to grab his jacket and hat. "I'm going outside for a minute," he said. "You need a little space after that heart-to-heart."

Did she? Part of her wanted him to stay right beside her, but as his words sank in, she also felt an internal earthquake taking place. It was like some sci-fi movie, where heavy walls started to move, only they weren't closing in and threatening her. They were opening, providing new space.

She could almost feel her heart and soul expanding.

She was also almost afraid to believe him. Could it really have all been Hector? That seemed unlikely. No one person was ever entirely at fault for a broken relationship....

That thought drew her up short, as if someone had jerked her. No one person was at fault? Then why had she been so convinced that *she* and she alone was at fault for what happened with Hector? Because she had certainly swallowed the idea completely.

But in reality...in reality maybe not. Probably not. Memories began to sift up through the sands of time, reminding her that Hector hadn't been the most devoted of partners in anything.

In fact, as she reflected, she realized she had ceded an awful lot to him, more than she had ever ceded before or since. Maybe she had been uncertain during her transition back to civilian life. Maybe she had been trying to relearn "normal" life, as distinct from her military life, and had lost her footing. But certainly by the time she got involved with Hector, she had been putty in his hands. Well, not entirely. But maybe too much.

She had refused to give up her job, or cut back on the hours. She had refused to give up her painting, too. Which had given him plenty of wedge to use against her about everything else. Maybe she had even been set up for that as a child, when she had been taught over and over that her wishes about anything didn't matter. That she wasn't even entitled to have any wishes.

Regardless, she'd left that situation to go into the military, which had given her tons of confidence in some ways, but had also taught her that her wishes and desires didn't matter. It had been easy for her to follow orders. Hell, that was how she had been raised.

So she had come back from a war, eventually gotten out of the service, gone through some therapy of her own to deal with the trauma, then moved out into the civilian world.

As a woman who still didn't feel she was entitled to any wishes or wants of her own.

Damn! Oh, she could get all tough and insistent about things she had learned to deal with in the military, like those guys across the valley, about not leaving a buddy alone, about not doing a solo recon, but when it came to anything else she couldn't even decide whether to have her eggs scrambled or fried, at least not when anyone else was involved.

She almost cringed to remember how many times she had said, "I don't care," or "Whatever you like," to Hector and her friends. Oh, man!

But before she cringed, she remembered that she hadn't ceded ground on her job or her art. Somewhere in there she still had a backbone.

So she must have seemed almost perfect to Hector, who wanted everything his way. A calm certainty settled over her. Hector *had* been selfish. Craig was right about that. But she had refused to give in on her work or her painting. No wonder he had gone looking for someone else, someone far more adoring. Someone much more malleable than she had turned out to be.

Understanding rushed through her, and it felt so damn good. She had strength, and if she had that strength she could grow more.

The kernel of determination that she had never entirely lost swelled and grew its first shoot. She *could* come back from this and get over it. She became sure of it.

The cabin door opened and Craig poked his head

in. "We've got company coming. You want me to keep them out here?"

"Who? And no, I'm fine." She said the last firmly, and with a real smile. "Thanks."

"I don't know who yet. I hear the engine." He came inside and reached for the gunbelt he'd left on the shelf. She watched him strap it around his narrow hips.

"Want me to get the shotgun?"

He didn't argue with whether she should, and she was grateful that he didn't treat her like some incapable ditz.

"Not yet. I want to see who it is first. I'll signal if I want backup. By the way, it's loaded." Then he vanished outside.

Backup. The word warmed her, and strength filled her. In some areas she had no doubts about herself, and apparently he didn't either. It felt like balm.

Rising, she picked a position where she could see out the window without being obvious to anyone outside, a position near the shotgun, a Mossberg autoloader. An excellent weapon.

Now she could hear the engine, too, even through the thick log walls. Moments later she recognized the official SUV of the Conard County sheriff's department. She saw Craig relax and relaxed herself.

Amazing, she thought. When first she had met him, Craig had seemed as relaxed as any person she had ever met. Apparently the Buddy thing was getting to him more than he let on. She bet he didn't usually respond this way to the sound of an engine.

Craig was a big man, but the deputy who climbed out from behind the wheel was even bigger. His Native American heritage was stamped plain on his face, and from beneath his tan Stetson flowed long black hair streaked with some gray. Not exactly a regulation cut, but she suspected that didn't matter to him, and probably not to anyone else he worked with. From the other side appeared a tall, young deputy, maybe about Craig's age. She went outside to greet them because it seemed friendlier.

Craig tossed her a smile. "Sky, meet Micah Parish." The huge deputy, a man who appeared to be in his late fifties, reached out to shake her hand. "Howdy," he said.

"And this is Doug Madsen."

The younger man stepped forward and shook her hand, as well. He had icy blue eyes but a warm smile.

"Come in," Sky said. "I'll make some fresh coffee."

The three men filled the cabin. It was good that Craig had rolled up the sleeping bags that morning, because there wouldn't have been room to stand. Once the coffee was done, they settled in, insisting Sky take the armchair. Craig perched on one bench, Micah on the other. Doug stood leaning against a wall.

Conversation had been casual, kind of bouncing around, but once they were all settled with coffee, things got serious.

"You know Gage was out at the Jackson place a few days ago?" Micah asked.

"Yeah, he said he was going."

"Well, our sheriff hasn't lost all his DEA skills. He came away with some photos."

Craig straightened. "Buddy let him?"

"Hell, Buddy didn't know. There are some really small cameras these days. Not that it matters. Buddy welcomed him and showed him around a bit. Plain view doctrine. No permission necessary. Gage got some interesting stuff here."

He reached into his jacket pocket and pulled out a

thick manila envelope. "He can email you any of these you want. Quality off the printer isn't as good. But we got one absolutely fascinating thing."

He pulled out a piece of paper, unfolded it and pushed it across the table. "Face recognition told us who this Cap guy is."

Craig leaned forward to read, and gave a low whistle. "Well, hot damn. I wonder if Buddy has any idea what followed him home."

Sky rose immediately. "What?" she asked.

When Micah hesitated, Craig said, "She's army, too."

"Too?" Sky repeated.

Craig answered. "Micah's retired Special Forces. Doug was a ranger. I think we're all pretty much on the same team here."

Then he handed her the paper to read.

Chapter 9

"They're not wants or warrants," Micah said as she scanned the paper. "But apparently Cap—Captain Les MacDonald—has a checkered history."

He most definitely did, Sky thought as she scanned the printout, starting with a dishonorable discharge from the army. After that, he'd apparently been on the fringes of a number of dubious activities, from illegal arms sales to drugs, but had never been directly implicated. He was a "person of interest" in past cases, but then his record went blank for four years. "He's dangerous," she said, handing the paper back and sinking into the armchair.

"So it would appear," Micah agreed. "Just how dangerous we don't know. Some things aren't there but Gage sniffed them out. He's been hanging around with a white supremacist group. Apparently only on the fringes. The guy is real cautious about not getting too deep into anything."

She nodded. "But he's learning."

"That's our feeling," Micah agreed. "A great addition to our county. I'm just wondering why he attached to Buddy and moved to the back of beyond."

"Takeover," Craig said. "Buddy must have talked too much to this guy at some point, and he saw an opportunity to move in and run the show. The question is what kind of show."

A silence fell over the cabin, punctuated only by the occasional drumbeat of rain on the roof and by the popping of burning wood in the fireplace.

Craig spoke again. "Do we know anything about his military background?"

"Sketchy," Doug answered. "He tried for the rangers and couldn't make the grade. Then he wanted airborne and didn't make it through jump school."

"So either somebody saw something in him that they distrusted, or he just isn't capable," Craig said.

Sky spoke next. "Failures like that can turn someone into a problem. They've got something to prove."

"He's not going to prove it here," Micah said emphatically. "We'll keep you posted. Gage is looking for a way to go over Buddy's place with a fine-tooth comb, but I doubt he'll get it. He talked to ATF, but they need more. So here we are. You two just be careful, hear?"

He checked to see if Craig wanted any of the other photos, but he declined. "There's nothing there, really. I need to see with my own eyes."

Micah stuffed everything back into the envelope. "Like I said, you be careful. Right now this Cap guy looks unpredictable. At some point he's bound to move from the fringes into outright action to prove something, as Sky here said. Let's hope he moves on before he does anything bad."

The two deputies left, and the heavens continued to weep. Back inside the cabin, Sky felt chilled, and not because it wasn't warm enough inside.

"Trouble," she said. "That guy is trouble."

"I agree."

"Buddy and his family could be in the most trouble of all."

Craig frowned. "Maybe. But right now I think the Jackson family is good cover for Cap and whatever he hopes to accomplish. Gage's visit achieved something else."

"Which is?"

"Cap now knows that the sheriff drops by from time to time. It would look really bad if a deputy dropped by and the whole Jackson family wasn't around, if you get my drift. So he needs the cover. Maybe they're part of his plan. Hell, at this point I can't even be certain Buddy isn't fully on board with whatever Cap might want. One thing for sure, I'm moving Buddy out of the perfectly-harmless-nut category. He might not be so harmless after all."

Sky didn't disagree. The cabin no longer felt like a cozy bulwark against the dismal day outside. Rising, she went to pull a cardigan out of her duffel and pulled it on, wrapping it tightly around herself. Inactivity didn't suit her, so she began to pace, no easy feat on the small amount of bare floor, hardly bigger than a king-size bed.

She was having a feeling that she recognized from Iraq all those years ago, when she had learned in the most unforgettable way possible that no place was safe, not for an instant, not for a moment, not even on a base.

Exaggeration, she told herself. This wasn't Iraq, and she didn't even know if there was an enemy. And Cap, while he might be looking to prove something, had no reason to prove it at the expense of Craig or her. No reason.

"He's got what, four guys?" she asked aloud.

"Cap? Three, maybe four. No army, that's for sure. We'll have to see if others show up."

"Yeah." A handful of men. A handful of men they could *identify,* which was extremely important as she had learned in a war where anyone could be a combatant and most didn't wear uniforms.

All of a sudden, strong arms wound around her from behind. Holding her snugly, halting her pacing. For an instant she wanted to pull away because the need to keep moving was powerful. A leftover instinct of some kind.

"Easy, Sky," he said. "It's going to be okay. It's a small group of fringe types. We can deal with it."

"I know." She forced herself to relax, releasing a sigh as she did so. "I know. But it still feels creepy."

"I agree with you there. But creepy isn't a threat assessment, is it."

In spite of it all, she had relaxed enough to laugh. A weak laugh, but genuine. "You're right," she said as she turned within the circle of his arms to face him.

He smiled down at her. "Remember, this Cap has failed at everything. And managed to anger somebody enough that he got a dishonorable discharge. I'd be more worried if it had been for medical reasons."

"Why?"

"Crazy."

She laughed again, more easily this time. "I didn't think of that. So we can be reasonably certain he's not that far over the edge."

"Yeah, it takes a lot to get discharged for mental ill-

ness. Hell, they wouldn't even let go of guys with se-
vere post-traumatic stress disorder. I figure Cap is a
guy with an inflated sense of himself. He's more apt
to screw up by thinking he's better than he is or by
overreaching."

"That's possible." But even as she answered, she realized that her uneasiness with the situation was slipping away, being rapidly replaced by awareness of the
man whose arms were around her. He held her loosely;
she could have moved away, but she didn't want to.

What had he said earlier, about her having warning signs that popped up? Had she been putting him
off without realizing it? Did she want to keep putting
him off?

No. The answer was clear in her own mind, in her
body, and it didn't carry one iota of doubt with it. She
might be making one of the worst mistakes of her life,
but she didn't believe it. Craig wasn't Hector, not in any
regard. Two men couldn't have been more different.

This man intuitively understood her land mines and
her scars. He probably even shared some of them, although he didn't talk about them.

Nothing could come of this, but she didn't seem to
care anymore. Just a fling. She could survive a fling.
There was, however, an imperative question she needed
to have answered: Was she a lousy lover?

Craig didn't think that was possible. He'd said so.
Lousy lovers were selfish lovers, and looking back at
her days with Hector she could see his selfishness. It
had been there in a lot of ways. So maybe she wasn't
the one who was flawed, and right now she desperately
needed to know.

If there was one thing she could put to rest, that was
it. One way or the other, she needed to know rather

than nursing her pain from Hector and never finding out if he was wrong.

If he was right…well, it could hardly hurt any worse than it already did, could it?

But more than the aching wound in her heart, she wanted Craig. He wasn't simply an answer to a question. She had been feeling and quashing stirrings of desire for him ever since she had first laid eyes on him. He'd said he was tempted by her. He'd told her he wanted to make love to her and stopped only because he felt her resistance.

That felt so good. Another sigh escaped her as she let go of something old and dark and turned her face toward something new, something that she desired, rather than denying herself out of fear.

But remembering what he had said about her off-limits signs, she realized he wouldn't take the first step. He wouldn't cross the barriers he'd sensed unless she invited him to. Because he was that kind of man, a good man, one who genuinely cared about taking care of everything he perceived as being under his protection. And whether he agreed she was capable of looking after herself, she had no doubt that he thought of her as falling under his protection.

A tremor of uncertainty and growing passion both rippled through her. It was as if she hovered at the brink of a cliff, wanting to soar, afraid of falling and unable to take the step.

But oh, how she wanted to. A tingling warmth was spreading throughout her. Her entire universe seemed to refocus, heightening her awareness of her womanhood. Even her breasts began to yearn for a touch. Anticipation became her friend for the first time in a long time.

But she had to take the first step. Seconds must have ticked by as she tried to find the courage to make a move. Even a simple move that would let him know.

Odd how she seemed to have forgotten even such an easy thing. But Hector, she realized now, hadn't welcomed overtures from her. Not ever. She'd had to wait until…

Ah, to hell with it, she thought. She raised her face, met those gray eyes squarely—they looked probing, she thought—then leaned into him and touched his mouth with hers.

"Ah, Sky," he breathed against her mouth. Then his arms became steel bands around her, pulling her close, holding her tightly to the length of his body.

His hard muscles against the softer curves of her body felt like heaven. She reached up to hang on to his shoulders as he deepened his kiss, taking care, so much care, as if he were testing how far she wanted him to go.

That had never happened before, she thought with hazy delight. Hector had always taken what he wanted however he wanted it. And why the devil was she thinking of Hector *now?* She wanted to banish him to the depths of a hell where he probably belonged.

She let her head fall back a little, her mouth opening even more, and Craig took her invitation. His tongue plunged into her, seeking out every sensitive place, some she hadn't realized she had.

Along her cheeks, over her tongue, then over her lips again until each nerve ending awoke to exquisite sensitivity and delight. She tried to respond in kind, to give him the same surprising pleasures, and loved it when he groaned quietly, deep in his throat.

Ah, this was good, so good she never wanted it to

end. Never had she felt that way about a kiss before. But then never had a kiss seemed to awaken her entire body.

He tasted like coffee, but even as she reveled in his taste, his aromas began to fill her nose: musky, manly, woodsy, a little damp from rain. Delightful scents, enticing scents. And as the kiss continued, the odor of musk increased, exciting her even more.

Everything else dropped away like dead leaves from a tree in a winter wind. Gone, it was all gone except for Craig and the passion he was stoking in her.

God, she tasted so good, Craig thought. Like coffee, yes, but with a hint of her minty toothpaste. Her mouth was warm, welcoming, making him want to enter her another way now.

He was as hot as a bonfire already, certain she must feel his hard, throbbing staff against her belly. Tinder to her spark. It was only with effort that he clung to his control. This was no time to go caveman. Not this time, although he could easily have lowered her straight to the floor and taken her with only the barest nod to necessities.

Fire licked at his groin, at the edges of his mind, but concern for her never entirely vanished. Not yet. She might become afraid again at any moment.

But having her cling to him this way and welcome him this way was enough to push him to the edge of madness.

He knew how scary this must be for her. He half expected her to stiffen, to try to pull away, and he wondered if he'd be able to let go.

But she didn't pull away. He could feel her growing softer against him, more yielding, more accepting, more hungering.

She was riding the wave with him.

Gently he pulled his mouth from hers and felt a surge of renewed desire as a soft moan escaped her. But he had another goal now, and without hesitation he found her ear, nipping gently, feeling the shudder pass through her, feeling the way her grip on his shoulders tightened almost painfully.

Then down her throat to the edge of the sweater she'd tried to hide in. The paint-spattered sweater. Those paint splotches that seemed to embarrass her but that he found somehow endearing. But he couldn't express that now.

No, nothing in him wanted to talk right now. Every single cell wanted to act, to pursue satisfaction, to find the answer to his manhood in her womanhood.

Risking breaking the spell he felt growing between them, he turned her a little in his arms. His mouth descended to the base of her throat, his tongue licking her warm skin, feeling her pulse beat rapidly. Then he boldly slipped a hand up beneath her sweater, beneath her shirt and found the bare skin of her midriff.

She froze, and for an instant he thought he had blown it all. But then a soft moan issued from her, a quiver passed through her and her fingers dug even harder into his shoulders.

She whispered his name brokenly. "Don't stop…"

Music to his ears, timed exactly to the throb of his entire body. The drumbeat of his blood nearly deafened him then, but those words, spoken in a broken whisper, resounded in his head. Don't stop. He wasn't even sure he could now and need hammered him ever harder.

He'd rolled up the damn sleeping bags, and even in his impassioned state he didn't want to take her on a wood floor. Splinters, roughness…anything but good.

He had enough presence of mind to lift her. Then he settled on the armchair. There was just enough room for her to straddle him. He saw her eyes widen with surprise, then narrow again as she realized what was happening.

She smiled sleepily, delighting him. She thrilled him even more when she leaned in to kiss him. Whatever her wounds, she had clearly decided to get past them.

Acutely aware of the burden that placed on him, momentary nervousness filled him. She took care of that in short order by leaning into him and wrapping her arms around his neck. There was no doubt this woman knew what she wanted, and that pleased him hugely.

Nervousness vanished. As he returned her kiss, he grasped her rump in his large hands and pulled her closer until their hips connected. He almost groaned as she pressed against his staff and her moist heat reached him even through two layers of denim.

He slipped his hands upward now, sliding them under her sweater and shirt, running his palms over her satiny skin. Edging steadily upward he sought the clasp of her bra, wanting to free her to his touch more than he had wanted anything in a long time. Women were no mystery to him anymore, but this one was affecting him as if she were a brand-new one, like the very first one, filling him with need and fear, anticipation and apprehension all at once. He wasn't sure she wouldn't change her mind. He wasn't sure he wouldn't disappoint her. Both kept him on exquisite tenterhooks of deepening hunger and inescapable uncertainty.

He found the clasp. She felt it and arched backward, almost as if offering herself to him. He quickly slipped his other hand beneath to join the first and when he released the hooks she gave a soft moan. His finger felt the bra pull open as it ceased to support. He didn't hesitate now, but slipped his hands around until he cupped both her breasts.

She groaned. He closed his eyes in absolute delight as she filled his hands, as he felt the hard, big pebbles of her nipples pressing into his palms. He now had no doubt she was coming on this ride with him, as hungry as he.

The pounding in his body grew harder and more insistent. His staff had stiffened until he felt it would explode, good, so good.

Running his thumbs across her nipples, he reveled in the shivers that ran through her, in the way she almost jerked at his each touch. He squeezed and kneaded, and even pinched her lightly, trying to wring every drop of pleasure out of this for both of them.

But most especially her.

She pushed hard on his shoulders, holding herself up, making her breasts available to his caresses. As she pushed against his shoulders, she brought her center even closer to his groin, and began a slow, steady rocking against him. He could feel her thighs tighten around his with each movement.

This was incredible, he thought hazily. Had it ever happened so hot and hard for him before?

They were going to reach a peak before he even unbuttoned their jeans, and damned if he cared. He rose up to meet her, savoring the pressure and her immediate response.

Finesse vanished. They were riding a sudden storm and with each movement of their hips the deep ache grew, goading them closer to the precipice.

Then, as if shot out of a bow, they flew. He heard her quiet keen, she bucked once hard, then collapsed on him weakly. An instant later, with one last upward jolt, he followed her.

He hadn't even started to catch his breath when the radio across the room started crackling, Lucy calling his name impatiently.

The sound of the radio was an unwelcome, unwanted intrusion. Sky straddled Craig's lap, sated, wanting to melt into him again, amazed that they had visited such heights in such a hurried fashion. Cripes, like kids in the back of the car, she thought. She might have been embarrassed except that she hadn't gone there alone. Craig had been right with her.

And that warmed the kernel of hope in her heart even more. The most basic of sex, and it had been good for both of them. No wine, no roses, no dinner, little foreplay, no romance and it had been exquisite.

Then the radio. She didn't even bother to stifle a groan of protest as she tried to find strength to lever herself off him. Long-ago training rose to take over: you didn't ignore a radio call. Ever.

He seized her waist and helped her to stand, standing with her at the same time. Then he eased her back into the chair.

"I'm going to kill Lucy," he remarked.

"Don't bother. She doesn't know."

He paused long enough to brush her hair lightly and drop a kiss on her mouth. "Wonderful," he said. "More later, unless you object."

Her cheeks flamed but she smiled. He returned the smile then headed for the radio, which sat on the shelf next to his hat and gun belt.

"What's up, Lucy?"

"Something's going on, Craig. Don is on his way. You're still at the cabin, right?"

"I was taking a comp day."

"Sorry, it's over. I'll let him know where to find you. Out."

He put the radio down and looked at Sky. "The comp day was over, except for you, since Micah showed up." Walking over to the window, he stood looking out at what had become a steady rain. "I wonder what the hell is going on."

"She didn't seem to want to say on the radio."

"No, she didn't."

They both understood what that meant. Whatever the news was, it wasn't meant to be overheard.

"There's too many forest service guys in the area," Cap said.

Buddy shrugged. "They're looking for a blocked stream. It's important."

"Well, *we* blocked the stream, so how do you think that's okay?"

Buddy bridled a bit. Sometimes he didn't like the tone Cap took with him. "This is *my* land. I can do whatever the hell I want on it. Those rangers can't even cross my boundary without my permission."

"You were sure eager enough to show that sheriff around."

Buddy glared at him. "You want to draw attention? The best thing to do when the sheriff pays one of his courtesy calls is to act like everything's normal. Be friendly. If I stop doing that, he for sure knows I'm up to something. Cut it out, Cap. He didn't see a damn thing he doesn't always see."

"You hope. He saw the new barracks and he didn't look like a dope to me."

"I told him it was because I needed more storage. There's no reason on earth for him not to believe that. He knows I got a lot of food stashed out here. Never made a secret of that."

"Well, maybe you should have." Cap frowned at him. "You're a little too open for a prepper, Buddy."

"I'm also too far out for anyone to care when the stuff hits the fan."

"You can't be sure of that."

"Well, that's what you're here for, right?"

Cap didn't answer immediately, which made Buddy nervous. He was seriously wondering if he'd made a mistake by inviting the man here. The questions seemed to grow by the day. Before Cap, he hadn't had any trouble with anyone.

"My men are out there working, Buddy. I told you that. The day is coming. They're already starting to come this way as they finish their jobs. But in the meantime, we're going to have to keep an eye on those rangers. If they find out we've diverted most of a stream to make a reservoir, they can tell you to remove the dam, right?"

"It's my land," Buddy said stubbornly. "They can't tell me anything."

"They're the government. I wouldn't be too sure of that. Anyway, we need to keep an eye on them so they don't get too close. What's going on here needs to be absolutely secret."

"What we need to do," Buddy said off the top of his head, "is make them less suspicious. You start following them around the woods with your patrols, and they'll get even more suspicious. We need a way to look like the good guys."

"Got any plan for doing that?" Cap asked sarcastically.

"I'm thinking on it," Buddy said stubbornly. "I'll come up with something. By the time I get done, we'll look like heroes and they'll leave us alone."

Chapter 10

Craig put on a fresh pot of coffee, apparently as much of a requisite for the forest service as it had been for the army. He also pulled out prepackaged sweet rolls to go with it, so full of preservatives they probably could have safely been stashed for the entire summer on that very shelf.

She understood, though: food and coffee, the essentials, especially when life lacked other comforts. On a day like this, Don probably wasn't very comfortable.

Because the rain had been so steady, Craig went out to check on Dusty, carrying a heavy wool horse blanket with him. "He may be waterproof, but he doesn't have a way to run around and keep warm out there," he explained. "I'll be a few minutes. I'm going to brush as much water out of his coat as I can and check the drainage. I don't want him standing in water."

On a day like this, Sky figured there was no way

to avoid standing in puddles. A little while later, she heard thumping. Curious, she grabbed her jacket and went outside.

Dusty stood near the side of the cabin, under the overhang, wearing his blanket. Craig, however, appeared to be using a shovel to dig a trench. The center of the corral had become a lake.

"Can I help?"

He didn't argue. "There's another shovel around back in the small toolshed."

Walking around back, she noted with amusement that Dusty seemed unfazed by all of this. He was eating grain and watching Craig's efforts with one eye.

It felt good to use her muscles for hard labor again, though, even though she was sure she'd probably feel it later. They trenched their way steadily toward a downslope just beyond the corral fencing.

Craig paused, wiping his forehead on his arm. "It's going to be muddy no matter what, but at least it should dry faster when the rain stops. I need to get some bales of hay out here to spread around if I'm going to be here often."

"But he's okay when you're moving around, right?"

"Sure. He can always find a dry place to stand and some shelter. It's just being cooped up like this that concerns me, and I'm probably worrying too much. It's only one day, and he's found a fairly dry place to stand. It's not like I'm going to leave him standing in water up to his hocks for a week."

She liked that he cared this much, though, even if he thought it might not be essential. "We could go scoop up armloads of pine needles from around here."

He cocked a brow at her. "Do you want to spend the rest of the day on that?"

Well, actually, no, she thought, quickly bending to start shoveling again. As wet as the earth was, it was easy to trench. There were other things she'd vastly prefer to do with the hours ahead. Damn, she'd had sex with a man and they hadn't even gotten naked. Think of that. Good sex, too.

They were just finishing the trench, watching the puddle vanish from the center of the corral, when Don drove up in a service pickup. He climbed out into the steady rain, pulling a bright orange poncho over his head.

"Why the hell aren't you two inside where it's dry?" he asked as he walked over to the corral. Then he saw the trench. "Oh. Afraid Dusty will melt?"

Craig just snorted. "Go on inside. I just made coffee. We'll be there as soon as we rinse off."

"Naw, it's more fun out here." He winked at Sky.

She quickly reached for Craig's shovel. "I'll put these back." The wink had probably been innocent, but after what she and Craig had just experienced, she didn't want to flirt, even casually.

"No, I'll do it," Craig said. "I need to lock up. You go on in with Don."

Exactly what she didn't want to do, but given no option, she crossed the corral and led the way inside. Much to her relief, Don didn't seem to want to go any further than that wink. He doffed his poncho, sat at the table with a mug of coffee and took a sip with a satisfied "Aah."

"We've got some sweet rolls, too. Want one?"

"I'd love one. Somehow this turned into a long day."

She tore the wrapper off the foil tray and put it on the table with a couple of paper plates. "You traded in Tragedy for the day?"

"I stabled him, more for my comfort than his."

Sky laughed. "It's a good day for that."

"I thought so." Don flashed a grin. Just then Craig came inside, stomping the mud off his boots before he crossed the threshold. Sky immediately poured him coffee and as soon as he dumped his rain gear, she handed it to him.

He sat with Don at the table, pushing wet hair back from his face. "What's going on?"

"I was out at the overlook this morning."

"Overlook Rock?"

"Well, of course."

Craig snorted. "Like we don't have a heap of scenic overlooks."

"But only one we call *the* overlook," Don retorted.

Sky sat, too, watching the men needle each other. Some parts of male interaction she would never understand, but whether she understood or not, she was familiar with it.

"So," Don asked, "you estimate that Cap guy has two or three others with him?"

"That's all I could see a few days ago."

"Multiply it. While I was checking around this morning I got some good views of the Jackson property and the surrounding area. He may have only three or four of these guys working on that new structure of his, but there are more of them out in the woods."

Sky felt her heart accelerate.

"How many?" Craig asked.

"I wish I could tell you. They're ringing the place like a defensive perimeter and keeping an eye on the woods around."

"What makes you sure they aren't just hikers?"

Don nearly rolled his eyes. "Oh, I dunno. They all

wear the same camouflage and they're all carrying AR-15s? They look like a damn army. They fanned out for a while, then pulled back. Like they were checking to make sure nobody—namely us—was poking around anywhere near Buddy's place. I wanted to think they were just playing games, but I kept remembering that hiker who turned up dead a month ago."

"He was four miles from Buddy's place. Anything could have happened, and we still don't have a definitive cause of death."

"I know." Don sipped more coffee. "These guys were out a few miles from Buddy's place. Just saying."

Craig didn't say anything immediately. Sky waited with an almost sickening sense of dread about where this might lead. The idea that Buddy might be building an army, even a small one, boded no good.

"They've got to do something wrong," Craig said finally.

"I know. I get it."

Sky spoke. "This hiker. How is it nobody is sure how he died?"

"The reality of a corpse left unburied in the woods. Between animals and decomposition, there wasn't a whole lot left. We identified him because nothing dined on his driver's license or credit cards."

"It doesn't take long," Don agreed. "You know that's one of the very real arguments about why we'll never find Bigfoot remains."

Sky did a double take. "Bigfoot? For real?"

Don laughed and Craig cracked a grin. "Rumors abound," Craig said. "Always."

Don kind of laughed. "Never seen one. But you know that's what they say. If the remains are buried, they'd be nearly impossible to find. If they're not buried, they'd be gone lickety-split."

"All bases covered," Sky said drily.

"You got it. Even bones don't last long in the woods."

"Scat," Craig said. "We'd see scat."

"Only if we know what we're looking at and it hasn't been buried."

Craig arched his brow. "Are you buying this, Don?"

"Who, me? I'm just trying to lighten an otherwise depressing conversation. A hiker died, there's good reason why it's so hard to determine cause of death. However, I'm not ready to say four miles from Buddy's place is too far. Not after what I saw today."

"How many did you spot?"

"I counted five. I watched for about three hours."

"Five." Craig repeated the number, frowning thoughtfully. "And that was only what you could see from the overlook."

"Exactamundo. Five. That side of Buddy's place. If I hadn't been so far above them, I wouldn't have known it. As it was, they emerged into clearings just often enough for me to get what was going on. There might have been more."

"Militia," Craig said.

"That's my guess. This isn't the kind of thing Buddy used to do. He was just a squirrel gathering acorns against a winter that would probably never come. He always struck me as harmless."

"Me, too." Craig sipped coffee, then rubbed his chin. A moment later he tore off a piece of sweet roll and ate it. "I guess Lucy isn't exactly amused by this."

"Hell, no. The boss was in fine form. She was *not* happy about a bunch of guys patrolling *our* forest with AR-15s, legal or not. Her first thought was that some visitor could get hurt. Thank God we don't have too many of them right now, but she's going to steer them as far from Buddy as she can."

"The ones who stop by the office, anyway."

Silence fell as Don ate and got himself some more coffee. Sky sat wondering what anyone could do about any of this. If it wasn't illegal for those guys to be out there, then...what?

"Anyway," Don said, "Lucy wanted to be sure everyone was alerted. You know we've been moving as many guys as we can to this part of the park for a few days. Now she's worried *we* might run into trouble."

"Not if we're careful. Imagine the flares they'd send up if something happened to one of us. Although, the more of us that are skulking in the trees around here, the more likely that gets."

Don nodded and reached for more roll.

"About the valley river," Craig said. "That's been my excuse for wandering around the area."

"Yeah, that's what we're all supposed to be checking out."

"I can't find anything on forestry land. That leaves Jackson's place. He's got one of the biggest of the feeder streams running through his acreage. If he were to divert a significant amount, we'd notice below."

"It's probably him," Don agreed. "So tell me how we prove it."

"I'm just thinking out loud," Craig said. "Ordinarily I'd say there's no reason for him to divert anything. He's always had a few small ponds to carry him through a dry spell."

"Unless he adds a bunch of people," Sky added.

The two men exchanged looks.

"Quite a few people," Don amended.

"So how many of these guys is he planning to bring out here?" Craig wondered out loud. "And more importantly, why? I guess I need to go have another talk with him."

Sky's heart slammed. "Not alone! Those creeps were following me in the woods. Don't you dare go over there alone."

"Following you?" Don looked worried. "Why in the hell? You're just a painter. Are they that paranoid? Damn it, Craig, we've got to get to the bottom of this before something blows up that can't be contained."

"Parameters would be useful. Some idea of what they're up to would help. Playing soldiers in the woods isn't illegal."

"Damaging a national forest by diverting water is," Don said.

"Prove it. That's why I'm going to have to talk to him again."

"Not alone," Sky repeated.

He looked at her at last. "Not alone," he agreed. "This time I think we might need to join up with our friend the sheriff."

Relief washed through her. "Good," she said firmly.

Don left a short while later, promising to get back to them after working things out with Lucy. Apparently they were now observing radio silence except for the most innocuous of things.

"It never," Craig remarked, "used to drive me nuts to be out here without phone or internet. The radio was more than enough. Now I'd give my eyeteeth for an internet connection."

"I can imagine."

"I should probably take you to town, make sure you're out of the line of fire."

"We don't even know that there's a line of fire," she argued. "What's more, those creeps know all they want to know about me now. They went through my things. Nothing but painting supplies. No guns, no ammo, no fancy spy cameras. Just my digital SLR camera with a bunch of lenses and a handful of memory sticks. I'm no one and they know it."

"So?"

"So I'm not going to be run off. I came here to paint, and as soon as the weather clears, that's exactly what I'm going to do. We sure don't want to do something that might alert them to the fact we know something is going on."

"I doubt—"

"Hush," she said firmly. "I'm not running, and I'm not leaving you out here alone. Period. I don't care how much backup you have. I'd never forgive myself for hightailing it."

He stared into those determined eyes of hers and realized he had a new team member whether he liked it or not. She had something riding on this, too, although he would have liked to know exactly what it was.

"What's more," she said, "I can keep an eye on things without being obvious as long as I have a canvas in front of me and a paintbrush in hand. I also want to take another walk to that gorge. It's beautiful."

Well, that was a confusing mix. He couldn't decide if she was throwing all this out in the hopes that if she tossed enough, something would stick. In spite of himself, he laughed.

"How will going to some gorge keep an eye on Buddy?" he asked. "Do you have a line of sight?"

"Well, I'll find out if they're patrolling this side of

the valley regularly. And if they are, I'll keep at least one of them preoccupied."

Still he hesitated. While he had no proof that this could turn dangerous, he had an ugly suspicion it might do exactly that. Men patrolling the woods with AR-15s were dangerous if only because they might use those weapons carelessly. One itchy finger was all it would take.

Every protective instinct he owned wanted her out of here. But when he took a mental step back, he realized that even if he dragged her to town, she was determined enough to just get in her car and come right back out here.

"Look," she said, "your people are going to be concerned with what's going on over at Jackson's. I can keep an eye out over here. If they're spreading out this far routinely, that's more information to evaluate."

At last something that made actual sense to him other than apparent stubbornness. Okay, then. At least she'd be on this side of the valley, probably safe from most of it.

Except that his skin crawled a little when he remembered she had been followed in the woods yesterday. He couldn't imagine why they would take that much interest in *her*.

"Sky?"

She raised questioning eyes.

"I can't help it. I'm worried that you were followed yesterday. It doesn't make sense."

"They just wanted to know what I was really doing. They found out. The guy must have been bored to tears. Anyway, now they know. I admit I was angry and a little disturbed at the time, but I'm not anymore. I pose absolutely no threat to them."

"At this point I'm beginning to wonder exactly what they think is a threat."

"Bigfoot?" she suggested.

She made him laugh again. One thing that was missing from his usually solitary existence, he realized, was laughter, and it felt so good to laugh now.

The radio crackled again, breaking the mood, and he went to answer it. It was Lucy.

"You know those guys we talked about hiring on for that special job? They're being hired. Expect the first of them to be there to help you in a day or two. In the meantime, enjoy your day off. In fact, take another. You'll have plenty to do once the new crew arrives. Out."

He stood staring at the radio. Sky went to join him, all of three steps. "Was that as cryptic as it sounded?"

He put the radio down. "Well, we weren't planning to hire anyone."

"So what does she mean?"

"I think she or the sheriff is bringing in some outside help on the Buddy thing. My guess is ATF."

"Well, it's about time."

"Maybe so. I wonder what lit the fuse."

"Don seeing those guys patrolling, probably." She perched on the bench and put her chin in her hand. "That and the Cap guy's background. His being here means something, and from looking at that information this morning, my guess is it doesn't mean anything good."

He crossed to her, squeezed her shoulder, then sat facing her. "It bothers me, too. For what it's worth, I'm not sure Buddy is in charge anymore. I know that guy. This is not the kind of thing he'd come up with on his own. He was always harmless before."

"So you said, but he's not looking exactly harmless right now. So maybe it *is* Cap's influence. Or maybe Buddy took a liking to the guy and now he has a tiger by the tail. Maybe it's even changed his thinking about all of this doomsday stuff. We'd have to be mind readers to know."

"I'd love to get a look at that new building of his."

"Don't even think about it. You've got help coming with all the surveillance aids you lack."

"I know, I know. I'm law enforcement, but not at their level."

"By design." She reached across the table, and after a moment he took her hand. She could easily imagine the struggle he was having. He was a former marine. Action was his forte. Finding himself limited by the parameters of his current job, by the equipment he lacked, had to be galling. He wanted to deal with this, not turn it over to someone else. She could understand that. If she didn't, she'd be packing and heading for town.

You didn't walk away from a fight or a problem, at least not of this type, not when innocent peoples' lives potentially could be at risk.

"That was interesting about the hiker," she said suddenly.

"The rapid decomp?"

"Yeah. And the resultant difficulty in figuring out cause of death. I'm not used to thinking in those terms."

"Few people are," he answered.

"I know, but that's not the point. The point is, if someone *does* know that, they could use it to their advantage."

It seemed to her he sat a little straighter. Then he swore. Evidently he'd just made the same connection.

"How long," she asked, "has that Cap guy been there?"

"I don't know. I usually leave Buddy to his own devices. I may stop by a handful of times during the year just to be neighborly."

He rubbed his free hand across his chin and mouth, making a small, frustrated sound. Then he swore again. "Maybe we need the big guns after all."

"What's the worst that can happen? ATF comes, does their surveillance, maybe even finds an excuse to question, then leaves. That's the worst. If there's nothing wrong over there, it's over."

"Unless they miss something. Then every ranger in this forest could become a target."

"That's not likely," she argued. "You said it yourself. If something happens to one of you, this place would be crawling with federal law enforcement. No, they're not going to touch you, much as they might want to."

But hanging on the air was the unspoken *unless they could make it look like the hiker...cause unknown.*

The shiver that ran down her spine felt glacial in its iciness.

She rose from the bench and went to look out the window at the weeping day. There was no sign the weather might change anytime soon. The sense of being watched hit her again, causing the hair on the back of neck to rise.

"Craig?"

"Yeah?"

She pointed to the window. "Those shutters outside. Do they close?"

"That's how we shut the place up for the winter."

"Let's close them now. I'm getting that feeling again."

He didn't answer immediately.

"Well?" she said finally.

"The question is whether it's more important to see out than to not be seen."

She didn't answer because it was a good question. "I need the facilities."

"I'll go with you."

He stood and went to don his gun belt. Then he picked up his Mossberg. She understood perfectly.

After Craig escorted her back to the cabin, he insisted she remain inside. "I want to do a little casual scouting, and it won't look at all casual if we both do it."

That was enough to salve her pride, apparently. He wandered the small clearing, shotgun slung casually over his forearm as if he weren't expecting to use it, but the strap was firmly settled on his shoulder to give him support if he had to use it fast.

Here and there he stepped a ways into the woods, checking the ground. The nice thing about all this rain was that it would be virtually impossible for anyone to move around in here without leaving tracks. Despite excellent mountain drainage, the earth had become mud. Not even the carpeting pine needles could conceal a footprint now.

If Sky had felt watched while standing at the window, he had no doubt someone or something was watching. The most inerrant of human senses, he had learned to trust it a very long time ago. Somehow, some way, people knew when they were being watched, whether by an animal or another person. The sense usually got tamped down because most people lived in situations where others would look at them often, but it got finely honed in places the military took a person.

Finely honed. And when you came back from combat, it wasn't easy to tamp it down again.

That sense had warned him when wolves were watching. It had warned him when bears were watching. He credited it with once saving him from a grizzly mama who was feeling hyperprotective of her cubs.

Dusty had the sense, too. A lot of people laid that to the door of scent, and maybe it was for Dusty. He always knew when danger lurked, and would get fidgety if he felt stalked.

He was looking pretty calm right now, though, standing blanketed under the overhang, appearing to be half-asleep. Much as he liked to get out for a good long walk, he didn't seem to want it today.

"Getting up there, boy?" he asked the horse as he passed the corral. Dusty blinked one eye at him. He was joking, of course. Dusty was nowhere near retirement.

Craig swung out again, piercing the wall of surrounding trees. He ventured into the nearly night-dark depths of the rainy woods, scanning the ground for disturbance of any kind.

He couldn't say he was surprised when he saw it: a depression, then another. Scanning quickly he saw enough of them to suggest someone had walked up to this point, stood a bit, then walked away.

Probably still out there, too, he thought. Not watching right now, but getting ready to watch again. The comings and goings today, starting with a sheriff's vehicle, probably had garnered some interest.

The watching was too intense, too coordinated. Pointless unless these guys were planning some kind of action. The question was what kind? Their secrets were well enough protected on Buddy's private land, so the only reason to fan out this way was because they felt there was a threat, and if they felt threatened, they'd act. With Cap there, Craig had absolutely no doubt. The only question was who they considered a threat and how far they were willing to go.

Hell. *Buddy, what are you thinking?* Although he was beginning to wonder if Buddy was thinking at all. Or if Buddy was the one doing the thinking.

He emerged from the woods again and stood looking at the cabin. To shutter or not to shutter. He was definitely of two minds about that. On the one hand, shuttering would give them more privacy and probably make Sky feel more comfortable. On the other it might be read as an indication they knew they were being watched and were preparing for attack. That might send an even more dangerous message to a paranoid bunch of armed men.

Damn.

He walked over to the corral and Dusty came out from under the overhang to nuzzle him. The rain still fell drearily and steadily, and the desire to get back indoors with Sky was filling him. It was a new feeling to him, at least for many years now, to actually want to be indoors with someone. Sky was making him feel a lot of things he'd almost forgotten.

He gave Dusty a few pats and scratches. "Think I'm getting confused, boy?" he asked the horse. "We know she's going to leave soon, right? The thing is, I can't seem to get worked up about avoiding the trouble that might bring. I just want to enjoy now with her. Guess I pay for that later."

Dusty nickered quietly as if he understood. Not likely, but it occurred to Craig that holding conversations with Dusty might be an indication that he needed more human interaction.

The crack of a laugh escaped him. Dusty seemed to like it, tossing his head and then nudging Craig playfully on the shoulder.

"Okay, okay. I'm just sorry I can't bring you inside, too."

Dusty made that oddly delicate little snort, one that barely ruffled his nostrils. It always struck Craig as gentle. In return, he gave Dusty a big, smacking kiss on the nose.

Dusty turned his head, eyeing him as if he wasn't sure he appreciated that, then trotted back over to his dry shelter under the overhang.

Which left Craig to look at the wood shutters. They were heavy, basically planks with crossbars, nothing fancy. But sturdy enough to stand up to the worst the weather could bring, which was the whole point.

Better, he decided, for Sky to feel unobserved. Only three windows needed to be covered, so he closed and barred the shutters quickly. One last stop to make sure they had enough water in the gravity tank, then he picked up an empty bucket and headed inside.

"What's that for?" Sky asked as she saw the bucket.

"Chamber pot."

She stood up from the bench. "Someone was out there."

"Someone definitely was out there. Who and why and what they were doing is anybody's guess. Regardless, nobody uses the outdoor facilities after dark. I'm going out to my truck to get some plastic bags for liners, and a few rolls of paper. We have just gone totally basic."

She surprised him with humor. "If I don't have to

dig a hole, it's not totally basic. Especially if we have liners."

God, that woman could both surprise him and make him smile. A great combination indeed.

Chapter 11

Don radioed that he wouldn't be coming back out that day. The two of them sat in the shuttered cabin, listening to the rain drum, in darkness except for the oil lamps. The woodstove held the storm's chill at bay.

Cozy, except that it felt like a bunker, Sky thought. That was her fault for wanting the shutters closed. All of a sudden she remembered what Craig had said about when he came home from the war and he couldn't stand a closed door even in his own apartment.

"Craig? Are these shutters making you feel uneasy?"

"Not really. I can't see much from the windows anyway. I'd have to patrol occasionally regardless."

"That's not what I'm talking about."

His gray gaze was steady, his eyes an exact match for the dark clouds outside. "I know. I'm fine. I'm luckier than most. I got past it."

But she wondered. "You chose a career that keeps

you in the middle of nowhere away from people most of the time."

His eyes narrowed and his face seemed to tighten. "I like it."

"I can see that. And you said you'd always been interested in forestry. But…what if they sent you to a busier place? Would you still like it as much?"

"I started in a busier place before I came here." His tone grew a little edgy, almost defiant.

"Okay."

He leaned across the table toward her. "What are you trying to say, Sky? That I've got a major hang-up?"

She felt herself blanch. "No. No, it never crossed my mind!"

"Then what's crossing your mind?"

The truth was, he was right but she didn't want to admit it. Only a few days ago she'd dissociated for no good reason for the first time in years. Renewed lack of trust in her own mind was leading her to question him, perhaps seeking reassurance that he, too, occasionally got bitten by the past. "I guess…well, you saw what happened to me. That hasn't happened for years now. Maybe I just don't want to feel so abnormal."

His expression altered completely, speeding from astonishment to concern. "You're not abnormal."

"How can I tell that?"

"You have to believe that. You've been in a war, you came back and you actually managed to put a life together for yourself. Some guys can't do that, yet they're normal, too. Damn it, Sky, can anyone go to war and come back unchanged?"

She knew the answer to that, knew it all too well. Her work with vets had even taught her how bad it could get, and how lucky she was.

"I don't blame you for being uneasy," he went on. "You got caught unexpectedly by something that you thought was behind you. That chips at your trust in yourself. I get it. But look at the past few days and how much has been going on. You haven't slipped away. In fact, you've stayed front and center. You're okay."

She remained mute, trying to accept his reasoning. The army had taught her a lot of confidence, but it was confidence in other things, things that didn't often matter in civilian life. Overall, though, apart from Hector, she'd built a pretty decent life for herself. Day by day, Iraq slowly faded into memory. It almost never surged up fresh anymore.

"It'll keep getting better," he said. "Man, I put a Mossberg in your hands the other day and you didn't flash back. What makes you so unsure of yourself?"

Plenty, she thought. Hector had undermined more than her womanhood, she suspected.

"I guess," he continued, "that some people might think I'm hiding out here. I don't feel like it. I feel like I'm doing something really important, protecting this forest, this habitat, this environment for future generations. This place is teeming with life and I love it. I love watching the seasons change, watching plants grow, watching boulders tumble and streams rush. I love learning how things interact with each other, and how interdependent life really is. Being out here is almost a form of enlightenment for me. It's a different kind of city, but every bit as important to our survival."

"Maybe more so," she agreed. With a sigh, she let go of the troubled feelings. "I love it here, too. More than once since I arrived I wished there was a way I could stay. There's a connection of some kind here that

I don't get in all the hustle and bustle of a city. There's even more time."

"Time?"

"Time to just experience without racing on to the next thing on some to-do list. I must have spent a couple of hours sitting in that gorge, just soaking it in. I'd never do that at home."

"Of course not. There's always something that must be done."

"Exactly." She gave him a crooked smile. "And plenty of guilt if you don't do it. I have a friend who says the best vacation she ever took was a cruise."

"Really? That's never appealed to me."

"Me either. But she said that while she was out on that boat she was completely cut off from her everyday life. There was absolutely nothing she could do about anything at home. She couldn't even get a phone call. She said it was the most free she'd felt in her life."

"I know that feeling, except I'm tethered by a radio."

"Electronic leashes. I work with a guy who says his cell phone is his electronic leash."

He smiled. "Good description."

"Anyway, I'm probably worrying about nothing."

"Well, that's the other side of being cut off like this. If worrying is your thing, you have plenty of extra time to do it."

He hesitated. "Are you sure you don't want me to take you back to town?"

She shook her head. "Then I'd really worry. About what's going on out here."

"Rock and hard place."

"Not really. I'd rather be here."

"Things could get dicey."

"Things are already dicey," she argued. "Someone

was watching the cabin. Someone followed me yesterday and went through my things. I realize I'm no expert, but none of this is striking me as innocent." In fact, if they wanted to talk about worries, Buddy and his friends would be right at the top of her list.

"The ATF is coming," he reminded her.

"Right. Like that's going to prevent something from going critical. Like you're not going to be in the middle of it."

"You're worried about me?"

"Why does that surprise you?"

One corner of his mouth lifted. "It's been a while since anyone worried about me. It's a nice feeling."

That spoke volumes to her, and she thought about what it might be like for him. His parents and one brother had abandoned the continent for distant shores. Life had taken all of that away from him just as it had from her, and then he'd chosen the kind of life that kept him mostly alone.

Oh, clearly his fellow rangers and his boss were friends, but from what she had seen they weren't the kind of friends he'd be spending a whole lot of time with. So he was alone with his forest, which had a lot of advantages but didn't provide the kind of companionship most people needed.

Of course, these were his choices. Maybe she ought to pay attention to them instead of sitting here trying to establish links with him. Instead of thinking about how much she wanted him to make love to her again.

Instead of realizing that she felt less alone with him than she did at home in Tampa with all her friends. Less alone than she had felt during her time with Hector.

Wow. That was heavy. Dangerous, too.

"Something wrong?" Craig asked. Damn his perceptiveness.

"I'm fine," she answered, keeping her tone firm.

For a few minutes they sat in silence, the puzzle still scattered on the table in front of them. One corner of one tower had begun to rise, and they had most of the edge done. Their efforts had been casual. No pressure. No demands.

The day had brought enough pressure and demands. And to think that earlier they had both thought they were going to have a vacation day in the rainy woods. It hadn't exactly worked out that way.

But when did anything ever go according to plan?

Craig stood up. "I need to feed us. I hope we have enough left since we didn't go to town today. Unless you want to run in and have dinner or something."

She thought of the long drive along the forest service roads in the rain, thought about returning to civilization and people, and shook her head. "If we can manage it, I'd rather stay here."

She caught the hint of a smile from him. "Let me go see what we have left."

They had plenty for tonight. Not all the ice in the chests had melted, and they yielded cold cuts and a small jar of mayonnaise. An unopened loaf of rye bread sat on the shelf. There were even a couple of tomatoes that were still firm.

Sky cleared one end of the table, remarking, "I suppose we ought to just put this puzzle away. It's getting to the point where we have to keep laying out the pieces."

"If you've had enough of it. I don't mind having to straighten them out again."

"Maybe we should have put it on the floor."

"Where?" he asked humorously. He brought some paper plates over, too.

She lifted one. "Conservation?"

"Recycled paper. Easier to toss it on the fire than try to wash up, especially come winter. It's also useful for starting a fire if someone gets stranded out here."

"True." She hadn't thought of that, but if people came out here to ski or snowmobile in the winter, and got into trouble, the forest service cabins might be all that stood between them and death. "Do you keep the cabins locked over the winter?"

"Absolutely not. Toolshed, yes, cabin, no. Not this far out. If someone gets in trouble out here, they're going to need every possible little edge."

"Does it happen often?"

"Once in a while. That's why it's so important to check in with the office before you come out here. If someone doesn't come back, we definitely need a starting point. Searching a few thousand square miles is no joke."

By the time they finished eating and had cleaned up, it was still raining steadily. When Craig went out to check on Dusty, she followed. The woods had grown so dark with the clouds and approach of night they almost looked like a ragged black wall.

She thought Dusty gave them a look that spoke volumes as he stood beneath the overhang. "He's sick of it," she remarked.

"Can't say I blame him. He likes to be moving. Mustangs will often cover fifty miles a day just grazing. He's not much different. He must feel like a prisoner."

Dusty watched almost indifferently as fresh feed was laid out. Craig spent a few minutes patting him and talking quietly to him, but as he turned away, something changed.

Dusty nickered, but not that one little friendly nicker. He did it repeatedly, bobbing his head and pawing at the ground.

"Bear?" Craig asked, looking at the horse. Sky immediately peered around them.

Dusty shook his head and emerged from beneath the overhang, trotting around the corral as if he was disturbed. Twice around, then he reached a point where he actually reared up and pawed the air.

"I'm getting my gun," Craig said. Apparently he didn't need to hear it again. "Come inside."

"I can help."

"I'm sure you could, unless it's a bear. If it is, we don't want to spook it. Nor do you know how to deal with one."

"From what I hear there's not a lot of dealing to be done."

"Depends. Just do me a favor and stay inside. I don't want it to escalate if this is a bear."

Reluctantly she took up a post in the open cabin door. "I'm at least going to keep an eye out."

"I can live with that. Grab a couple of pans. If you see us come running out of the trees, start banging them."

She could do that. She grabbed the frying pan and the saucepan, then resumed her post. He left with his Mossberg and a strong flashlight.

She was surprised when Craig came around the corner from the corral riding Dusty bareback. She didn't have a lot of experience with horses, but riding without a saddle or stirrups struck her as risky.

But she *was* glad he wasn't going on foot. Dusty

made him appear a lot bigger and might prove to be more help by far than she could be. If it was a bear.

She didn't want to think it was a human threat. Although Dusty wouldn't have responded to that, would he? He hadn't reacted earlier.

Then she wondered why Craig was even checking it out. If it was a bear, wouldn't it be wisest for them both to remain inside?

Dusty, she realized. He didn't want the horse out there by himself if a bear was hunting. TV animal specials popped up in her head. Bears wouldn't be hunting at this time of year. Didn't that come later in the summer, after they'd fattened up on berries and stuff? But what if this were a grizzly? From what she understood about them, they didn't need a whole lot of reason to kill. Maybe that was wrong. She cursed her lack of knowledge. All she knew for sure was that if some bear was hanging around it might well have cubs, and that was a big problem.

Minutes stretched by as her nerves grew more taut. Where had they gone? How could they see anything in this lousy light? Well, he had taken that flashlight, although she wondered how he was going to juggle everything. Riding bareback, no holster… Maybe he could control Dusty with his knees?

Yeah, as long as the horse didn't rear. But maybe Dusty wouldn't rear with Craig astride him, and being free to run from a threat. Maybe he'd only done that because he was confined, or because he was trying to warn them.

God, she didn't know the first thing about horses either. She'd come out here with all a tourist's knowledge, which was to say zip, into an alien world as blithely as if she were taking a stroll down a sidewalk back home.

The forest was beautiful, but she was kidding herself if she thought it held no threats of its own.

Just as she considered banging the pots to relieve her own tension, Craig and Dusty emerged from the trees. Craig rode the horse around the clearing in the rain, apparently letting him work out any remaining restlessness. Then he came to the small porch.

"Bear," he said. "Gone now."

"Will Dusty be safe?"

"Let's just say all mama wanted was her cub, and they weren't thrilled to see me. They took off. I'll be right in."

He leaned down to pass her the shotgun and flashlight, then touched Dusty with his heels. She watched them disappear around the corner again, then realized she was trying to juggle too much: a shotgun, a flashlight and two pots. Sheesh.

She hurried inside, dropped the pots on the table along with the flashlight, then checked the shotgun to make sure the safety was engaged. It was, so she put it back on the shelf.

He was crazy, she thought. He'd gone out there in the dark looking for bear. Crazy. Except how could she judge? He understood these woods and probably had an encyclopedic knowledge of bears. He knew what he was doing.

But he was still crazy.

She didn't have to wait long after she put everything back. He strode through the door after shaking his slicker off and hung it from a hook on the back of the door.

"A bear," she said. "A bear with a cub. And you went out for a nice little chat?"

"Only to persuade her not to forage around here, at

least not right now. I think she was drawn by Dusty's grain. If no one's here and we leave a sack outside, it often goes to the bears and other critters. No big deal."

"No big deal," she repeated. "A mama with cubs is no big deal."

"Not as long as you don't get between them." He sat at the table and flashed a grin. "It was okay. We had a meeting of minds." Then his smile faded. "It was strange, though. She was an awful long way from her cub. Like something had disturbed them. I'm wondering if the cub let out a distress howl and that's what set Dusty off."

"Like something had disturbed *them?*" She put her forehead in her hand. "What the hell would…" She trailed off. "Oh. Buddy's friends. Well, I hope he got mauled by mama."

"As a rule," Craig said, "black bears don't cause unnecessary trouble. Unless someone actually threatened her cub, she'd try to lead him away or scare him off, then go back for her cub. As a rule."

"But not always."

"No. And she may be headed for trouble, because right now the smell of humans around here must be thick, and she shouldn't have come so close. Or maybe all the rain masked the human scent. Regardless, we'll have to keep an eye out, but for the moment, I'm not worried. She took off with her cub once she knew she'd been spotted. That makes her a smart bear who should live a long life."

Sky supposed she should be glad about that. "How's Dusty?"

"Better now that he got some exercise. And now that he knows the bear took off."

"One more question."

"Yeah?"

"Who the hell leaves grain outside in bear country?"

He broke into a laugh so hard she could see his eyes moisten.

"What's so funny?" she demanded.

"You just surprised me. That question was spot-on."

"Then explain it."

"Sometimes someone gets forgetful. Right now, though, since I've been corralling Dusty, there's enough feed out there to draw attention. My guess is mama and cub started coming this way a day or two ago, browsing as they went."

"I still don't see what's funny."

"Only because you have no idea how many times I've had to explain to hikers and campers why they shouldn't sleep close to their food, why they should hang it from trees and so on. Endless explanations. Nobody explained it to you, but you got it right immediately."

"It just seems obvious to me." She was surprised how much it relieved her to be certain he didn't see her as silly or stupid. And it reminded her of how often Hector had made her feel that way. Not constantly or she would have walked out. But often enough that she remembered it. God, what had she ever seen in that man?

"You have no idea how *un*-obvious that is to most people. Are you mad at me?"

"No, not really. I was just so worried when you went out there. I guess I'm wound up."

"Everything's fine."

"Now, sure. So you think somebody was out there again?"

"It's possible." The last of his smile faded. "The list

of things that would worry a she-bear is pretty short. It can't have been wolves because she'd be dealing with a pack and wouldn't leave her cub's side. We haven't reached mating season yet, so it's unlikely a male would be anywhere near. That leaves humans. What really bothers me, though, is that the cub wasn't up a tree. I wish I could find out if it's hurt."

"Don't even suggest going back there to find out. Not alone."

"I won't. But if I find out somebody hurt a cub, there'll be hell to pay."

Despite the warmth inside the cabin, Sky felt chilled and rubbed her upper arms with her hands. "I had no idea a small vacation in a national forest could turn so adventurous. Call me naive."

"I can escort you back to town."

"No!" She was vehement. "I'm not letting those creeps run me off, and I'm not leaving you here alone. They seem to have an interest in one of us. Most likely you."

"So what's your plan, then, Sky?"

She thought she read more in his eyes than simple curiosity, but she couldn't be sure. "I'm going to go out as soon as the rain passes and do what I've been doing. If I can keep one or two of those guys busy, that'll help. After today it's obvious they're interested in a lot more than what's happening at the edges of Buddy's property. In which case, me carrying on like there's nothing to worry about might lull them."

He nodded slowly. "Maybe. Especially after they've seen we're hanging out together."

"Exactly. So tomorrow, assuming the rain lets up, we carry on as if we've forgotten all about Buddy and Cap."

Boy, did she wish she could forget all about those guys. She wished this was just an ordinary vacation, that she'd met Craig under ordinary circumstances, that they could tell the world to go hang and spend the rest of the day exploring the burgeoning attraction between them.

That's all she wanted. A little peace and quiet to find out what it would be like to be with Craig fully, to find out if he could take her to those heights again when they weren't constricted by clothes. To find out if she could take him there again.

Even with all that was going on, that need was growing stronger by the minute. The need to love and be loved.

It was, she thought, staring down at her hands, as primal as questions of life and death.

Craig caught the flicker of heat in her gaze before she became fascinated with her hands. Damn, his body surged in response just from that look. He'd damn near forgotten he could respond to a woman like tinder to a match. One look and he was raring to go.

The whole world seemed to narrow to that cabin and to the woman sitting across from him. He was only human, after all, and his most essential nature was waking to possibilities, desires, needs. The smell of the hot woodstove dominated the cabin, but beneath it he could detect the very faint odors of woman. They called to him as much as her eyes had.

Oh, he had it bad.

He tried to think about threats, tried to think about the fact that he was fairly certain somebody had checked them out at least twice today, and that level of interest indicated that Buddy and his friends felt threatened. Feeling threatened could lead them to act.

He'd have loved to find an innocent reason, but there didn't seem to be any.

Right now, though, he didn't give a damn. Once he barred the door, they'd be safe from everything except fire, and given how wet it was out there, the only fire would have to be started in here.

And what a fire it would be, he thought, looking at Sky. She'd made him feel young again, surprising in itself because he hadn't realized he was feeling old in some ways. But she'd made him feel eighteen and full of all the hunger as if it were brand-new again.

He wished Buddy and his friends to the devil, then realized it didn't matter what they did today. If they were up to something, he couldn't stop it single-handedly. If they weren't, then he'd find out soon enough.

The day he'd intended to spend relaxing with Sky, the private adventure he'd been hoping for for the two of them, had damn near evaporated between two visits and a bear. Was he going to let go of what remained of this day?

No.

Rising, he walked around the table and held out his hand to her.

"Still thinking?" Cap asked sarcastically.

Buddy figured Cap was in a rotten mood because of the weather. His guys had fanned out, seen damn near nothing and one of them had just limped back in with a nice bear wound down the back of his butt and leg.

"That guy needs a doctor," Buddy remarked, ignoring the question. "Bear claws are filthy. Infection'll kill him."

"To hell with him."

"What was he doing screwing around with a bear cub anyway?" Buddy asked, using his own best sarcastic voice. "You guys grow up in a city?"

"Shut up, Buddy."

"I'm serious, Cap. You don't mess with cubs. The mother is never far away. Trying to get himself a bear claw? Deliver me from idiots."

"He's paying for it."

No question of that, Buddy thought. "He's lucky he ain't dead already. How'd he escape?"

Cap visibly gritted his teeth. "That damn ranger came riding into the woods. The bear headed back for the cub."

"Guess he owes Craig his life," Buddy said with more than a little satisfaction.

"Watch it, Buddy. You don't want to make me mad."

"Whose property is this?"

Cap glared at him.

In spite of his apparent bravado, Buddy wasn't feeling all that brave. Four armed men had grown to eight. How many more were coming? He once again wondered if he'd made the biggest mistake of his life by inviting Cap here. Sure, the guy had big plans, and Buddy wasn't opposed to them. The cataclysm was coming, and giving it a nudge wouldn't make much difference.

But having Cap run the entire show afterward didn't appeal to him.

"So what's the plan, Buddy?" Cap asked again, mockingly. "Your big plan for getting them off our back until we're ready. I'm still waiting."

"The woman," Buddy said. "The artist. She's out there alone a lot. We disappear her."

Cap raised a brow. "Thought you didn't have the stomach for killing."

"I'm not talking about killing her. We just arrange a little accident to keep her out of the way. She disappears, the whole damn service and the local cops will be looking for her."

"So?"

"So we help with the search. But we know where she is. So we save her and we're the good guys. They'd leave us alone after that."

Cap looked thoughtful. "Easier to kill her."

"That'll just cause more trouble and we won't look like the good guys."

"So we help with a search and rescue, save the bitch, everybody thinks we're wonderful and leaves us alone?"

"That's it."

Cap frowned into his beer. Time slipped away, but Buddy could see the wheels spinning.

"It has possibilities," Cap said. "Real possibilities. Let me think about it."

Satisfied, Buddy sat back and reached for another beer. Cap wasn't the only one who could make a good plan.

One last qualm rippled through him. "Just make sure you don't kill her. On top of that hiker last month, they might get suspicious."

"Accidents happen out here all the time, and we didn't do that hiker."

"Right." But Buddy didn't quite believe it. He took a long swig of beer, trying to deaden his doubts. Another bottle or two and everything would be fine.

Chapter 12

Sky looked at Craig's hand, her heart starting to pound, then up at him.

"Come lie with me," he said so quietly she could barely hear him above the drumming rain.

She caught her breath. Never had anyone asked her in that particular way, and for some reason the way he phrased it was as exciting as any touch might have been. Her entire body leaped in response and she took his hand.

An almost wistful smile appeared on his mouth as she rose. He drew her into his arms, gave her an amazingly gentle kiss, then released her.

Disappointment was barely born before she understood. He pulled the bedrolls from the corner and spread them on the floor, one atop another for cushioning.

Shyness threatened her as he turned back to her, but he was still smiling in that oddly wistful way, as if he

felt she might slip away before they answered the long-
ing. Or as if he were certain the end was written even
before the beginning.

Without a word, he stood in front of her to sprin-
kle kisses on her face as he held it between his warm
hands. After each kiss, he paused an instant to look
at her, but with each kiss her eyelids seemed to grow
heavier, as if her mind wanted to focus inward, on the
feelings he evoked.

A slow, steady throbbing, in time with her heart,
drew her awareness to the apex of her thighs. A heaviness grew, a good heaviness, that verged on an ache.

His hands left her cheeks and moved downward. She
caught her breath as he tugged her sweater from her
shoulders. She had no idea where it went, and no time
to wonder as he began to release the buttons down the
front of her shirt. One by one she felt them give way
and he followed his progress with lightly brushing fingers that set her skin aflame.

Then, tugging it open, he began to kiss her collar
bones, her throat, her breast just above her bra. She
gasped, unable to prevent herself from throwing her
head back. As she did so, she reached for his shoulders
to steady herself and arched toward him.

Primal impulses controlled her now, and in some
way seemed to set her free.

He gently tugged her hands down, then she felt her
shirt slip away. Only the wisp of her bra remained, and
she caught her breath, hovering on the brink of exquisite anticipation.

"You're stunning," he murmured. She hardly heard
him over the blood that rushed in her ears.

He found the snap on her jeans and twisted it open.
The sound of the zipper going down became almost

deafening, suddenly seeming louder than the hammering rain. She couldn't open her eyes as she felt denim and cotton panties sliding down over her hips. Revealing her. Exposing her. Making her so vulnerable.

She loved it. She wanted to burst free of all constraints and follow the lodestar of desire.

She knew he'd knelt only when she felt hot, moist kisses across her belly. Her ankles were wrapped in denim, she couldn't move a step and she didn't care. Nobody had ever treated her this way before, as if he wanted to worship her.

Warm hands closed on her rear, drawing her snugly against his stubbly face. That prickly roughness excited her even more, and she swayed, needing support for a body that no longer wanted to do anything except fall in an excited, pliant heap.

Then his hand slipped up from her bottom to release her bra. The fabric fell away and her eyes opened, just a little, to see him looking up at her, drinking her in. Had she felt shyness at first? No longer. His approving, hungry gaze drove all hesitation from her.

He stood, then lifted her right off her feet and put her on the sleeping bags. Standing over her, he raked his eyes over her as he began to strip himself.

Part of her wanted to help him with that, but her legs were still tangled, and she felt so soft right now she was halfway to being a puddle.

Except that ache between her thighs. That was growing harder and more demanding.

She managed to keep her eyes open because she wanted to see him, too. And what she saw made her catch her breath again. He was smoothly muscled all over and perfectly formed.

"You're gorgeous," she managed to say.

His smile widened a shade. "I'm supposed to say that to you. And you are. Gorgeous."

He kicked away the last of his clothing, his boots giving him only a minor struggle that made her almost giggle. How odd to feel like giggling when every cell in her body was focused on passion. Somehow it seemed right, though, as if laughter could be part of this intimacy.

But before the giggle could escape her, he bent over her and tugged away her shoes and pants, leaving her free to move any way she liked.

He stood a moment, looking down at her, his eyes almost blazing with heat. She could feel it as if it sprang from him to her. "I wish we had more light. Someday I'm going to make love to you under the sun."

The remark scattered her last intelligent thought. The thought of making love to him in a sunlit valley, or on that flat rock in the gorge she had found, outdoors in the midst of nature, swamped her in fresh heat. She raised her arms in mute invitation.

But he paused again, driving her nearly nuts until she saw the plastic bag he tossed down beside the sleeping bags, and saw the box of condoms half spill out of it. He had thought to protect her. Never would she speak of what it meant to her that he had bought those recently, that he wasn't pulling some battered packet out of a pocket or wallet.

"So we get a dozen tries?" she asked weakly.

Then he laughed. It was a nice laugh, a genuine laugh, and somehow it burst a bubble of tension inside her, one that needed to burst.

He lowered himself to lie beside her. "Haven't you heard that laughter is one of the top ten reasons that people stop making love?"

"I'm sorry."

"I think they were talking about another kind of laughter." He propped himself on one elbow and smiled down at her. "Nothing's going to stop me except you."

"I don't want to stop you."

"Then laugh whenever you feel like it. This should be a happy time."

Wow, what a concept, she thought, just before he stole all thought by stroking his hand right down her front, between her breasts and over the exquisitely sensitive nest of hair between her legs. She drew a sharp breath and lifted toward that touch.

"Easy, woman," he said with gentle humor. "I'm ready to pop my cork."

"So am I," she said breathlessly before opening her mouth to him, to the electric sensations his tongue sent running through her, almost as if there was a wire between her mouth and her womanhood.

His hand found her breast, kneading her until she ached, then he teased and twisted her swollen nipple, adding to the sparks that were zapping through her now. She reached up for him, wanting more than anything to give him what he was giving her. She found smooth, warm skin, felt the ripple of the muscles beneath, then at last came across one of his small nipples. It was pebbled, too, and while she had never tried it before, she brushed her palm over it, then squeezed it gently.

The groan that answered her taught her something new. Hector had never wanted such touches. In fact, Hector had wanted to be touched in only one place.

She banished Hector the instant he popped into her thoughts, and instead focused on the feeling of power her new knowledge gave her. With that sense of power came confidence. She could make him feel good, too.

He surprised her by suddenly wrapping his arms around her and rolling them both over. The next thing she knew, she straddled his hips, looking down at him.

"Help yourself," he said huskily, his heavily lidded gray eyes almost sparkling. Then he reached up and cupped her breasts, sending her to the moon.

She felt his staff between her legs, hard and ready. Immediately, she started to rub herself against him. He groaned but quickly slipped his hands down to still her hips.

"Me, too," he said. "Me, too. But I want to take at least some time…"

Gently, he lifted her so that she was no longer riding him. The movement forced her forward, and she reached out to steady herself with a hand on his shoulder. That left one hand to explore him with and she took advantage of it, finding out that he was as sensitive as she. He liked it when she stroked his neck, so she leaned down to kiss his throat. A long sigh escaped him, and she felt his hands tighten on her hips. Encouraged, she trailed her mouth lower, trying to give him the sensations he gave her.

When she sucked his nipple into her mouth, a deep moan was torn from him and he arched, giving her a taste of what she craved.

So good, she thought hazily. So good to make him groan. The sound rippled through her in the same exciting way his touches did.

Then his hands slipped around on her hips, and she cried out quietly as his fingers found sensitive flesh from behind, lightly stroking in the most maddening way. She couldn't have felt more exposed, and the feeling was exquisite, unlike any other touch she had received ever.

His hips held her wide open even as he denied her what she most wanted. The contrast, the near helplessness lit a hot, fast fuse, pushing her higher, pushing her close to the brink.

She retaliated, nipping his nipples and making him twist beneath her. Then she slipped her hand down and closed it around his silky, hard staff. He jerked and swore under his breath.

Suddenly she was on her back again.

"Damn," he muttered. "You kill my control."

Exciting warmth zapped through her in response. She killed his control? She liked that and smiled.

"Look pleased with yourself," he muttered as he scrambled for the bag and pulled out a condom. "You deserve to."

She watched him roll on the condom, and far from being a distraction, it only kicked her passion into higher gear to see him touch himself that way. Damn, her whole body flamed with hunger now, and each passing second seemed like one second too many between her and satisfaction.

He put a hand between her knees and they parted as if they had a mind of their own. She wanted to feel his weight on her. Even more she wanted to feel that exquisite sensation of him entering her, stretching her. Just the thought of it was driving her crazy.

He knelt between her legs, but didn't give her what she wanted immediately. Instead he stroked her there, lightly brushing against hairs until her hips rolled and she was ready to scream for something deeper.

Then he parted her petals, and his fingers unerringly found the hardened nub. The sensation was powerful, right between pain and pleasure, in some hinterland that nothing else could simulate.

"Craig…" She groaned his name. "Damn it…"

A short, thick laugh escaped him. Leaning forward, he slipped his hands beneath her hips, lifting her to him.

Then that exquisite, breath-stealing moment when he slid into her, filling her, answering an ache nothing else could answer. Reaching up, she grabbed his shoulders, tugging him down to her.

He propped most of his weight on his elbows and sucked one of her nipples as he drove into her again and again. She grabbed for his hips, urging him to harder strokes. Her hips rolled up to meet his, faster and faster.

Everything in the world vanished except him, his mouth on her breast, his manhood within her. Every muscle and nerve in her body tightened as she rose higher and higher. Sounds escaped her but she hardly heard them.

She was racing through the stars, hurled out to some distant place beyond imagining.

Then everything within her clenched in a spasm so intense it nearly hurt. Moments later she tumbled into satisfaction, her entire body throbbing with pleasure as galaxies exploded behind her eyelids.

He was only a second or two behind her, unleashing a deep groan as he stiffened.

Then he collapsed on her, heavy, hot and welcome.

She hated the instant when he pulled away, but she understood. He wasn't gone long, and soon he was beside her, throwing his leg over hers, wrapping his arms around her, holding her close and tight.

Hector would have already rolled away and given her his back, ready to sleep. She didn't want to think about him right now, but the comparison was inevitable.

Craig dropped a kiss on her forehead, then shifted

her head to the hollow of his shoulder. He made a nice, if firm, pillow.

"You are something else," he murmured, running his hand over her hair, then down her shoulder and side. "Something else indeed."

"So are you," she confessed.

"Just wait. There's lots more to explore."

She smiled into his shoulder, liking the sound of that.

"In fact," he said, "I'm feeling a little cavemannish right now. Fast and hot is nice, but not for a first time."

"I kinda liked it myself."

"Thank goodness."

She slipped an arm around his waist and squeezed. "I liked every bit. In fact I more than liked it."

He gave her a squeeze and another kiss. The musky scents of their lovemaking surrounded them, and she felt a trickle of renewed desire.

Yes, she'd more than liked it. She had loved it. For the first time in her life, all that anticipation, need and yearning hadn't fizzled like wet fireworks. She wondered how she could explain that to him, to let him know how wonderful he was, but words wouldn't seem to emerge. She just knew that in relatively short order he'd helped her on a journey of self-discovery that was going to leave her changed forever. In a good way.

"I'm afraid to ask, but how long are you going to be here?"

"A month. Maybe more."

"Aah, that's not enough time. Maybe more? You can extend your vacation?"

"I work for a mental health and rehabilitation center. My mental health matters, too, so if I need a longer break I can take it."

"Take it," he suggested.

God, that warmed her. She tilted her head, trying to see his face, but got a view of his chin.

Maybe that was for the best. Wrapped in this glow, she suspected they weren't being entirely realistic. They hadn't known one another that long, an incredible number of things could go wrong. These moments would pass and reality, with all its hard edges, would return.

Besides, he liked his isolated forest. She doubted he would ever want to leave. Her life was more than half a continent away. She had patients she needed to return to. Friends she would miss.

But for now it was just fine with her to live in the spell of the moment. Time enough later to deal with all the hard edges.

"I should feed us," he remarked. "Make us some coffee. Find something to cover you. Rebuild the fire."

She listened to the list and didn't know whether to laugh or groan. She didn't want him to move away. She didn't want food, and the cabin was still warm enough.

Lying naked with him, all tangled together, felt incredibly good and she didn't want to let go of the feeling.

Apparently he didn't either, because he stirred only to wrap them closer together.

The ceaseless rain continued to hammer on the roof, making Sky feel as if they were ensconced in a cozy cocoon. Having Craig wrapped around her only enhanced that feeling.

"I could get used to this," she remarked.

"Me, too. Too bad life doesn't operate that way."

"Well, sooner or later we'll *have* to get up."

He laughed quietly. "We'd look pretty funny mummified like this."

She laughed, too, experiencing for the first time in her life being able to laugh with her lover after sex. It added to the glow she was feeling, and she wished she could hang on to these moments forever. Knowing that couldn't be, she tried to engrave them permanently in her memory, the sound of the rain, the smell of the cabin, the way her skin felt all over, the way he felt against her, his strength.... Oh, she hoped she would never forget even the least detail.

He turned toward her, sprinkling kisses on her shoulder. "And with that, darlin', I'm going to have to get up. Some things just can't wait. But don't run away. I have devilish plans for later."

She hated to let go of him, and when he rose, she didn't want to move. He went to his saddlebags in the corner, and pulled out a flannel shirt. With a smile, he spread it over her. "I hated to do that, but you may not have noticed it's getting chilly in here."

It was, and he was right, she hadn't noticed until he'd removed his heat from beside her. That man was practically a furnace.

He tossed some more wood into the stove, then, much to her dismay, began to dress. "Dusty," he said. "I didn't give him much of a chance to stretch earlier, and by now he's probably run around the corral enough to have six inches of mud on each hoof."

The things she didn't think of. Sitting up, clutching the shirt around her for warmth, she watched him finish dressing, then head outside as he pulled on his slicker.

She realized she needed to do something, too. The idea of lazing all evening was an attractive one, but not one suited to her. Even when she was holding still, she needed to accomplish something, usually painting, sometimes reading.

She dressed, opened her art case and pulled out a sketch pad and some charcoal. She might not be able to paint in this light, but she could draw.

Almost before she knew it, she was sketching Dusty and Craig as they had appeared the first time she saw them. Quick lines created the shapes and the feeling of movement. She propped the pad up and stepped away from it, debating whether to add shadows and more detail, or leave it minimalist.

Right now it looked like a quick Picasso sketch, though of course she would not put herself in that kind of class. Picasso had a magic she could only wish for.

She decided to go for more detail. Why not? She had time and it would occupy her far better than sitting here thinking of newly budding hopes and dreams that scared her.

She had to be practical. For all she was enough of a dreamer to pursue her art, she remained at heart quite practical in dealing with most things. Practicality said she was enjoying a marvelous interlude that had to end. She could enjoy it, but she didn't dare lose sight of the very real limits on these days.

She carried her pad back to the table, pulled the one burning oil lamp closer and picked up her charcoal. As soon as she began to fill in more detail, she drifted away from her surroundings into a creative surge. She might as well have gone deaf, and was blind to everything except the sketch in front of her. She loved these times when art just took over, making her feel more like a conduit than a creator.

"That's really amazing." Craig's voice startled her out of her preoccupation. She blinked, amazed to find he was once again inside with her.

"I didn't even hear you come in!"

"So I gathered." He'd already dumped his slicker and moved until he stood over her shoulder. "Hope you don't mind."

But she did. She didn't like people to look at her work before it was done, and she truly hated to work with someone peering over her shoulder. Still, she didn't want to tell him to get lost. The mood was broken anyway.

"That's really phenomenal," he said. "So few lines and you captured so much."

Pleasure touched her. "Thank you. But it's not done." She began to put her charcoal back in the box, and Craig moved away.

"I'm sorry I interrupted you," he said.

Something in his tone dispelled the last of her fog. "What were you supposed to do? Stand out in the rain? It's okay."

He reached for the coffeepot and began to refill it.

She stared at his back, wondering if he'd caught her momentary irritation at the interruption or the way she'd felt when he'd looked over her shoulder.

Seeing him respond this way after what they had shared such a short time ago hurt. An almost physical pain speared her. "Craig? What's wrong?"

"Nothing. I bothered you, and I'm sorry."

It sounded like nothing, but it didn't feel like nothing. She continued to stare at his back and wondered how to deal with this. A sense of near desperation filled her, but she didn't know if she was overreacting. Maybe she was assuming he was troubled when he wasn't. Hector, she was discovering, was a bad guide.

Finally she said the only thing she could think of to try to get a conversation rolling. "Craig, I'm sorry."

He turned immediately. "For what?" He looked genuinely surprised.

"For…I don't know. Making you feel unwelcome?"

"Aw, hell," he said quietly. He rounded the small table in two strides and sat beside her on the bench, wrapping his arms around her. "You have nothing to apologize for."

"But I felt…like you were offended by something I did."

He shook his head, catching her chin so that she had to look into his face. "I wasn't offended. I felt bad because I interrupted what you were doing. I felt bad when I realized that looking over your shoulder made you tense. I mean, idiot that I am, I know that looking over someone's shoulder isn't always a good thing to do. But I wasn't thinking. I was so struck by what you were drawing.…"

He leaned in and kissed her hard. "I won't look over your shoulder again."

She seemed to have lost her breath. After a beat or two she rediscovered her voice. "It *does* bother me when I'm working," she admitted. "I'm used to being alone most of the time when I paint or draw. But you have nothing to apologize for."

"Then let's forget it. I'm not offended and I won't look over your shoulder again without an invitation."

She answered his smile with one of her own. "How's Dusty?"

"Like I thought, he'd picked up a lot of mud. We took care of that. Tomorrow I'm going to bring some hay out here. A thick layer of it will allow the vegetation to grow back and keep his hooves dry if he has to be out there again. But right now? He's okay for right now."

"Good. I like Dusty."

"I think he likes you, too. I don't, however, think he likes this weather much. He may be tame, but I don't think he's truly domesticated, if you get my drift."

"Not exactly."

"Well, he's a great horse and a great companion. But he's also used to spending hours every day roaming this forest. He's not your corral sort of horse."

"Ah. What about the winter?"

"We still spend a lot of time out here, unless it gets brutally cold or we get a blizzard. You should see how shaggy his coat gets. I swear he's half woolly mammoth."

She finally released the last of the tension, a tension that she had built herself out of pieces of her previous relationship. She needed to be wary of that. She certainly ought to know as well as anyone just how much past experience could color the present.

They made sandwiches again for dinner and sat facing each other at the table.

"We need to go to town early tomorrow," he said.

"What for?"

"Um, how about food? And ice? And maybe one of Maude's fantastic breakfasts?"

"And hay," she reminded him. "But what about Dusty? You don't want him to stay in the corral another day."

"He won't. I'll either ride him down to HQ or we can lead him with the truck. They have a bigger corral down there and after the fifteen-mile walk it won't seem so bad to him. He'll probably even get to see a few of his friends."

"Do horses have friends?"

"Believe it. They're herd animals. Every so often they need to socialize with their own kind. God knows what they talk about. How irritating we are in the saddle? Who's got a better rider? Whether the hay is fresh or the oats good?"

She laughed. "I wish I could listen in."

"Sometimes I just wish I could read their tail flicks and their ears better. I swear, a horse can express volumes with his ears."

"And their eyes," she said, remembering how Dusty had looked at her when he decided she was okay. "Your horse has the most expressive eyes."

She almost added *as do you,* but when she met his gaze the fire she saw there rendered her breathless. As if passion had been waiting patiently in the wings, it burst forth onto center stage.

Later she would have only the haziest memory of how they came to be lying naked together on the sleeping bags. She would only vaguely recall them pulling at each other's clothing, not even remember the moment when they tumbled to the floor.

But she would never, ever forget his weight on her and the powerful way he drove into her, as if he wanted to bury himself completely inside her. She would never forget the spasms of hunger and finally delight that ripped through her. Nor would she ever forget how he managed to bring her to the peak and topple her over the edge repeatedly.

And she would always remember how, later, they slowed down and made love again, taking their time with each touch and caress and kiss, until he lifted her over him. Or how it felt to ride him to the stars.

Those things became branded in her heart.

Chapter 13

Dawn brought a perfectly clear sky with light so breathtaking and crystalline that Sky ached to paint. Craig had managed to distract her for a while—well, it was easy now that she had discovered just how good sex could be—but finally there was no escaping the day's requirements. He kissed her over and over again, as if he didn't want to let go, and she pretty much felt the same way.

Except that letting go was inevitable. Impending sorrow lanced her heart but she tried not to let it show. If there was one thing she had learned, life was what it was, and sometimes it hurt like hell.

She reminded herself that he had asked how long she could stay, but he hadn't even hinted that he didn't expect this to end. It was just a fling. She needed to keep that in mind and simply enjoy it for what it was. Living in the moment was a skill she had learned in Iraq.

Looking forward and looking back changed nothing, enhanced fears and pain, and made you miss the good things right in front of you.

"I'm taking my car," she said as they left the cabin. She carried her painting kit.

"Why? I can bring you back after the shopping."

She shook her head. "I'll meet you here later. This light...I can't waste this light, Craig."

He looked up at the sky as if it might reveal the answer to a mystery, but he didn't see light the way she did. He probably noticed that the rain had left the air so clear that everything seemed sharper and brighter, but he probably couldn't grasp what that meant to her. Not since she had arrived here had she seen light like this, and at home the higher humidity often affected the way things looked.

There she didn't often see light like this, so fresh it might have been poured unused from a bottle.

"You're going to paint," he said.

"I need to. I can't waste this light."

"I heard that part." He sighed, looked at her and apparently concluded she was determined. "All right. Just stay on the hillside in the open and keep the radio with you. I'll do the grocery shopping as fast as I can. No point in both of us going into town."

She touched his arm. "I can take care of myself, Craig. If anyone bothers me, he'll regret it, okay? They've got to know by now I'm just a painter. Neither of us have done a thing to make them nervous. They'll probably just stay clear."

"Probably." He clearly didn't feel he had a good argument against that. "I may be a little while. I have some things to take care of."

"That's fine. I'll probably be back here by noon or one, because the dust will start filling the air again."

"If you're not," he warned, "I'll come looking for you."

"Fair enough." She laughed, gave him a quick kiss, enjoying the fact that she could do that so freely now, and went to climb into her car.

It didn't strike her until she was setting up her easel on the hillside, hunting for the firmest ground, that he had said he had things to do.

What things? Surely he wasn't going to confront Buddy again? Or take a look at those trip wires?

No, of course not. It was daylight now, and Craig was nobody's fool. She spread her tarp and settled in.

"She's painting again," Cap remarked, looking through binoculars from one of the new watchtowers.

"So?" Buddy asked, standing beside him. "That's all she ever does."

"True," Cap admitted. "That and hanging out with the ranger at that cabin."

Buddy sighed. Cap had begun to seriously irritate him. "The ranger's not a problem. He hasn't even been back over here. If he's got the hots for her, so much the better. He'll be thinking about everything else but us."

"What about your plan to turn us into heroes?"

Buddy shifted uneasily. It was a good plan, if they did it right. He was just worried that Cap might go too far.

"As long as she just gets lost and we can find her, it's a good plan. If you kill her, this place is going to be crawling with Feds after that hiker. It won't just be Craig. It'll be the damned FBI. That wouldn't be smart."

"Depends." But Cap lowered the binoculars. "Okay, I'll play along. We'll cause her a small accident today. Then when the search starts, a few of us join up."

"Me included. They know me. If I don't show up, it'll look weird. The important thing is to make them forget about us. To look like the good guys to them."

"It would help," Cap said.

Buddy looked at him, feeling that Cap was agreeing with him without meaning it. He knew Cap had big plans, but in simple fact, Buddy couldn't imagine how starting them here in this isolated place would make a damn bit of difference. He remembered Idaho, damn it.

"The thing is, we look innocent. They leave us alone and we can keep planning the big action."

Cap nodded and let the binoculars dangle from his neck. "I'll send one of my guys out to set up a problem. Then maybe he can lure her into that gorge again. You can live with a broken leg, right?"

The tone was almost scornful. "I just don't want her dead. Neither should you if you're half as smart as you seem to think."

Cap frowned at him in a way that made Buddy climb down from the tower and head for his own cabin. His wife, Vera, was looking worn and tired these days, probably because she and the girls were having to cook and clean up after so many more. He felt a twinge of conscience.

But he also knew something else. If Cap went too far, he didn't want his family in any potentially dangerous crossfire. Not like what happened in Idaho.

"Stay close," he said to her. "You and the kids. The minute anything seems to be going cockeyed, you get to the safe room and don't leave it."

Weariness gave way to fright. "Buddy, what's going on?"

"Nothing yet. You know what I told you to watch out for. You keep them kids close, hear?"

Craig loathed leaving Sky behind. No, there was no specific threat. No, he couldn't point to a damn thing except there were new people haunting these woods carrying AR-15s, which wasn't illegal, and if they were just playing at being soldiers he couldn't say a whole helluva lot about any of it. There'd been no overt threat. He didn't like that one of them had followed her the other day, but on the other hand she was probably right: after checking out her kit they'd have to realize she was exactly what he'd told them she was, a painter.

Except that the increasing amount of surveillance they seemed to be under was making him jumpy as a cat. It was almost like the tightening of a noose. Which didn't make sense. Why the hell would they care about a painter?

So they shouldn't pay Sky any further attention. Did he like that one of them may have been lurking outside the cabin yesterday? Definitely not. But it wasn't like he could prove it was one of them. People wandered these woods all the time, and while the numbers weren't huge, there were still about twenty or thirty hikers and campers out here at any one time. Then there were the poachers. They probably constituted a bigger threat than Buddy and his friends.

In fact, it could well have been a poacher who mixed it up with that bear yesterday. That was more likely than that it had been one of the toy soldiers.

Sky wouldn't have a thing to fear from the poachers. They didn't like attention, and the only people who could cause them trouble were the rangers.

So... He blew a long, loud breath between his lips and told himself to calm down. He usually wasn't one to get worked up, but since Sky's arrival he'd been getting worked up a whole lot.

She awakened his every protective instinct, and he seemed to have a whole lot of those. Worse, he had figured out that she desperately needed affirmation in every way. She had been a trained soldier. Hector had undermined her in a lot of ways. She was struggling to regain her confidence, and to have argued with her about her ability to look after herself would have been wounding.

He couldn't do that to her.

And to think that such a short time ago he would have thought her perfectly safe in that clearing, just sitting there painting. What had been the threat to her then? A bear? Not likely when all she was doing was sitting there. The smells of human and those oil paints would have kept any sensible bear quite a distance away.

So why was he so certain that things had changed? Because that Cap guy had been hanging around on the fringes of so many radical groups that espoused terrorism? No reason they would pick on one woman.

But then there was the hiker. Much as he'd tried to minimize that when talking about it with her, it still nagged at him. A lot of things could kill you out there alone in the woods. No question. A fall, a stumble, hypothermia if you got caught in the rain...yeah, whole lot of reasons. And no good reason to tie it to Buddy and Cap.

He stopped in at headquarters, let Dusty loose in

the corral with a few other horses and spoke for a few minutes with Lucy.

"I'll make sure someone goes that way at least once before you get back," Lucy promised him. "We'll keep an eye on her for you. I just wish I knew what was coming down. Or if something even is."

So did he. Climbing back into the truck, he headed into town, determined to stop and see Gage and find out about this ATF move. As law enforcement himself, he had a right to know.

Then he was going to stock two coolers and hightail it back up there.

Because for some reason he kept seeing those trip wires he hadn't been able to check out last night. Tonight, he promised himself. Tonight he was going to make sure they were innocent...or not.

Having an action plan settled him a bit. He knew he ought to insist Sky stay in town until this was over, but he figured he wouldn't get very far with that. That woman was stubborn.

And for some reason that made him grin. Her arguments might sometimes seem to be all over the map, but he had figured out the gist: Sky had something to prove, and to her that meant sticking this out and being his sidekick.

Okay, then. They'd deal with it.

The back offices at the Conard County Sheriff's department had turned into an ad hoc operations center.

Gage greeted him with "We're getting ready for the ATF."

"What are they going to do? Knock on Buddy's gate?"

"I don't know. I just found out that first sheet we got

on Cap McDonald wasn't all of it. He's on a terrorist watch list and has been for a while."

"Whoa."

"Yeah, that's what I thought. That and what the hell is he doing at Buddy's place. Buddy's no terrorist. He likes to dream about it, but he wouldn't do it."

"No, he just wants to survive it. I'd bet he doesn't know much about Cap."

"Apparently not. But while you and I will distinguish, I'm not sure about ATF."

"They won't want another Idaho."

"Damn, I hope not. The Jacksons have always been on the fringe around here, pretty much keeping to themselves. At least since I moved here a couple of decades ago. But they've always been harmless fringe. You know that."

Craig nodded. "I've talked to him any number of times over the past three years. I wouldn't have pegged him for trouble. So maybe we need to be worrying about *him*. Just suppose Cap sees Buddy's place as a base of operations. What if Buddy gives him trouble?"

"Then Cap had better move on because it won't go unnoticed for long."

"Sure it would. They never go to town. Who'd notice if they just disappeared?"

"You for starters," Gage said. "My wife for another. Vera Jackson borrows books from the library on a regular basis to help teach her kids. Emma, my wife, lets her keep them for a month at a time, rather than two weeks, but she'd notice if Vera didn't show up."

"And you'd hear about it?"

"Believe it. I wouldn't get a decent night's sleep until I went out there to make sure Vera and the kids were okay. Cap may not realize that. He might think nobody would notice."

Craig rubbed his chin. "Then maybe Buddy's got a whole lot to worry about."

"It's possible. We don't know all about what's going on out there, though. As for the ATF...you're senior officer on the forest lands. I'm going to make sure they understand that very clearly."

"I'm not at their level. The kinds of crimes I investigate don't rise to that level."

"But you know the forest. You know the Jacksons. And it is your job. If nothing else, they'll have to keep you in the loop."

That didn't exactly make Craig feel any better. He was a federal law enforcement officer, yes. But he also knew the limits of his experience: poachers, the all-too-frequent idiots who thought the isolated forest would be a great place to raise some cannabis, and other miscreants.

But he understood what Gage was trying to do. He was trying to keep a federal officer in the loop to protect the Jacksons...unless they were in it up to their necks.

The more he thought about it, the less likely it seemed to Craig. Gage was right, the guy was a bit of a nut, but so far he'd been a harmless nut. If he crossed that borderline, it would most likely be the result of Cap's influence.

On the terrorist watch list? The thought sent chills down his spine and he hurried to pick up ice and supplies.

Sky might be safe out there, seeing as how she posed no threat to those guys, but he was incapable of understanding the mindset of a terrorist. They struck him as no different from any other mass murderer or serial killer, except they cloaked it in some political reason.

He didn't get those guys at all.

And that made him fear for Sky.

Well before noon, the breeze had begun to stir up enough dust that the light lost its clarity. Edges that had been sharp earlier began to blur ever so slightly. Sky sighed contentedly and started to put her brushes away. She snapped enough pictures earlier to have captured the transparency of the light, and digital cameras were far better for that than film, which softened everything just a bit. Not so much that most people would notice, but she did.

She had just finished putting her brushes in a plastic bag along with a little cleaner to keep them soft when she heard something from the woods.

Glancing over, she saw something dart away. She froze, almost certain it had had the shape of a man. She hadn't felt watched most of the morning, so she tried to talk herself into thinking she must have seen something else. Fifteen minutes later, packing all the while, she was still trying to talk herself into believing it was nothing, and since she didn't catch sight of anything else, it should have been easy to believe.

But if there was one thing she trusted, it was her eyes. They were tuned the way a musician's ears were tuned, to a level of exquisite perception. She didn't mistake shapes.

She wrapped a rubber band around the bag holding her brushes and tucked them into her kit while she debated what to do. Craig had told her to stay here. But if something was going on in those woods, he needed to know it.

Then she heard a cry. It came from quite a distance, toward the gorge, but it sounded like someone had gotten hurt. There was no longer any question.

She jumped up, grabbed the radio and tried to call Lucy to tell her what was up. All she got was crackling static.

That was weird. She knew this model of radio and she should have been able to bounce a signal off a satellite and talk to anyone around here on the same frequency. Maybe the battery was dying? Or maybe some atmospheric thing after the storm of yesterday. She could go back to her car and drive down to the station.

But the cry haunted her. If someone was seriously hurt, time could be of the essence. How long would it take to get to the station, then send out a search party?

She keyed the radio again, and through the static was glad to hear what she thought was Lucy, although the signal was breaking up so badly she couldn't be absolutely certain.

"Lucy, it's Sky. It sounds to me like someone just got hurt in the woods. I heard a scream."

A broken answer came back. The only words she could make out were "mountain lion."

Did Lucy mean mountain lions could sound like someone in pain? Or was it a warning to watch out for them? Keying the radio again, she told Lucy which direction she was heading but got no response. She hoped like hell her message had gotten through.

In the meantime, she picked up everything that could conceivably be useful from her canteen to her palette knives. She'd just keep trying the radio, but she couldn't ignore that scream.

Then she trotted toward the woods. She would go no farther than the gorge, she promised herself. She could find her way back from there without any trouble. Wandering around wildly with nothing to guide her wouldn't be smart. She paused frequently to check the pocket compass she carried, making sure to keep her bearings straight and true. From time to time she picked up a few dry sticks and left a trail marker, just in case.

The path she left behind disappeared swiftly as water-filled grasses sprang right back up. When she hit the forest floor, it was a little spongy, but it, too, rebounded. Ten minutes later it would have been hard even for an experienced tracker to follow her trail.

She never dreamed that someone was following her, removing the trail markers and all other signs of her passage.

Craig stopped at headquarters to let Lucy know what was coming tomorrow. But Lucy diverted his news about the ATF almost immediately.

"Sky called. The signal was all broken up, so all I know is that she heard someone scream. I told her it could be a mountain lion, leave it alone and leave the area."

"I hope she listened."

"I don't know. We lost signal again, damned if I know why. Probably a bad battery. I asked Don to go check on her, but he's all the way to hell and gone because we lost another hiker. Most of our people are out there searching. Don said he'd head her way, though."

Craig's skin began to crawl with uneasiness. "Where are they looking for a hiker?"

"Up in Murfree's Pass."

"Great." At the far end of the forest. "All right, I'll check on her."

Lucy half smirked. "I kinda thought you would."

"Did anybody ever tell you that you think too much?"

Lucy's laugh followed him out the door.

Dusty welcomed him gladly, and seemed more than ready to be tied again to the pickup. Making sure not to move too fast for the horse, Craig picked his way up the service road as quickly as he dared. Dusty trotted in the grasses alongside the road, beside the truck, tossing his head as if he enjoyed the clear, sunny day. After all that rain yesterday, he probably did.

"Damn, Dusty," Craig said, "women cause a lot of trouble. You know that? No, how would you know that? They gelded you before you had a chance to find out."

Dusty snorted but didn't break stride.

"I mean, Sky is a grown, capable woman, right? So why the hell should I be worried? She went out to paint, the way she was doing before she even met me. She was doing just fine on her own without me. She even has combat experience and training, something most women don't have. So I'm stupid to be all worried, right?"

Dusty didn't answer. Of course.

"Just because something weird is going on over at Buddy's doesn't mean she's in any danger. Hell, Don saw those guys playing their little games in the woods, but there's absolutely no reason they should go beyond that, not unless they're hunting for some serious trouble. Are they *that* stupid? I doubt it."

Again no answer from his companion. Talking to a horse had its advantages, in that he didn't get any back talk, but sometimes it was seriously unsatisfying.

Then he asked himself probably the most important question of all: Would he be nearly as worried about any of this if Sky weren't in the equation?

The answer: no. Most definitely no. He had confidence in his ability to deal with damn near everything that life delivered his way. So why shouldn't he give the same courtesy to Sky? She might not know the forest the way he did, but she sure as hell knew a lot of other stuff that could be useful, even out here. She was trained, damn it. She hadn't just walked off a street like a lost lamb.

That settled him down some and he eased up on the pedal a bit, giving Dusty a breather. Not much farther now to where Sky usually parked.

Her car was still there. Good sign? Bad sign. He cussed, parked right behind her and got out to saddle Dusty. Dusty stood perfectly still for him, his flanks almost quivering in anticipation.

Craig patted him. "You like a good ride, don't you?"

Of course he did. It wasn't just running around and working off energy that Dusty liked. Craig had long since figured out that the horse liked feeling useful, too.

When he was sure he had everything, he mounted Dusty and headed along a narrow deer track that would take him to the place where Sky liked to paint. Overhanging limbs kept him from moving too fast, and his heartbeat seemed to increase with every little delay.

If Sky thought someone needed help, she wouldn't hesitate. He was sure of that, as sure as he was of anything about her. She dove right in, wanting to be helpful and part of any solution. Wanting to protect. That seemed to be as strong in her as it was in him.

He hoped like hell that she'd listened to Lucy about the possibility she'd heard a mountain lion. They didn't make the sound often, but he'd heard it on occasion: it sounded just like a man screaming, very different from their usual roars and growls. It could fool someone who hadn't heard it before.

He worried, too, because an experience like Iraq seemed to burn most normal fears and cautions out of people. Well, of course it did. You had to do things that ordinary folks would never do. You had to learn to stifle spine-chilling fear in favor of action. And then it just seemed to burn out, as if you grew dead to it.

So she wasn't going to stand there wringing her hands and she clearly hadn't returned to her vehicle.

He swore quietly and watched Dusty's ears prick. Leaning forward, he patted Dusty's neck. "Not you, boy. Not you."

It seemed like a lifetime passed before he reached the clearing, and what he saw jumped his concern into high gear. Her painting kit lay in the grass. Her radio was gone as was her tarp, and maybe some other stuff. She had evidently taken off to investigate the scream.

It was exactly what he would have done, so he couldn't blame her.

From horseback he couldn't see any signs of where she had gone. Dismounting, he scanned the area around her painting supplies and couldn't glean anything either. Grasses full of water sprang back quickly, and on this slope the water had drained too fast to leave muddy ground that would record depressions.

He cussed again and reached for his shoulder microphone. "Sky? Sky, do you read?"

Atmospheric static answered him. He tried three more times before Lucy broke in. "I told you. Her radio's out. They found that hiker, so everyone is heading your way now. Any idea which way she went?"

"None. It's like she was beamed out of here." That

meant he needed to stay put until the others arrived. Coordination in a search was essential.

"She's probably all right, Craig," Lucy said almost gently.

He didn't need gentleness, he needed action. "Yeah. But I'd like to see for myself. How long since she tried to talk to you?"

"An hour, maybe a little longer."

"Hell." An hour. Easy enough for her to have walked three or four miles in almost any direction. And with every minute he waited, she could be going farther. Or she could be coming back. Regardless, someone had to be planted right here until she returned or others arrived.

He looked at the sun, realized that in little more than an hour or so it would sink behind the western peaks, dimming the light, making it harder.

The only thing going for her right now was that he was certain she had good navigation skills. He didn't know if she had a compass, but she knew how to mark her own trail so she could follow it back. All the military training would stand her in good stead, even if this turned out to be nothing but a stroll.

Damn, she must have been propelled by the sense that someone was in serious need of help, because he could count at least a dozen reasons not to go haring off alone in what might be a dangerous situation.

Then he remembered the gorge she had told him about discovering. That meant she had gone into these woods alone before. Maybe he needed to have a good talk with her about the dangers out here. This wasn't Iraq and it wasn't Tampa. Something as simple as a twisted ankle could kill someone who was out here alone.

Dusty started grazing on the greened-up grass and Craig squatted, waiting, using his binoculars, surveying the area all around for any sign of her passage, an indication of which way she might have gone.

He found nothing.

Sky heard the cry again, and she could make out the word: *help.* It sounded fainter, weaker, but it pulled her directly to that gorge she had discovered the day before yesterday. In the thick woods, she might be mistaken about the source of the sound and she knew it, but it was the only direction she had. She tried the radio again, but couldn't get a decent signal.

Damn. Well, to the gorge and no farther. Craig would probably have plenty of words for her about doing this solo, and she wouldn't blame him. But she couldn't ignore that cry, either. Mountain lion? No way. Somebody was hurt.

But she was also aware that she was no woodsman and had no illusions about her ability to find a single person in such a large area with such heavy growth. There was just so far she could take this. If she didn't find anything by the time she reached the gorge, she was going to have to head back and hope that Lucy had summoned help.

She heard water rushing ahead of her now and realized she had almost arrived. She quickened her pace, intending to stand on the edge of the ravine and call loudly to see if anyone answered. The roar of the water, the river engorged by yesterday's rain, would probably make it difficult for her to be heard even a few feet away, but she had to try it. Besides, she might see something.

She reached the edge of the ravine and put her hands to her mouth, calling, "Hello? Hello?"

The roaring water deadened the sound, preventing even an echo. Regardless, she tried a couple more times.

She was just about to turn around and head back when something caught her eye. It looked like orange fabric, the kind a lot of people wore in the woods so they wouldn't be mistaken for a deer—probably a wise thing even when it wasn't hunting season, given what Craig had said about poachers. She was willing to bet people tried to hunt all kinds of things out of season here.

She walked a few more steps to a place that looked like she could climb down without too much trouble. Turning around, she hooked the radio on her belt, then knelt and backed up until she could feel the edge. Lying on her stomach, she pushed back until she bent at the waist and could feel rocks beneath take her weight. She eased downward, feeling her way, sure there were enough protruding rocks to make it safely. It wasn't that steep, after all, and getting down was always the hard part. Coming up was ever so much easier, although what she would do if she found someone in dire need remained to be seen. Well, there had to be easier ways out of here, and she could always go for help once she knew.

Her arms were over her head, clinging to the lip of the gorge while her feet felt for another place to support her. Just then, the rock she was hanging on to gave way.

She barely had time to realize she was falling. Her awareness filled with blossoming pain as she tumbled, hitting sharp rocks. Then she came to an abrupt halt. The pain that erupted in her leg turned the world black.

She passed out.

Chapter 14

Sky woke slowly, her head throbbing, but worse, when she stirred, she felt a warning grinding in the bones of her shin. Before she even opened her eyes she knew she had a broken leg.

She lay there, letting the waves of excruciating pain roll through her, hoping it wouldn't put her into shock. She was in enough trouble now.

When at last the agony had become familiar enough that she wasn't totally focused on it, she cussed herself for being a damned fool. What the *hell* had she been thinking?

Yeah, she had thought somebody was hurt. Maybe they still were, and now she was useless because she'd been stupid, stupid, stupid.

She should have guessed the rain could have loosened some of those rocks. She should have realized that any accident at all out here, with no one knowing where she was, might cost her her life. Even more damning, she had come out here without a working radio.

Wincing until her jaws hurt, she felt for the radio and tugged it off her belt. She keyed it and heard more static. Forcing her hand into the pocket of her jeans, she pulled out her cell phone. Even if there was no cell tower, maybe, just maybe they could pick up her GPS signal? But then she remembered that depended on a cell connection, too. Her phone hadn't worked but once the entire time she'd been in these woods, and then only for a couple of seconds.

She made sure it was on anyway, then took in the rest of her situation. It was dark in this gorge because of all the overhanging trees, but the light was no longer green. Twilight was coming on, and soon after it, a very chilly night.

Pain notwithstanding, she needed to do something for herself and do it quickly. The only blessing she could see at the moment was that she hadn't fallen into the water. Being dry might save her when the night chill moved in.

What the hell had she been trying to prove? And who had she thought she would prove it to? Craig? Herself?

She forced herself to dissect her own thinking, her own urges, in part because it distracted her from the pain in her leg that roared anew with every movement.

Even the act of sitting up was almost enough to make her pass out again. Breathing steadily, moving slowly, she propped herself on her elbows.

As long as she had some light, she needed to act. Splint the leg. Find some cover for warmth. Maybe some tree limbs to pull over herself. Maybe a niche in the rocks that would at least prevent all her body heat from escaping.

There had to be a way.

Looking around, she saw some dry tree branches. Probably brittle, but better than nothing. Unfortunately, they were about six feet away.

Turning over, even onto her side, seemed like a dangerous thing to do given the way her leg screamed at every movement. Using her good leg and her elbows, ignoring the agony, she pushed herself toward those branches while she tried to figure out what clothing she would sacrifice to tie the splint.

And wondered what the hell she had been trying to prove.

The answer that came to her was quite simple, though. She couldn't ignore that scream. Alone or not, she had learned in tougher situations than this to rescue those who were hurt. How could the threat of the woods possibly compare to what she had faced in the army?

It couldn't. So she had done the ingrained thing. She wouldn't be questioning herself at all if she'd found someone who needed help.

Get on with it, she ordered herself. Just get on with it. If she survived this, there'd be plenty of opportunity to figure out whether she'd acted on training or for some other reason.

Pain exhausted her by the time she reached the scattered tree limbs. She lowered herself to her back, stared up at the boughs that darkened above her and sought some energy.

This was no time to flag.

Her groan was smothered by the rushing water as she forced herself to sit up and select some branches that might work. When she had found four of them, she pulled off her sweater, blouse and undershirt. Chilling air gave warning of the night to come. She quickly pulled everything back on except the undershirt, which she started tearing into strips. It wasn't easy to get the rips started, but once she got them going, they tore freely.

Then, nearly blacking out, she leaned forward to move her leg until it was on top of one of the sticks with strips of cloth lying beneath it. Tying them in place was going to be just as bad. She bit her lip until it bled and set to work.

Night was moving in no faster than usual, but to Craig it seemed to be advancing like a speeding car. Various other rangers had appeared and set out to cover patterns on the search grid laid out on a map on a folding table. The helicopter overflight would probably have to end shortly. In these mountains the darkness and the dangerous drafts as day changed to night would make them useless.

Pretty soon he'd set out himself, once he made sure that everyone who arrived was assigned a grid section. He hated waiting here, he wanted to march off into those woods, but he grasped the fact that doing so would probably not be the best thing for Sky.

But with each passing hour he worried more. Her last contact with Lucy had been around midday, six hours ago. Even the long twilight wasn't going to be much help in a few more hours. Search teams would have to come back in when night settled. Time was running out.

For the first time in a very long time, he felt terror. He kept it tamped down by focusing on the demands of getting the search going, but he hadn't been this afraid since his early military days. It dawned on him that of all the things that mattered to him, one of the most important was that Sky be alive.

He didn't care that she'd be leaving in a few weeks. He just needed to know that wherever she went she was still breathing and healthy.

Every wish and want he might ever have had narrowed to that one simple thing: *please let Sky be okay*. He'd give anything, his own life, if it would help make that so.

It chafed the hell out of him that so far he hadn't been able to do a damn thing except organize the search. Yeah, that was essential, but it left him feeling like a caged tiger.

Just when he least needed it, Buddy and his friend Cap showed up with another guy. Craig watched their approach stonily. He didn't need this crap now.

But Buddy surprised him. "Hey, Craig."

"Hey."

"I hear that painter lady is lost in the woods hereabouts. Me and these guys, we came to help look."

For a mere instant Craig felt gratitude. Then suspicion surged. Buddy maybe, but Cap, the guy on the terrorist watch list?

"Kind of you, Buddy."

"It's what folks do, right? I feel bad about yelling at her. Besides, I wouldn't feel good about myself if we didn't do nothing."

Craig thought Buddy looked fairly sincere, but he wasn't so sure about the other two. Especially since they were carrying those damn rifles.

"What's with the firepower?" he asked point-blank.

Cap shrugged. "One of my guys got raked by a bear."

That immediately set off Craig's alarm bells, considering the bear and cub he'd found yesterday, so oddly separated as if mama bear had been chasing off an intruder.

But could he in good conscience turn down an offer of help? And there was honestly no reason to think these guys would do anything else. No reason except for instinct, anyway.

He started to look at the map, deciding which way to send them when Cap punched his finger on a sector that didn't have a red mark on it. "We should go this way. We know that area pretty well."

Craig couldn't come up with a single valid reason to tell him no, but the way Cap moved in to select part of the search grid put him on high alert. Even his fellow rangers took whatever assignment he handed out. This guy was beyond enough.

"Great," he said, managing a smile that didn't quite make it. "Appreciate the help. Be sure to grab one of the emergency kits to take with you, and a radio. The search team frequency is already set. And get back here by dark. We don't need to be searching for you, too."

He watched the three men pick up the packs containing everything from survival blankets to first-aid equipment and food, then head out to the south.

He heard footsteps behind him and pivoted to see Lucy. "Sheriff's bringing in some people, too. Buddy, huh?"

"And his best friend Cap."

Lucy's face settled into a frown. "Nothing yet?"

"Not a damn thing. I can't imagine where she would have gone. If she's got the sense I thought she had, she should be back here by now."

"People get lost," she said soothingly.

"Not this woman. Army trained."

"Oh." Lucy's frown deepened. "What do you want to do?"

"I want to follow those three guys. Cap was a little too eager to pick a sector."

"He picked one?" Lucy evidently caught the possible ramifications of that. "Okay, you go. I'll stay here to hold down the fort for you. Bring her back, Craig."

"I sure as hell will if I can find her." Unfortunately, he had plenty of experience that told him how long that could take. "Listen, I'm going to switch to another frequency if those guys do anything suspicious. You monitor it?"

"You bet. Use the auto distress call so I don't miss it."

He nodded, zipped his jacket and picked up one of the emergency kits. Then, after a moment's hesitation he added his shotgun, slinging it on his shoulder. He was already wearing his pistol, but they had AR-15s.

"Good idea," Lucy said. "You want me to get somebody to follow you?"

He shook his head. "I can deal with them if I need to. I'd be more worried if we didn't do a good enough search because another one of us went haring off after these guys."

"I know. But when the sheriff's people get here, don't be surprised if I send one of them along. Mark your trail."

"Always."

Then he was off, not wanting to lose track of Buddy and company in the darkening, dense forest.

Sky had begun to feel chilled, probably because she wasn't moving much. She pulled a power bar out of her sweater pocket and took another bite before wrapping up the rest to save for later. She was getting thirsty, too, but dragging herself to the water seemed insane. Her plastic canteen had shattered in the fall.

Every time she moved, grinding pain nearly paralyzed her. Even with the splint reaching down beneath her heel, she hadn't been able to completely insulate her lower leg against all movement. Sometimes when she slid along, it was tolerable agony. Other times… well, she had nearly blacked out briefly a couple of times.

At least her thirstiness wasn't extreme, which meant she wasn't bleeding internally. She'd been worried about that, but apparently, other than her leg, all she had was a bad goose egg on her head and a bunch of bruises. All things considered, she'd been lucky for a damn fool.

If everything weren't so wet, she would have tried to gather wood and tinder for a fire, hoping to be able to strike a spark with her palette knife and rock. But if there was anything dry on this mountain after yesterday, she couldn't find it. So that meant finding a way to insulate herself against the cold.

So far she'd had little luck. The stream was still engorged with runoff, but checking around persuaded her that it had probably scoured its banks pretty well yesterday. She'd been lucky to find sticks for a splint caught in cracks among a few rocks. Something as light as pine needles wouldn't have made it, most likely, and if any leafy branches had fallen down here, they seemed to be long gone.

Conserving body heat had become her only priority. She had to get through this night. She was sure the rangers had begun to search for her, but she couldn't afford to believe they'd find her tonight. Maybe tomorrow if she was lucky, but probably not tonight. Given the radio trouble, they might have no idea which direction she had headed, so the search area was huge.

If they didn't run across her trail markers, it could be a long time. God, why hadn't she thought to leave a message with her painting stuff? At least an arrow of some kind?

Because she'd been all hot to trot to the rescue. Because for some reason she had ignored some very basic principles, such as making sure someone would know where she had gone. Well, she had hoped Lucy had heard her, but it was apparent now that she hadn't. Therefore, she'd been a fool.

Trying to prove what? She was still struggling with that. Had she been trying to prove something, or had she just kicked into high gear because she thought someone needed help? Back and forth her thoughts ran like a caged rat. Bottom line, the reason didn't matter anymore. Now she was in trouble, she hadn't helped anyone and she'd made her situation worse by not using her mind before giving in to the immediate rush of adrenaline and need to help.

Fools rush in... The old aphorism came back to her. Absolutely true, she thought now, but she was getting too tired to keep worrying about why she had done this. She needed to deal with the facts and save the personal debriefing for later.

Right now she had to find a way to stay warm and nothing else mattered.

Then it occurred to her she hadn't heard that cry for help again, and even in the lousy light when she looked across the stream she could see the orange that had drawn her down here was nothing but a torn piece of cloth. One that hadn't been here the other day. Probably washed up here by the storm.

A prickling sensation started crawling up the back of her neck as it struck her that, yes, that cloth might have washed up here yesterday, but combined with the cries for help... What if this had been an ambush?

That might have been a wild thought for most people, but not for someone who had served in the war. There ambushes had been a daily fact of life. Just because she was in the civilian world didn't mean they couldn't still happen. When she remembered what they had learned about Cap, maybe she had good reason to be paranoid, although she was damned if she could figure out why he'd come after her.

Stop it, she told herself, even as she looked up and surveyed the rim of the gorge as far as she could see it. You need to stay warm, get warmer if possible. Even if this hadn't been an accident, that was the only thing that mattered now.

Once again she surveyed a depression in the wall of the gorge. It wasn't huge, but right now it offered the only possibility of protecting at least part of her body from heat loss.

Biting her sore and swollen lip, hoping she'd make it, hoping she'd find something better to use along the way, she began to drag herself toward it. The pain in her leg had become so familiar now it merely provided a background.

Craig soon realized he had one advantage: Buddy, Cap and the other guy didn't see any need to be surreptitious. After all, they were searching, not being hunted. So they called out from time to time and didn't bother to be at all quiet. Scuffing along the ground, they even left quite a trail in places.

On the surface, it appeared quite natural, the way people would actually search. Distrust wouldn't leave him alone, though. In fact, it was gnawing at him.

Local people often turned out to help with searches, especially when time started lengthening. If they didn't find Sky tonight, he'd expect to see a lot more than sheriff's deputies out there come morning.

So if it had just been Buddy and maybe even the other guy showing up, he wouldn't have thought much about it. But Cap's presence…well, Cap's résumé didn't exactly suggest he was the rescuing sort. Far from it.

And the way he had moved in to select the area he wanted to search raised a whole bunch of red flags. At this point, Craig would have bet a great deal that Cap had a pretty good idea where Sky was.

The thought didn't comfort him a whole lot. In fact, it increased both his anger and his fear until his ears were damn near humming with it. If Cap knew where she was, then maybe he'd killed her.

Except that somehow that didn't add up. If Cap had killed her, he wouldn't want to lead them to her body. So maybe she was still alive, hurt or trapped somehow. As possibilities ran around inside his head, his senses ratcheted to the highest alert level he had felt in a long time. Sort of like entering a cave in Afghanistan.

He wanted to hear what they were saying, but periodically they'd turn and scan the whole area and he had to duck. Good practice, even when conducting a search. Nothing that could itself be called unusual.

Except that Cap was out here, and he was wondering what the hell Cap hoped to gain. Did he want to look like a hero, hoping it would divert suspicion from what he and his guys were doing? Hell, that sounded more like Buddy than a guy who'd managed to get himself on a watch list.

But why pick on Sky? She hadn't done a damn thing except sit on the side of a mountain and paint. And take photos, which wouldn't disappear just because she did.

Why not go for him? He was the one who had gone over there to talk to Buddy and then prowled around the perimeter of Buddy's land. He'd be the obvious one to eliminate.

And maybe that was the problem. Maybe they figured that was too risky. Knocking out a federal ranger usually resulted in enough law enforcement presence to be like a suffocating blanket.

Okay, that made it unlikely they'd come after him or one of the other rangers. But why in the name of all that was holy had they picked Sky?

With angry, worried questions buzzing around in his head like furious wasps, he almost got too close. He dropped to the ground just in time as they paused to scan around the area again. He noted that they had stopped calling for Sky. That was about the most informative thing they'd done yet.

Certain now that they knew where she was, and that they were probably somehow involved, the question became whether to keep following them or confront them. He decided to follow, because there was no guarantee they'd simply tell him where she was. No, they'd probably deny all knowledge.

They started moving again, making no attempt to be quiet. They certainly seemed to feel they were alone out here, as he could hear laughter from time to time. That laughter scorched his soul, and a chilly, killing rage came over him, unlike anything he had felt since the war.

The ice, though, clarified his head. It drove away the angry wasps of thought, and focused him intently on one goal: to follow them to Sky.

Despite the growing chill, perspiration dampened Sky's skin by the time she made it to the hollow in the cliff face. Water loss was not a good thing. Still, if she could scrunch herself into that niche at least half of her would be protected, and the rock should capture her body heat, eventually reflecting some of it back. It certainly wasn't likely to drain her as fast as the air as long as she didn't press right up against the stone.

She rested a few minutes, allowing her skin to dry, studying her scraped and bloody palms. That crawling had done her few favors. She suspected that her elbows weren't doing much better.

She'd saved some strips of her undershirt in case she needed them for the splint, but now she wound a couple of them around her hands before she attempted to contort herself into that niche. She took another bite of the power bar and looked longingly at the stream, so close and yet so far. No, she couldn't afford to drag herself over there, nor would it probably be wise to drink icy water, which would only cool her down more. She had a day or two before thirst should become a serious problem. If she wasn't found sometime in the morning, she'd have to crawl to the stream. Simple but important choices.

She just wished she was sure she was thinking clearly. Given fatigue, a blow to the head, hunger and now thirst, she couldn't be sure. She had to count on training she hadn't needed in a long time to carry her through.

As soon as she felt the handful of calories from the energy bar start to hit, she began the painful process of twisting herself into that niche. Agony. Every single movement had become sheer agony.

Something interesting had happened. The quickstep march of Buddy, Cap and the other guy had slowed down. They made no pretense of continuing to search. In fact, having left a very obvious trail to this point, they had become suddenly quite interested in leaving none at all.

Proof they had come in here, but no proof of where they went next.

They gathered in a knot and began talking. Craig couldn't hear them, and the lack of noise they were making now made it hard for him to creep any closer. He reached for the volume on his radio, and turned it all the way down to make sure no errant sound alerted them. Although, to his dismay, the damn radio had been utterly silent. Soon, though, given the growing lateness of the hour, searchers were going to start sending messages back and forth that they were heading back to the command post.

His heart squeezed as he thought about Sky possibly having to make it through this night. But he didn't focus on that for long. Right now he had a more immediate problem: What were those guys talking about?

Moving with stealth, aided by the wetness of the forest floor, which kept leaves and pine needles from crunching, he crept closer.

"…just wait another hour or so and head back," Cap said.

"You can't…" Buddy's voice grew muffled, making the rest inaudible.

"Look," said Cap, sharply, "the hero thing you wanted to do? It works as good for us if we find her dead in the morning as if we find her alive now."

"No," Buddy said. "No! You know where she is, and we can't leave her to die. Damn it, Cap, it's not like she knows anything. She'll be as grateful to us as anyone."

"Dead or alive makes no difference. Why do you think I brought us this way?"

"What are you talking about?"

"I came this way so we could make sure no one else finds her, Buddy. Time to grow up, man. You want a revolution? Then prove you're tough enough."

Craig's blood curdled in his veins. He waited for Buddy to object, but the man didn't.

"No one else is coming this way," Cap said. "That's obvious now, and we've been steering away from her anyway. We're covered, no one will find her and in the morning we can be heroes."

"What if she's not dead, Cap?" the other guy said. "She might make it through the night."

"If she does, we can take care of that."

"That's just wrong," Buddy said hotly. "Damn it, she's not an enemy. She's just a painter."

"How do you know that? She may have been put there to watch us."

Once again Buddy fell silent. Moving silently, Craig punched the distress signal on his radio, sending out the beacon Lucy would be watching for.

Damn, he couldn't believe what he was hearing. All of this to make them look like heroes, and so much the better if Sky died?

He began planning ways to take them out. He calculated angles of attack. Three of them wasn't too many, but unfortunately they were better armed. He'd need surprise. Big-time surprise.

He began to circle around them to the one direction from which they wouldn't expect anyone to come: ahead of where they'd been walking.

Keeping low, shotgun carefully cradled in his arms, he sought the moment and the opportunity.

"You didn't tell me you wanted her dead," Buddy said unhappily.

"But it was your great idea anyway," Cap said sarcastically. "Man up, Buddy. The revolution has no room for wimps."

Craig heard the most chilling thing then. Buddy said, "You're right."

So the argument was over. These guys intended to leave Sky out overnight, regardless of her condition, and if she wasn't dead by morning, Cap was going to take care of it somehow. Hell, he'd probably make Buddy roll a boulder down on her.

The absence of Sky had convinced him of one thing: she was hurt or she'd have long since returned. How badly, he didn't even want to imagine.

Anger thrummed steadily now, trumping even worry, but his head remained absolutely clear. He just needed his opportunity. One little sliver of time to act.

Sky had wedged herself into the niche, trying to minimize body contact with the rock inside, and while she could physically feel that it was capturing warmth on that side of her, the other side seemed to be losing it just as rapidly. The pain in her leg rose and ebbed like a tide, reaching crescendos that made her groan, then easing just enough to unlock her brain again.

She had to stay awake. She remembered that. Hypothermia was far more likely to get her if she allowed herself to sleep. But exhaustion was dragging her down despite an agony that should have made sleep impossible.

She ate the last bit of the energy bar and scanned the gorge around her, hoping to see a person, any person. But no one appeared. Her hands, which had been throbbing, now started to grow numb and she tucked them under her arms, willing sensation to return.

Not much longer till dark, she realized. At least down here in this gorge. Would they call off the search with nightfall? Probably. She couldn't imagine that it would be wise to wander around these woods with only flashlights.

Then it occurred to her that the rushing water drowned most sounds. How could she call for help? Looking around, she sought some rocks. Maybe if she found a couple, she could bang them together. Maybe that sound would penetrate the water's rush better than a voice.

It gave her something to do. Since she absolutely, desperately needed to stay awake, it was a welcome idea. It busied her, trying to find some rocks that she could reach without moving too much.

Because she had expended so much effort to reach this niche, she was afraid to leave it for any reason before morning. She was running on willpower now, and had no way to gauge when the last of her physical strength would desert her.

Movement helped keep her warm, though, so without abandoning her niche, she started to feel for rocks.

* * *

The sound of rocks banging reached the knot of men in the forest, and Craig, as well. He tensed, readying his shotgun.

"Well," said the third guy, "she must still be alive and kicking."

"How bad is she?" Cap asked.

"Her leg's broken. I watched long enough to be sure. She's not going anywhere."

"Okay." Silence. "Gaff, maybe you ought to go take care of her now. She could die in a rock fall."

That did it. Craig quit looking for the best opportunity. Gun at the ready, he stepped out of concealment, aiming at the three men.

"Don't move."

They swung around and saw him. Immediately Cap lifted his rifle, aiming at Craig. Before he could shoot, Craig stepped behind a tree, making sure to keep his line of sight. Buddy and Gaff both lifted their own rifles to the ready.

"I can take you all out with one shot," Craig said. "Advantage to the shotgun, and I'm loaded for bear. Literally."

Cap took a shot anyway, and the bullet hit bark just above Craig's head.

"No!" Buddy shouted. His rifle, which had been pointing in Craig's direction, suddenly swung around and fired at Cap. Cap fell. Gaff lifted his own gun, aiming at Buddy, but before he could take his shot, Buddy fell to the ground. Craig seized the opportunity and sent a blast toward Gaff. The result wasn't pretty.

Buddy, lying on the ground now, yelled, "I won't shoot."

Craig didn't think he would. He'd seen Buddy shoot Cap. "Keep your rifle on Cap. He may not be gone."

"Okay, okay!"

Craig waited until Buddy rolled onto his stomach and took a bead on Cap.

Then he shoved another shell into his shotgun and stepped out again, moving toward them. As he got closer, Cap suddenly stirred. He fired but heard the report of Buddy's rifle at the same instant. Cap went still.

Game over.

Except for finding Sky. That's when hell grew even colder.

"I don't know exactly where she is," Buddy said. He was now standing with his hands up while Craig debated whether to cuff him. "I just know Cap was going to arrange for her to have an accident in the ravine."

"So this was your bright idea?"

Buddy looked down. "Yeah. I didn't mean for it to go this far." He glanced at Cap's body. "He wasn't who I thought he was."

"Maybe I'll want to hear about that later. Right now I want just one thing."

Buddy, looking hangdog, nodded. "She's in the ravine. That's all I know."

Craig heard the distant crack of rocks hitting each other again. "You don't know how damn lucky you are that she's probably still alive."

Buddy looked at the barrel of Craig's shotgun, unerringly pointed right at his middle. "Believe me," he said. "I know. Let's quit wasting time and find her."

Craig keyed his radio on the search frequency. "She's in a ravine south of the command center, Lucy. I haven't reached her yet, but start sending rescue this way. She's badly hurt from what I just heard."

"You got it. Cavalry's on the way."

"We got a couple of bodies out here, too. They aren't pretty, so warn anyone who comes through the woods."

He looked at Buddy. "Grab an emergency pack. You're going to get to be a hero after all."

It was getting harder and harder, but Sky kept banging the rocks. She thought she heard gunshots, but couldn't be sure. Babbling brook my foot, she thought as the waters rushed nearby, determined to swallow any other sounds. Washing them away as surely as they washed away any other debris.

She had begun to shiver, despite the effort she was expending, and she could feel her body's growing need for rest. A rest that could prove fatal.

So she banged the rocks again and deliberately moved her leg to send another tide of agony racing through her.

Stay awake. Just stay awake.

Apparently she didn't succeed. The next thing she knew, jarring pain roused her. Craig's voice reached her as if from down a long tunnel. Something crinkly was being wrapped around her, and at some point she vaguely registered growing warmth.

Red blossomed behind her eyelids and she opened them to see a flare burning nearby. With a loud pop, another one ascended upward.

"You're going to be okay. You're going to be fine. I'm here."

I'm here. Those words in that voice were the best she'd ever heard.

Craig could have cheerfully added another killing to the list he carried, but it wouldn't serve any purpose now. He took one of Sky's roughly bandaged hands between his own, willing warmth into her icy fingers. "Stay with me, Sky. Stay with me." The flutter of her eyelids gave him his only hope.

She was so damn cold, probably only a short way from succumbing to exposure and her injuries. Cap had done better than he thought. She wouldn't have survived till morning. He just hoped she had enough body heat left for the survival blanket to do her some good.

The radio crackled to life. "Sheriff says the rescue chopper is on the way. You have another flare?"

"Yeah."

"I'll let you know when to release it. Meantime I've got a dozen guys running your way with a basket and backboard in case the chopper can't do it."

"The chopper better do it. She's cold as ice."

"Working on it." No-nonsense Lucy. If he hadn't known her well, he would have wondered if she even cared. But Lucy cared. She cared naturally about everyone and everything.

"Craig?"

He almost didn't hear her, but he snapped around. Her eyes were open halfway. "I'm here. Rescue is on the way."

"Cool. Wanna talk."

"Save your energy. We can talk all day tomorrow."

He thought he saw the whisper of a smile on her lips. Hope, real hope, began to rise in him.

"Craig?" Lucy on the radio. He keyed his mike.

"Yeah?"

"They're almost there. Get that flare ready. Guys on the ground estimate five minutes to reach the ravine."

They must be running despite the darkness. Warmth toward them penetrated the chill in his heart. Good men and women, racing to the rescue through darkened woods.

He felt Sky's icy fingers move, then squeeze ever so slightly. "I'm here," he said. "I'm here. Just a few more minutes and we'll have you out of here."

"Thirsty," she mumbled.

"Not for much longer, darlin'. Just a little longer."

The radio came to life. "Give us that flare now."

Moments after the flare reached the peak of its arc, blinding light flooded down from above. Though he couldn't really hear the rotors, he knew what it was.

Thank God.

Chapter 15

Sky awoke with difficulty. Sleep kept wanting to drag her back into darkness, into a jumble of images she couldn't evaluate for their reality. A flash of twisting in the air, another flash of being dragged through a door into the belly of a beast.

A woman's voice: "This will prick." She never felt the prick.

And now she was hot. So very hot. She struggled against the muzzy thickening in her head. "Hot," she managed to croak.

Something lifted from her, and she immediately felt cooler. A hand touched her brow.

"You're coming out of anesthesia," a woman's voice said. "Morphine for pain. You're going to be just fine."

She let the darkness take her again.

The next time waking was easier. Pain pounded in her leg, but much reduced. With effort she opened her eyes and saw a ceiling. Curtains. Hospital. It was over.

A sigh escaped her. Somehow she had made it. "Sky?"

Her eyes tracked to the right and she saw Craig leaning toward her. She felt him squeeze her hand. "Relax, heal. I'll be right here."

"My leg?"

"It's reset. It was a bad break, but they didn't need to insert a pin. You'll be up and about in no time."

"What..." But exhaustion claimed her again. Exhaustion and meds.

Bright western sunlight streamed through the window of her room, golden in the late afternoon. In the distance she could see the purpling mountains.

"Welcome back."

She turned her head the other way, ignoring the throb the movement induced, and saw a very weary, unshaved Craig sitting beside her in a dirty, wrinkled uniform. But he smiled and leaned toward her, brushing the lightest of kisses on her lips.

"I had to fight with them to be here," he said. "Some stupid rule about family only. And then you've got a waiting room full out there. Those vets you gave that talk to? There's a lot of them out there keeping vigil. Even though you're going to be fine, they seem to want to see with their own eyes."

"Wow," she murmured. "Water?"

"I don't know, but there's ice chips here. Want some?"

He tipped a cup to her lip and she held the chips on her tongue, enjoying the way they moistened her mouth. She didn't feel thirsty, but her mouth felt like desert sand.

"More?"

She took a few more, and finally the roof of her mouth let go of her tongue. "What happened?"

"Beginning where? If you're tired, I'll give you the short version."

"Long version." She winced as she tried to lift herself higher on the bed.

"Hold on. That's what they make these handy dandy buttons for." He passed her the control that was dangling from her headboard and put her thumb over a button. "This should raise your head. Do it slowly. I don't know how it's going to make your leg feel."

She hardly felt it in her leg at all, but stared down to discover she now sported a cast from toes to knee. It was propped on a couple of pillows.

"Okay. Please pass me the ice and tell me."

So he told her. She gasped but wasn't completely surprised when she learned that she had been set up to have an accident. "So they could be heroes? Amazing."

"I agree. Apparently one of them called for help, and when you started to climb down, someone else kicked a rock loose and you fell."

"Nice of them."

"Well, Cap and one of his guys are dead now, and four others are in custody. We're piecing it together."

He sketched her rescue by helicopter, and told her how impressed everyone was by the way she'd splinted her own leg and taken care of herself.

"Survival," she said, dismissing it. "Anyone would have."

"Not everyone would agree with you." His tone was gentle. "Regardless, you're here, you're alive and you're safe. That's what matters most."

He squeezed her hand and she clung to it, but a few

minutes later, a nurse shooed him out. He promised to come back as soon as they let him.

She didn't hear him return, as fatigue claimed her yet again.

Three days later she was released with crutches, a cast, a sheaf of directions and some pain medications. Craig helped her into his truck, then asked where she wanted to go.

"The cabin," she said immediately. "I know I'll be useless, but if you don't mind…"

"I don't mind. I'm on vacation. If I can make you comfortable there, I will."

"I'll be fine." In the back of her mind was a job offer she had received from those same vets who had kept vigil in the waiting room. They wanted her to stay on and work with them, and were offering a tiny salary. It might be just about enough if she was careful, and it would let her paint more. The idea was tempting.

But if there was one thing she knew for certain, it was that she wasn't going to stay here if Craig had lost interest in her. Right now she couldn't tell.

Some kind of wall seemed to have grown between them. She had been feeling it even as he had hovered at the hospital. Maybe he felt this wouldn't be a good time to ditch her, given her injury. Or maybe it was something else.

"I was so stupid to run off into the woods like that," she said, voicing the concern that had plagued her almost as much as wondering about him. "I know better."

"We often know better but do things anyway. You thought someone was hurt. I'd have done the same thing."

"But you aren't a city girl."

"Neither are you, not really."

"I should have at least left some indication of the direction I'd taken. I *did* mark my trail, though. Is that how you found me?"

"If you marked your trail, someone was at pains to remove them all. No markers. That surprised me."

"God! Who would have thought?"

"Anyway, I followed Buddy, Cap and this other guy. That's how I found you."

"Why'd you follow them?"

"Because Cap was too damn eager to select his own section of the search grid."

"That would do it." She turned her attention out the window, watching town disappear behind them, then watching as they steadily climbed into the mountains, passing the ranger station and climbing upward.

"How's your leg doing?" he asked.

"Sore, but not that bad." The kind of question anyone would have asked. Damn, she was starting to feel teary, but what had she expected? Declarations of undying love? He hardly knew her. Maybe she should have stayed in town instead of inflicting herself on him. Somebody else could look after what little bit she would need.

"I'm sorry," she said. "If it's too much trouble, just take me back to town."

He jammed on the brakes, skidding on the gravel. She looked at him, startled.

"Cut that out," he said tautly. "Just cut that out. We're going to talk, but not while I'm driving. Damn logging trucks..."

She wondered what kind of explanation that was. He needed to concentrate and anything they discussed would distract him? That didn't make her feel good at all.

Never before had he been sharp with her, and that caused the growing crack in her heart to deepen. She blinked back tears, telling herself she was just down because of the recent physical trauma, that she'd be fine and that she couldn't possibly have fallen for a guy so soon after Hector.

Craig was a loner anyway, she reminded herself. A guy who preferred the solitude of the woods to human companionship. She had to admit she couldn't blame him. Everyone was different, and he seemed to have chosen a solitary path through life.

So buck up and press on. She'd gotten past worse things.

She tried instead to think about the nice offer that veterans group had given her. They'd even promised her that there'd be more of them because once word got out that they were doing more than chewing the fat together, others might start coming to meetings more often. She liked their optimism. Certainly they'd seemed to like her brief introduction to art therapy. They'd even confided that they'd contacted the VA about getting her transferred here. That would have been sweet.

Somebody wanted to keep her around, anyway.

But she wasn't going to stay. Craig was clearly wrestling with something, and she figured if he wanted her to hang around he wouldn't be wrestling with anything at all. No, the hard thing was telling someone to get lost. Or, putting it more nicely: go back home.

Back at the cabin, he steadied her until she was safely seated in the armchair, then he went out to his truck and returned with a few pillows. Pulling over a bench, he propped up her leg.

"Thank you."

He gave her a smile that almost seemed to reach his eyes. Almost. She hated being unable to help as he built a fire, then started carting in coolers, blankets, a…was that a foam mattress?

She stared at it, wondering. Well, of course, she'd opted for the cabin and he was just protecting her leg. A kind, caring man who did kind, caring things, that was all.

But at last he was done, and had started a pot of coffee. Then he pulled the second bench over and sat near enough to reach for her hand.

"Now we can talk."

Here it came, she thought. The pain in her heart suddenly rivaled the pain when she had broken her leg. "Yes?"

"It's no problem for me to have you here. Far from it. I can't tell you how glad I was when you said you wanted to come out here."

Glad? Her heart lifted a tiny bit and she tried to squash it back down. Getting her hopes up was only going to make this harder.

"Damn, Sky, is the world really ending?"

"What do you mean?" God, she loved looking into his gray eyes.

"You look ready to cry. I know you're tired. You're probably hurting like hell. Do you want to leave this until later?"

"Leave what? Just talk to me now." She braced herself.

He glanced away for a moment. "I'm not usually a chicken."

"That doesn't sound good." Her heart cracked even more, and grief began to seep out around the edges.

His gaze pierced her. "That depends. It's just that

I've never even wanted to give my heart to someone. I didn't know how difficult it could be." He paused. "Well, hell, I've already given you my heart. The question is what you want to do with it."

Astonishment deprived her of speech. Anticipated grief didn't want to give way to hope. Hope was dangerous.

"Look," he said, "I know I live the kind of life most women would hate. I get it, I've heard it often enough. I'm the kind of man who will be gone for days at a time. I won't be around a lot, at least not in the summer, and I couldn't possibly claim that would make me the best friend or companion. Then, I know you've got a whole life down in Florida. Why in hell would you want to give that up to live in the middle of nowhere with a guy who's gone a lot? But the simple fact is, I can't stop hoping that you might see some reason, any reason, to want to hang around. I love you, Sky. If I wasn't sure of it before, I was convinced when I almost lost you. It's really selfish, I know, but I'd rather not spend the rest of my life without you."

Joy began to blossom within her, at first almost painful as it shot her from the depths to the heights faster than a rocket. "Selfish?" she repeated stupidly.

"I know it's selfish. What can I offer? A lot of solitude and a cabin in the woods. Most women would run from that in a heartbeat. I mean, if I weren't selfish, I suppose I'd be offering to follow you home, but honestly, Sky, I'd feel crushed by the crowding and then I'd make you truly miserable. I'm recognizing my own limitations here. It's not easy."

She needed to stop him before he put himself down any more. She tugged his hand until she pressed it to her heart. "Sh," she said.

He sighed. "I know. I'm sorry. This isn't fair to you."

"Cut it out," she said, repeating his words. "Can I talk now?"

He nodded, clearly bracing himself.

"I love you, too. I want to stay here. In fact, I've even got a job offer from the veterans group. It would be just enough, and I'd have more time to paint. But most importantly, I could be with you."

She watched emotions race across his face. "Really? Even though being with me would mean not being with me for days at a time?"

"I'm pretty self-sufficient. I can handle it. What I can't handle is losing you."

The next thing she knew, he'd leaned into her, wrapping her in a crushing bear hug, his cheek against hers, his mouth against her ear.

"I love you," he murmured, sounding choked. "Dang, I never thought this would happen. But I love you. Just promise me you'll tell me if you change your mind. Promise me."

"I promise." It was an easy promise to make, because she knew she'd never have to keep it. Her heart soared, and she lifted her arms to wrap them around his powerful shoulders. "I love you, Craig. Always. I promise that, too."

He pulled back a bit, then swallowed anything else she might have said in a kiss that reached her heart and soul both.

"I love you." The first words on life's best journey.

* * * * *

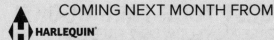

REQUEST YOUR FREE BOOKS!
2 FREE NOVELS PLUS 2 FREE GIFTS!

HARLEQUIN®

ROMANTIC suspense

Sparked by danger, fueled by passion

YES! Please send me 2 FREE Harlequin® Romantic Suspense novels and my 2 FREE gifts (gifts are worth about $10). After receiving them, if I don't wish to receive any more books, I can return the shipping statement marked "cancel." If I don't cancel, I will receive 4 brand-new novels every month and be billed just $4.74 per book in the U.S. or $5.24 per book in Canada. That's a savings of at least 14% off the cover price! It's quite a bargain! Shipping and handling is just 50¢ per book in the U.S. and 75¢ per book in Canada.* I understand that accepting the 2 free books and gifts places me under no obligation to buy anything. I can always return a shipment and cancel at any time. Even if I never buy another book, the two free books and gifts are mine to keep forever.

240/340 HDN F45N

Name	(PLEASE PRINT)

Address		Apt. #

City	State/Prov.	Zip/Postal Code

Signature (if under 18, a parent or guardian must sign)

Mail to the **Harlequin® Reader Service:**

IN U.S.A.: P.O. Box 1867, Buffalo, NY 14240-1867
IN CANADA: P.O. Box 609, Fort Erie, Ontario L2A 5X3

Want to try two free books from another line?
Call 1-800-873-8635 or visit www.ReaderService.com.

* Terms and prices subject to change without notice. Prices do not include applicable taxes. Sales tax applicable in N.Y. Canadian residents will be charged applicable taxes. Offer not valid in Quebec. This offer is limited to one order per household. Not valid for current subscribers to Harlequin Romantic Suspense books. All orders subject to credit approval. Credit or debit balances in a customer's account(s) may be offset by any other outstanding balance owed by or to the customer. Please allow 4 to 6 weeks for delivery. Offer available while quantities last.

Your Privacy—The Harlequin® Reader Service is committed to protecting your privacy. Our Privacy Policy is available online at www.ReaderService.com or upon request from the Harlequin Reader Service.

We make a portion of our mailing list available to reputable third parties that offer products we believe may interest you. If you prefer that we not exchange your name with third parties, or if you wish to clarify or modify your communication preferences, please visit us at www.ReaderService.com/consumerschoice or write to us at Harlequin Reader Service Preference Service, P.O. Box 9062, Buffalo, NY 14269. Include your complete name and address.

HRS13R

Turning his back on Gabby, Trevor strode out of the living room.

The moment he did, Gabby immediately followed him.
Since the area was still crowded with people, she only managed
to catch up to him just at the front door.

Trevor spared her a look that would have frosted most people's
toes. "Where do you think you're going?" he asked.

He sounded so angry, she thought. Not that she blamed him,
but she still wished he wouldn't glare at her like that. She hadn't
put Avery in harm's way on purpose. It was a horrible accident.

"With you," she answered.

"Oh no, you're not," he cried. "You're staying here," he ordered, waving his hand around the foyer, as if a little bit of
magic was all that was needed to transform the situation.

Stubbornly, Gabby held her ground, surprising Trevor even

though he gave no indication. "You're going to need help," she insisted.

Not if it meant taking help from her, he thought.

"No, I am not," he replied tersely, being just as stubborn as she was. "I've got to find my daughter. I don't have time to babysit you."

"Nobody's asking you to. I can be a help. I *can,*" she insisted when he looked at her unconvinced. "Where are you going?" she wanted to know.

"To the rodeo."

That didn't make any sense. Unless— "You have a lead?" she asked, lowering her voice.

"I'm going to see Dylan and tell him his mother's dead," he informed her. "That's not a lead, that's a death sentence for his soul. You still want to come along?" he asked mockingly. Trevor was rather certain that his self-appointed task would make her back off.

Trevor was too direct and someone needed to soften the blow a little. Gabby figured she was elected. "Yes, I do," she replied firmly, managing to take the man completely by surprise.

Don't miss
THE COLTON RANSOM
by Marie Ferrarella

Available July 2013 from
Harlequin Romantic Suspense
wherever books are sold.

HRSEXP0613R

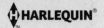

HARLEQUIN®

A *Romance* FOR EVERY MOOD™

Love the Harlequin book you just read?

Your opinion matters.

Review this book on your favorite book site, review site, blog or your own social media properties and share your opinion with other readers!

Be sure to connect with us at:
Harlequin.com/Newsletters
Facebook.com/HarlequinBooks
Twitter.com/HarlequinBooks

HARLEQUIN®
A *Romance* FOR EVERY MOOD™

Stay up-to-date on all your
romance-reading news with the
Harlequin Shopping Guide,
featuring bestselling authors, exciting new
miniseries, books to watch and more!

The newest issue will be delivered right to you
with our compliments! There are 4 each year.

Signing up is easy.

EMAIL

ShoppingGuide@Harlequin.ca

WRITE TO US

HARLEQUIN BOOKS
Attention: Customer Service Department
P.O. Box 9057, Buffalo, NY 14269-9057

OR PHONE

1-800-873-8635 in the United States
1-888-343-9777 in Canada

Please allow 4-6 weeks for delivery of the first issue by mail.